DEATH of a DAPPER
S

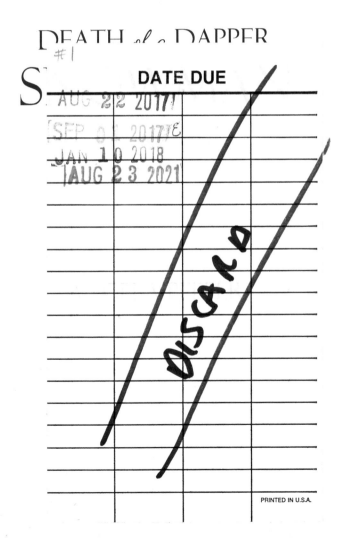

CHAPTER 1

STORMY DAY

THE HAND-PAINTED SNOWMAN on the vase kept his coal-black eyes trained on me. Sweating and breathing heavily, I was getting my morning workout by pushing the accent chair from one side of the living room to the other.

I stepped back to assess my handiwork. The room was still off-balance and bare. The little snowman looked embarrassed to be there as the sole decorative item in my new-to-me house.

The doorbell rang.

I picked up the vase and turned it around on the coffee table, so the snowman faced the window, and only the painted mountains would be visible to my guest. That tweak made all the difference. One lone Christmas decoration would be pathetic, but a single piece of ceramic art made an elegant centerpiece.

I opened the door and invited in the perky blond real estate agent who'd sold me the place.

Samantha Sweet glanced around the interior as though appraising the value added by my decorating, or the lack thereof. She was frowning. I had a table and four chairs, plus a sofa, accent chair, plants, and lamps, but no curtains, no art on the walls, and nothing personal other than the vase.

"Good start," she said with enthusiasm.

"I know it needs softening up," I said. "Everything's square, and I need more roundness, more texture."

She said, "Stormy, you could get a pet."

"To decorate? That seems a bit selfish, to buy a pet just to accessorize my living room. Then again, fluffy white cats and dogs look great with everything. Or should I go brown? What colors are in style these days for pets?"

Her mouth pinched. Sadly, her lack of appreciation for my particular brand of irreverent humor immediately took her off my shortlist for potential new friends. That narrowed my list down to zero, which was a shame. I tried not to let my disappointment seep into my voice as we continued to make small talk about throw pillows and decorating.

She took a seat on the upholstered living room chair, refused coffee but accepted water, and we got down to business.

I'd already bought the house we were currently sitting in, as well as an established retail business on Broad Avenue. Both were sizable commitments, but when managed well by yours truly, they promised to be cash-flow positive. That left me with enough capital to acquire a few more investments, possibly a nice round ten. If I had ten, there'd be security. Even if a few flopped, the diversity of my portfolio would spread out the risk.

Samantha's green eyes had nearly popped out when I'd told her my intentions. She was no slouch and had gotten to work immediately, scouring the town for more deals.

For today's presentation, she had three prospects, each in its own folder. I sat kitty-corner to her, on the sofa.

Samantha opened the first folder and composed herself with a professional smile that didn't quite extend to her eyes.

Before she could speak, I said, "Pass."

She gave me a wounded look. "But I haven't even told you what it is."

"I can see you've only got five sheets of paper in that skinny folder. You and I both know this one's no good, which is why you're presenting it first. Classic sales technique. Let's make a deal. I'll be honest with you, as long as you promise not to play the usual games."

Her lips pinched again. She set the first folder aside. "You're right," she said. "It was for a micro-brewery they've been trying to unload for years. Nobody else wants it, either."

"I saw it listed online," I said. "The building has some value, but the equipment's outdated. The beer itself is decent, but I'm guessing the margins are wafer-thin." I nodded to the other materials on her lap. "What's behind door number two?"

She opened the next folder, tipping her head from one side to the other as she handed it to me.

"Katrina Court is a three-story, twelve-unit rental block," she said.

I closed the folder after a cursory glance and set it aside. "Pass."

She sputtered, "Bu-bu-but you said you were interested in more residential rentals."

"I'm not some overseas investor taking properties by the bulk, sight-unseen. I've been inside Katrina Court. If the cash flow looks good, it's only because of deferred maintenance. The current owners keep patching pinhole leaks in the pipes to delay repiping, and I'm sure that's just the tip of the iceberg. A lack of spending may help today's income statement, but they're devaluing the infrastructure, which is where the only value is because that land isn't zoned for redevelopment, as I hope you would already know."

She blinked, her green eyes professionally inscrutable. "Of course."

"What else have you got?" I leaned forward, reaching for the final folder. My lower back was stiff from my furniture-pushing workout, and my hand moved jerkily upward.

Samantha flinched away from my hand, as though I'd been about to slap her.

"The last one's no good, either," she said. "It's no use. I'm sorry."

I took the final folder and looked over the contents. "Samantha, this is a low asking price for a retail business with such high volume. What makes you think this coffee shop won't be of interest to me?"

She bit her trembling lower lip. "Just a hunch. Honestly, I don't know. I'm much better with houses, not other investments."

"You can learn the basics, though."

Her hands flew up to her face, and within seconds she was wracked with sobs. "It's no use," she cried. "I'm terrible at math. I have to use a calculator for everything, even for splitting a stupid lunch bill. They should take away my license."

I perused the contents of the final folder, waiting for her to pull herself together. A minute later, she was still sniffling and rambling about her incompetence, eyes hidden behind a chipped manicure. At first I'd been mortified, embarrassed on her behalf, but with each passing minute, I softened. Her purse was open enough to reveal the stuffed animal that likely belonged to one of her young children. She was trying to raise a family while building a career, and she had found her breaking point, in my new living room.

"Samantha," I said gently.

She continued to berate herself, sobbing, "Last week I put a contract into the system with a comma instead of a decimal point, and I nearly blew the whole deal."

I handed her a tissue. "Mistakes happen."

She blew her nose and dabbed her eyes dry. "I'm the mistake. This whole career is a mistake."

"How much sleep did you have last night?"

She looked as if she might start sobbing again.

"Sleep helps," I said. "But the real issue is Imposter Syndrome. It's surprisingly common, from academia to the business world and pretty much everywhere in between. It's that fear you got where you are by the skin of your teeth, and everyone's going to find out you're a phony."

She swallowed hard. "That's me."

I shook my head. "That's most of us. And the only cure is to know your stuff, inside and out."

"But I don't know anything," she said, the water welling in her eyes and ready to go again.

"You weren't born knowing," I said. "So you have to learn. Educate yourself, and that feeling will go away." I took the papers from the folder and spread them across the coffee table between us. "For example, this place has a low asking price because it has no intangible assets, no competitive advantage. They don't even have a single secret recipe because their baked goods come from a supplier. They're in a great location, sure, but I see here the lease is up for renewal next year, and the demolition clause is not in their favor."

I flipped through the papers, picking out numbers and doing quick calculations on the pages, even though I could have done them in my head.

She nodded, almost smiling as it sank in. "So, you're saying secret recipes would be a valuable asset, along with, um, customer goodwill?"

"That's right," I said, flipping over a sheet to write a list on the back. "Here are some good books you might want to check out."

When I finished and closed the folder, Samantha was leaning back in her chair, a stunned but pleased look on her face.

"Thank you," she said. "You're not so scary after all."

"Someone told you I was scary?"

Her eyes widened, and she mumbled something about being on her way.

"Your last name is Sweet," I said. "You're married to Michael Sweet?"

She nodded begrudgingly.

"High school was a long time ago," I said. "I've changed a lot since then, and I don't throw food on people anymore. Not even if they're bullying little kids in the cafeteria."

She said, "That was all that happened?"

"Yes. Michael more than deserved a tray full of mashed potatoes and gravy in his lap."

Her posture stiffened. "He says you dumped food on him several times."

"Your husband was a slow learner."

She tipped her head to the side. "True enough."

"How's he treating you these days?" I chuckled as I sipped my coffee. "Do you need me to come over and talk to ol' Mikey about anything?"

She met my smile with one of her own, a genuine grin. "Things are great, thanks. He's a wonderful husband and a great father to our kids. I shouldn't have let your reputation get to me, since you've always been as nice as pie in our dealings."

I raised my eyebrows. "My reputation?"

She jerked into motion, tapping the electronic device on her wrist to check either the time or her messages or both. "I'll be in touch again soon," she said. "I'll read those books, and I'll get better. Is there anything specific I should keep an eye out for?"

I handed her the folders. "Let's look wider," I said. "Let's not limit ourselves when there are plenty of other towns nearby that are equally good, or better."

"Better?" Her voice rose up sharply. "Better than Misty Falls?"

I walked her over to the door and passed her the wool winter jacket she'd worn in. It smelled of sweet perfume and was the same green as her eyes.

"Let's broaden our search," I said.

We exchanged a few more details about pricing and other criteria, and she left.

I finished my coffee and jotted down some errands for the day. My stomach felt unsettled, even after eating a healthy breakfast muffin.

When I'd suggested looking wider for investments, Samantha had been crestfallen, as though I'd written off the entire town. She wasn't wrong. The idea that I had a reputation in Misty Falls as anything other than a savvy young businesswoman rankled me.

Why would I keep trying so hard to fit into a place that wouldn't love me back?

CHAPTER 2

BROAD AVENUE RUNS through the center of picturesque Misty Falls. Like the main streets of other charming small towns, Broad Avenue is lined with colorful storefronts topped by hand-lettered signs and striped awnings. Above the shops, Oregon's snow-capped mountains rise majestically to frame the sky. If you're standing in the center of town when snow is falling, and you squint your eyes just right, you'll feel like a tiny figurine inside a snow globe.

Snow had started falling by the time I steered my car onto Broad Avenue. I turned off the radio to better enjoy the view and the tucked-in-bed feeling of fresh snowfall.

My employee had already opened my store that morning, so I was in no rush to get to Glorious Gifts. I parked behind the building and took a leisurely stroll up Broad Avenue to get a takeout coffee. Things did not go well at the cafe because the little bundle of evil known as Chad had been working. Then I burned my tongue on the latte, but I was determined to look on the bright side for the rest of day.

With a smile on my face, I walked into my store and greeted my employee, Brianna, with her beverage of choice: a mocha.

Brianna squealed and declared, "Stormy Day, you're the world's greatest boss! I award you this prize." She took from the shelf a ceramic mug decorated with the phrase World's Greatest Boss and handed it to me.

"You shouldn't have!" I clutched the mug to my chest for a moment before returning it to the shelf. "I'll keep it right here, with my other ones."

A trio of customers came in. Brianna went over to see if they needed help. I checked that everything up front was in order, and then went back into the small office to receive the recent orders into the computer's system. The shop's inventory wasn't entirely computerized yet, but I was working my way through the huge undertaking. I anticipated the job being lighter after the busy Christmas season, when much of the existing stock had been sold through.

I'd lost myself in a soothing stream of numbers when a sound startled me. I sat up straight and listened while a loud woman in the store made unreasonable demands.

Her shrill tone carried all the way back to the office with perfect clarity. "When was the last time you dusted this top shelf?" she demanded.

I rubbed my temples and listened as Brianna said, "I'm sorry, ma'am. I'm too short to see the upper level, so I didn't realize it needed dusting. I'll get to it right away."

"Being short is no excuse," the woman said. "Get yourself a ladder. Chop chop."

I heard the ladder squeak as Brianna put it into action. Slowly, I rotated my swivel chair to face the door of the office. So much for my attempt at an enjoyable day. There wasn't enough room under the desk for me to hide, and soon she'd be coming for me.

The woman in the shop wasn't just any local know-it-all. She was my father's girlfriend, Pam Bochenek. The two had met earlier in the year, at a fundraiser where she was handling the decorating. The relationship hadn't been serious until an injury had him immobilized at home, and Pam moved in "temporarily" to help him with errands. We both thought she'd move back out once I returned to town, but it hadn't happened yet.

I'd accepted that maybe this was a sign from the universe, and it was finally time for Finnegan Day to settle down with a woman. I would have preferred that woman not be Pam Bochenek, with her wild mood swings and her strange ideas about what types of foods were best pickled, but there was no point in denial. Pam was part of our lives, and I could fight and make things worse, or try to befriend her.

Or I could sneak out the fire exit.

I tiptoed to the office door to check the line of sight to the back door.

"Stormy!" Pam yelled.

Busted. I shook my fist in the air.

She called out, "I know you're here, so stop screwing around. I saw your car parked in the back. Don't you think that car is awfully flashy for Misty Falls? People will talk about what a big city hotshot you think you are."

"And a good morning to you, too," I said with a pasted-on smile as I emerged from the office.

Pam threw her spindly arms in the air in mock surprise. "She's come out of her cave!"

"You say that like I'm some hibernating bear."

Pam squinted at my face. "Have you been sleeping? You have bags under your eyes. That new haircut really draws my attention to them."

I rubbed the back of my head, my fingers moving easily through my new pixie-cut hairstyle. After years of fighting my naturally curly hair and spending vast sums on straighteners, I'd finally found the haircut that suited me. Unfortunately, it didn't meet Pam's approval. Never mind that her own light brown hair was barely inches longer than mine.

"I'm fine," I said. "How about you? With my father off to Portland, are you bored? Should we wander over to the paint-your-own ceramics place again?"

"I'm busy." She picked up a plastic pet carrier and set it on the counter with an angry clunk. "I have to get the cat fixed before she goes into heat."

I peered into the cat carrier, expecting to see her new Russian Blue cat, but the container was empty.

"I'm afraid it's too late," I said to Pam. "Your cat has slipped into invisibility mode. The vet won't be able to fix her if they can't find her."

Pam gave me a blank stare. "That sounds like something your father would say. You people are so weird."

"I'm weird? You're the one with an invisible cat."

"Obviously we'll have to catch the cat first. I need your help. The stupid thing won't listen to me. I've been yelling for her to come home for the last hour."

I suppressed a smirk. "I can't imagine why that didn't work."

Pam shoved the pet carrier along the counter toward me. "Your father should have taken care of everything before he took off on his trip. He's got a lot of loose threads he needs to tie up before he goes gallivanting around."

I bit my tongue. My father hadn't "taken off" on anyone. He'd left town the day before to get a hip operation done in Portland. He would be laid up in bed for the next few days, hating every minute of it, but to hear Pam talk, you'd think he was off gambling and watching showgirls.

Pam stepped away from the counter and pulled on her winter gloves. "We'd better get moving. The cat is due at the vet right now."

Again, I bit my tongue. Most people in want of a favor have the decency to ask nicely. Pam, however, had helped me get a discount on my new furniture a month earlier, and ever since, she'd been acting as though one phone call had been an immense sacrifice, and I owed her countless favors.

I patted the plastic carrier. "Don't worry about the cat," I said. "I'll drive over to the house and take care of this. Then we'll be even for you getting me the discount on the furniture. It's the least I can do to repay you."

Her nostrils flared as she eyed me with suspicion. A moment passed. I held my ground in silence.

The ladder squeaked as my employee dusted the upper shelves and pretended she wasn't listening.

Finally, Pam emitted a sharp acquiescence. "Fine." We had a deal. She walked toward the exit, calling back over her shoulder, "I just wish other people would take their promises and obligations seriously."

I followed her outside, onto the snowy sidewalk.

"Trust me with this," I said. "I can get one little cat to a veterinary appointment."

She held up one gloved hand and cut me off before I could bring up my credentials. "Just get the cat. Don't go snooping around."

"Snooping around?"

She cleared her throat, as though she was about to say something.

I waited.

The snow that had begun falling an hour earlier was getting denser. The snowflakes were thick, delicately weighty on my eyelashes. White crystals settled on the top of Pam's head, like a melting coronet. She was pretty, which was probably what initially drew my father's eye. In the soft diffuse light of the snowy day, with the feathery decorative collar of her jacket becoming frosted, she reminded me of a regal character in a fairy tale.

I brushed away the snowflakes on my eyelashes. "Pam, when it's snowing like this, do you ever feel like you're a tiny figure inside a snow globe?"

"No." Without further comment, Pam turned around and walked up the street, muttering about errands and unfinished business.

I returned to the store for the pet carrier and my jacket, rolled my eyes at Brianna, and left to fulfill my part of the bargain. I had to chauffeur a cat to the vet. How much trouble could that be?

CHAPTER 3

THERE'S NO PLACE like home, and there's no street quite like the one you grew up on. For me, it was Warbler Street, named after the small, vocal birds. One Christmas, my sister and I were given a beautifully illustrated encyclopedia of local birds. I loved looking at all the warblers and picking which one I felt the street was named for. My favorite was *Dendroica petechia*, the Yellow Warbler, a bright harbinger of spring.

Spring and summer could never come fast enough when I was a kid. I steered the car past the corner where my sister and I had once sold lemonade by the glass on hot, sultry, endless days. Warbler Street was our jungle gym. We'd play until dusk, hiding and seeking, marking the sidewalks with chalk, refusing to come inside until my father threatened to put out an APB and have us arrested.

Now, the trees and houses seemed to have shrunk. With a blanket of snow over everything, my sunny memories seemed even more precious.

I parked in front of my father's house. The interior lights were off. Knowing he wasn't there, inside the home, gave me an uneasy feeling, like a preview of some future I didn't want to consider.

I pulled my phone from my purse and called him. We'd spoken before my meeting with the real estate agent, so while the phone rang and rang, I worried he'd turned off his phone in preparation for surgery.

He finally answered with a cheerful greeting, his voice colored by his mild Irish brogue. "Talk fast. They're coming to wheel me away."

A lump in my throat road-blocked my words. Hospital noises echoed in the background. Someone asked if he was warm enough or needed a blanket. The mental image of my brave, strong father in a blue-green smock, being wheeled into an operating room, took me by surprise. Painful emotions surged through my chest.

"You still there?" he asked. "Stormy, you should have seen the look on the old doc's face when I gave him his gift, a brand new measuring tape. I told him I wanted both legs the same length, or else every anniversary of the surgery, I'll come to his house and kick him with whichever leg's longest."

"Oh, Dad." I shook my head and let a laugh ease my pain.

"Don't you worry about a thing. This doc has a good sense of humor, and he's got an excellent success rate. I'll be fine. What's going on with you?"

"I'm parked in front of your place."

"The house is still there? Pam hasn't burned it down?"

I quickly told him about that morning's visit and my current mission. "Remind me, Dad, what's the cat's name?"

He chuckled. "There's no point in naming something that doesn't come when you call it." He told me to hang on while he spoke to someone there with him. "Showtime," he said when he returned to the line. "Thanks for taking care of Pam for me. I owe you one."

"Good luck." I would have told him I loved him, but he was already gone.

I put the phone in my purse. My chest ached if I held still, so I seamlessly moved on to my next task, grabbing the pet carrier and supplies. Everything would go well, I told myself. He was strong and healthy, plus the orthopedic surgeon had a brand-new measuring tape.

The cat was sitting on my father's porch, looking pretty, all long legs, sleek gray fur, and elegant jade eyes.

I opened the pouch of cat treats as I approached. The goodies had a strong salmon aroma. I blew over the pouch as I shook it, sending the smell to the cat's sensitive nose. The gray tail swished, but the cat stayed in place.

"What's the matter? Cold feet? The snow must be cold on your little toes."

The cat yawned, bored with my simplistic patter.

"Cut me some slack," I said. "At least I'm not yelling at you, like Pam would."

The cat's eyes narrowed at the mention of Pam.

"Not a fan? You and me both," I said under my breath.

I glanced around, feeling embarrassed about talking to a cat. I saw nobody, but the back of my neck tickled as if I was being watched. I opened the door of the pet carrier, sprinkled a few snacks inside, and got closer to the porch.

The cat's dark gray ears twitched. It ignored me and looked off at something else.

I followed the cat's gaze over to the neighbor's yard. A creepy face, pale and round, stared back at me. Startled, I dropped the pet carrier with a clatter. But there was no pale-faced person watching me. Just a snowman. He wore a formal top hat and a jaunty red scarf, like the classic snowman you'd see on a greeting card.

While I was distracted, the cat whipped past me in a streak of gray, darkly visible against the bright snow.

I grabbed the carrier and gave chase, stumbling through the overgrown hedge between my father's yard and the neighbor's. The cat led me straight to the dapper snowman, scaling its body in bounding leaps. The cat scrambled up, toppling the snowman's black hat and then taking the hat's place, right on top of the head. From its new vantage point, about six feet above the ground, the cat surveyed the neighborhood and began licking one elegant front paw.

Undaunted, I put the pet carrier on top of my head and proceeded calmly. Sniffing the salmon-flavored treats, the cat strolled right into my trap. I closed the cage door and pumped my free hand in a fist.

I set down the carrier and picked up the top hat. Feeling whimsical, I plopped the hat on my own head and pulled out my phone for a snazzy self-portrait. This would be the perfect image to show my ex I was having a great time and had made the right decision in walking away from everything we'd built. In the photo, I looked rosy-cheeked and happy. The snowman, however, had a crooked grin that made him seem creepy.

I decided to take a better picture once I'd fixed his crooked grin. I rearranged a few of the pebbles that formed his smile, but that wasn't enough. It wasn't his grin that was off-kilter but his whole head.

Meanwhile, the cat had finished the snacks and meowed impatiently inside the carrier.

"Just a sec," I said. "I'm giving this snowman a face-lift, so to speak."

I grasped the base of the perfectly round ball forming the snowman's head and pushed up. The head didn't budge. The cat meowed again, sounding irritated.

"I know we don't have time," I muttered to the cat. "But I want my old friends to see that my life is perfect, and a crooked snowman face doesn't cut it."

I gave the snowman three firm karate chops to the neck, through the red scarf. The ball jiggled as it came loose. I grabbed hold and gave it a solid tug up. The snowy ball split in my hands, revealing a core that was definitely not snow. Stunned, I dropped the two hollowed-out halves.

Sticking up from the upper body was another head, a human head. I blinked in astonishment. This had to be a prank by neighborhood kids. Some clever brat had re-purposed a Halloween costume to give someone a scare.

But rubber masks usually resemble famous people, not my father's cranky neighbor, Mr. Murray Michaels. This face was highly detailed. It even had eyelashes. The chill in my hands spread through my entire body. This wasn't a Halloween mask that looked like Mr. Michaels.

Frozen inside the snowman was the actual Mr. Michaels.

I stumbled backward, sucking in air, preparing to run or scream or both. But I didn't scream, and I didn't run. Something propelled me forward, slowly. I reached out and gently touched the man's cheek. The flesh was cold, frozen solid, and he was not just dead but very dead. If there were such a classification as very dead, Murray Michaels would be in that group, along with mummies from Egypt and those cadavers that are plasticized for scientific display.

His face showed no bruising or marks, and no blood was visible on the surrounding snow. I carefully brushed away some of the snow around his neck, jerking my hand back when I touched something unexpected. It was just the collar of his shirt. I shook my head at myself for being jumpy before leaning in to examine some dark purple lines on his neck.

Behind me, a man yelled, "Hey, lady! Get away from there!"

CHAPTER 4

I WHIRLED AROUND, and something dark came at me. I jumped back, raising my arms in a defensive posture against what, a split-second later, I realized was just the top hat tumbling off my head.

The man yelled again, "What's going on?"

He stood on the walkway, only fifteen feet away. He wore a blue uniform and looked familiar. I couldn't recall his name, but I assumed I must have met him through my father. He was reaching under his dark vest, about to pull something from a pocket or holster.

"Don't you dare shoot me," I said.

"Why would I shoot you?" He made eye contact with me briefly before shifting his gaze to the frozen face I stood beside.

The man in blue's jaw lowered slowly, his eyes bugging out at the same speed, as though all his facial features were attached to one control switch. He fumbled the object he'd been reaching for, which wasn't a gun at all. It was just a phone, and he dropped it in the snow. With a mild curse, he got down on his knees, which were bare. Despite the winter weather, the man wore knee-length shorts with a dark stripe on the outside seam.

Being the daughter of a police officer, I should have known better and recognized the man's uniform as that of the US Postal Service, but I'd been so shocked by the discovery of the frozen head. The mail carrier continued to fumble his phone, chasing it clumsily through the snow.

Without looking up, he asked, "Lady, is that who I think it is?"

I looked directly at the head, just to be certain.

"Yes, I believe it's Murray Michaels. I just saw him two weeks ago, when my father threw a party. Mr. Michaels came over to complain about the noise."

I stared at the lifeless face, searching for some clue in the fuzzy memory of our last interaction. Mr. Michaels had been cranky that night, but that wasn't out of the ordinary for the grumpy loner who never said anything nice to a neighbor, unless he was trying to get a bargain at a yard sale. That night, my father had asked him to come in, but he declined, to nobody's surprise.

"Well?" the mail carrier said.

"I should have invited him to the party," I said with sadness. "We could have been nicer."

"I'm calling the police," the mail carrier said, locking his eyes on mine. "That is, assuming my phone still works."

He didn't look down at his phone. He stood motionless on the walkway, blocking the exit route to my car.

A minute passed, and neither of us budged.

"Go ahead and call," I said.

His blue eyes stayed coolly locked on mine. "Maybe you should make the call. Go ahead."

A terrifying thought blossomed in the back of my mind. What if this man had yelled at me to step away because he knew the body was there? What if he was the killer?

The fair-haired mailman was a big guy—tall, with a surprisingly husky figure for someone who walked all day. By comparison, I was much smaller and weaker. My best option was to run. If I stayed, I would need a weapon, but the pointiest thing within reach was the snowman's nose, down by my feet, and I didn't think a carrot would do much for defense, even when frozen.

"You look twitchy," the mail carrier said. "How do I know you're not dangerous?" A bead of sweat rolled out of his sandy-blond hair and ran down the side of his round face.

I replied, "You're the one who looks nervous. You're sweating all over the place."

He pulled out a kerchief and mopped his brow. "Lady, this is normal," he said. "I run hot."

"That would explain the shorts," I said.

Something pulled on my jeans. The young cat, who didn't sense the gravity of the situation, had reached through the lattices of the pet carrier's door and snagged the leg of my jeans with sharp claws.

The mail carrier's jaw dropped. His eyes bulged again, this time at the plastic pet carrier.

He demanded, "What are you doing to that poor cat?"

I picked up the carrier. "We have a vet appointment."

"Isn't that Mr. Day's cat?"

"Good eye. It certainly is. Mr. Finnegan Day is my father."

He gave me a sidelong look. "And what's your name?"

"Stormy."

He nodded knowingly, as though he'd gotten the confirmation he was looking for. He finally used his phone, jabbing the screen while his face reddened.

"Congratulations, lady," he said to me, holding the receiver of the phone below his double chin. "You've just incriminated yourself. This is my route, my street. Mr. Day's daughter is named Sunny. You got the name wrong, you criminal."

"Sunny is my sister. There are two of us."

His eyes twitched, but he didn't soften his glare. He spoke into his phone. "Hello? I need to report a homicide, as well as a suspect."

I objected, "Suspect? I'm a witness, same as you."

His nostrils flared, and he kept talking. "Yes, the suspect is a medium-sized white woman. She was wearing a top hat when I arrived at the scene, but she's taken it off now. She's also kidnapping a cat." He paused before adding, "No, I haven't been drinking."

I took one more look at Mr. Michaels. This time, I caught details I hadn't noticed before, including the narrow crescent of one eyeball, visible through relaxed-looking eyelids. He seemed to be on the verge of waking up. My stomach lurched. I pitched forward and tossed up that morning's muffin and coffee.

The mail carrier kept talking on the phone, describing the scene and giving dispatch the address.

Now that I was lighter by the weight of one modest breakfast, the urge to run away hit me hard. My vehicle was nearby.

My father always taught me to be safe, and if my instincts told me to run, I should run, and never mind the possibility of being rude or hurting someone's feelings. He always talked about how some attacks happen partly because the victim is too polite to bolt, and while he wanted me to be a polite person in general, it ought to never put me in danger.

I ran to my car and opened the door. To my surprise, I still had the pet carrier in one hand. I placed it on the passenger seat as I scrambled in. A minute later, I was driving, on the run, but from what?

The cat meowed, demanding to be let out of cat prison.

I turned the car left and then right, my mind a swirl of paranoia, panic, and bizarre thoughts. I didn't want to believe a person in Misty Falls had been murdered, so my imagination offered up alternative possibilities. What if Mr. Michaels had been hiding in the snowman to play a prank on someone? What if he'd climbed in there and then had a heart attack? Or fallen asleep and froze to death?

No, that was crazy. I'd heard of people going through major personality changes in their older years, but I couldn't imagine a shift that dramatic, transforming a cranky man into a prankster.

The cat meowed again.

"I know," I said. "Today has turned out horrible."

I kept driving, my eyes on the road but my mind elsewhere. Who would kill Mr. Michaels? After his brief appearance at my father's party, there'd been some discussion of the man. He'd been squabbling recently with my father over the property line, which was part of a battle that had been carrying on for the better part of two decades. Pam had mentioned Murray Michaels becoming, in her words, an old nuisance. She said he'd been stirring up trouble with some of the downtown businesses, causing problems at several places, from the costume rental shop to Ruby's Treasure Trove. He hadn't been into my gift shop that I could recall, so I didn't know what the fuss had been. She also mentioned him seeing a woman, a scandalously young woman who worked at the Olive Grove. An old friend of mine worked at the same cafe, so I could ask her about it, or pass the information along to the police.

The cat meowed again, sounding even less impressed about the interior of the pet carrier.

"Did you see anything?" I asked. "Did you see this young woman Mr. Michaels was wooing? I think Pam said she was a blonde."

There was no answer, but it felt good to talk, even if it was to an animal. The cat meowed plaintively.

"What about you? Do you have an alibi? Can anyone vouch for your whereabouts?"

The cat reached one paw through the gated door and swatted air.

I'm innocent, the cat meowed. I have an alibi, I swear!

I let out a small laugh, feeling better as I imagined what the cat could be saying.

Look at my sweet little gray face! Do I look like a criminal to you?

"If it wasn't you, that doesn't mean you weren't the brains behind the operation. Maybe it was all the neighborhood cats, working as a group. Wasn't Mr. Michaels notorious for yelling at you cats? He never grew anything in his garden, but he didn't appreciate anyone else digging in there."

The cat meowed again.

"You're right. He wasn't the most enjoyable person on the block."

Another meow.

"No, I wouldn't say he was a bad person. Just cranky and ornery, and that's no crime. In fact, some people might say the same things about me because I keep to myself."

The cat didn't meow but seemed to be listening.

"I'll stop hiding when summer comes, maybe, or I might move again. I don't really fit in here. I feel like a puzzle piece from another puzzle."

The cat reached a gray paw through the door and waved it, as if to tell me to keep going.

"You know, I shouldn't speak ill of the deceased, but Mr. Michaels should have moved, or tried something. He didn't fit in, either. I think he had a girlfriend once. Or maybe it was a sister."

I went quiet, imagining a younger version of the man, opening the door of his house for a lady visitor. In my earliest childhood memories, he'd have been around the same age I currently was. Thinking about him being my age made me empathize with him more than I ever had.

The sudden clarity of the tragedy hit me like a solid blow to the backs of the knees, emotionally buckling me.

I had to stop the car, put on the parking brake, and focus on breathing.

Mr. Michaels wasn't just part of the Misty Falls scenery, that scowling curmudgeon every small town has, always complaining about lineups at the post office or the need for more traffic lights. He was a person, with bills and taxes and plans for the future. He suffered from gout but was grateful his health wasn't worse. He had a television but no cable. He loved old Western novels, re-reading the same ones until they were falling apart. Maybe he had upcoming plans for Christmas, or maybe he didn't. Now he was gone.

The postcard view in front of me, of snow-peaked mountains framing in colorful streets, blurred as my eyes filled with tears.

Mr. Michaels wouldn't be getting any more second chances.

A car honked. The traffic light in front of me was green. I thought I'd pulled over to the side of the road, but I was in the middle of an intersection. I raised my hand in an apology wave and stepped on the gas.

The veterinary clinic was up ahead. I'd driven there on autopilot, the list-making, organized part of my brain still working despite my lack of awareness. I pulled into an empty parking space and turned off the engine.

I grabbed some tissues from the glove box to clean up my face. Sirens blared nearby. Were they coming to nab me for leaving the crime scene? I instinctively hunched over, hiding as the police car drove past. I kept my head down, my face near the front of the pet carrier.

The cat seized this opportunity to reach through the lattices and smack me on the nose for wrongful incarceration.

CHAPTER 5

THE CALICO VETERINARY CLINIC was warm inside and held a pungent symphony of aromas. The heaviest of the odors was food-like, either canned beef stew from a staff member's lunch being microwaved, or top-quality pet food. The scent made me the opposite of hungry. Hitting me second was a mix of antiseptic and cleaning fluids, which was neither good nor bad. Finally, there was a floral air freshener, mixed in with a person's perfume or cologne.

The powerful smells were very effective in bringing this moment into focus and pushing the snowman to the back of my mind.

Across the counter, an apple-cheeked woman with unnaturally red hair greeted me. She had an inch of blond roots showing underneath the primary shade, and her natural hair was blond, straight, and thick. Her name tag, affixed to a teal smock she wore over a black turtleneck, read Natasha.

Natasha cooed at the cat, "Hello, good looking. What a lovely Russian Blue you are." She flicked her eyes to me. "What can we do for you?"

"The appointment should be under Bochenek or Day. I'm here to get this cat fixed."

Natasha chirped back, "Fixed? Why? Is your cat broken?"

"Not that I know of."

She laughed. "Of course I knew what you meant. Just a little veterinary humor to lighten the mood for Miss Kitty."

"I'm sure Miss Kitty appreciates the playful banter before you drug her and rip out her reproductive organs."

Natasha held her finger to her lips. "Shh. Not in front of the patient."

Someone behind me chuckled in a low, masculine voice. The man's laugh seemed to be teasing me. I didn't want to give anyone the satisfaction of rattling me, though, so I didn't turn around.

Natasha leaned down to look into the cage, frowning.

"This is not going to work," she said.

I let out a heavy sigh. "Now what?"

"We can't do the spaying procedure you requested. This cat is a male."

"No, she can't be."

The guy behind me chuckled again. I started to turn my head but stopped myself.

Natasha opened the pet carrier door. The cat sprang out and into her arms. While the cat swatted her crayon-red hair, she pointed the animal's back end at me. "See those?" she asked.

I was too surprised to do more than murmur, "Yes."

Natasha explained, “Female cats don’t have these parts back here. Are you familiar at all with basic male anatomy?”

The guy behind me snorted.

“Yes,” I said through gritted teeth. “I’m familiar with basic male anatomy, and I see your point. Girl or boy, the cat still needs to be fixed.”

She gave me a grin that bordered on pure evil. “Why do you keep saying fixed? Is your cat broken?”

The guy behind me could no longer control his laughter.

“Listen, I’ve had a rough morning,” I said to Natasha. “How much do I pay you to deliver the deluxe spa treatment, or whatever you call it, to this cat?”

“It’s actually cheaper for males,” she said. “But I do have some concerns. Are you absolutely sure this is your cat?”

“No,” I admitted. “Let’s check the tag on the collar.”

She hugged the gray cat and stared at me as though I was the worst human on the planet. I reached out and checked the tag on the collar. I found my father’s address and phone number, but there was no name for the cat. My father, in his usual eccentric way, had listed its name as THE CAT.

I felt a sudden sense of solidarity with the cat. My father had given both me and my sister play-on-word names, his never-ending personal prank on us both. The cat deserved better. I stared into his green eyes, and the name popped into my head as though sent there by the cat himself. It was the perfect name.

"Jeffrey," I said. "Put his name down as Jeffrey. Jeffrey Blue."

The newly-christened Jeffrey Blue stared back at me with wide green eyes, as if to say, please don't make me have this deluxe spa treatment, which may or may not involve me getting fixed, which I'm guessing is not a good thing.

I assured Natasha that I was running an errand for my father's girlfriend, with a cat I had only met once before. She warmed up and told me it wasn't that uncommon for people to mistake male cats for females before things started to pop out. Natasha told me to take a seat while she brought him back to the veterinarian for a preliminary exam.

She backed away with him in her arms, and Jeffrey meowed as if to say, Where am I being taken? Hey, there are cats in cages back here! Help! Get me outta here!

Natasha disappeared into the back with Jeffrey, and I understood, for the first time, how those mothers must feel when their kids go off to their first day of school. I'd only been Jeffrey's guardian for less than an hour, but I was feeling some very parental concerns.

Poor Jeffrey. I heard him meow pitifully in the other room, and I got the urge to barge into the back and rescue him. Jeffrey and I had been through so much together, from the discovery of the body to our little heart-to-heart in the car ride over, and now he was on a cold examination table.

A big hand gently patted my shoulder. "There, there," the man who'd been chuckling said. "You're having a rough morning, aren't you?"

At the touch of human kindness, I nearly fell apart but didn't.

"I'll be okay," I said with a stoic lift of my chin. "It's Jeffrey I'm worried about. Between you and me, he's been working too many hours prowling the neighborhood. Plus up until today, he thought he was a girl kitty."

The man walked over to the waiting room's water cooler.

"Sounds rough," he said. "Can I buy you a drink?"

"Better make it a double," I said as I took a seat.

"A double." He grinned, as though my asking for a double water was the most delightful thing he'd heard all week. He was tall, mid-thirties like me, and had plenty of dark hair, wavy on top and trimmed around his face in a thick yet tidy beard. If I'd known the man was so ruggedly handsome, I might have turned around at the first chuckle.

He filled two waxed paper cups to the top and sat on the end chair, leaving one empty chair between us. He smelled as good as he looked, which, I thought, was really nice for his wife, whoever she was. A man that attractive had to have been snapped up by someone. His left hand probably bore a wedding band. I leaned forward as I accepted my water, trying to get a peek, but he seemed to be aware of my investigation and tucked the hand into a coat pocket. His jacket was the shabby army-surplus type favored by teens carefully cultivating an appearance of not caring about their appearance. Paired with the green jacket were equally tattered jeans, frayed at the knees. He appeared to be a drifter, one of the temporary workers employed at the local furniture factory. My interest in his ring finger faded.

"I'm Logan," he said, passing me the cup of water in lieu of a handshake.

"Of course you are." I swigged down half the water, which was warmer than I expected and slid down easily.

"Interesting," he said. "You don't know your cat's name, but you know mine."

"You look like a Logan," I explained. "All woodsy and stuff, like logs."

His blue eyes twinkled with amusement as he waited for me to introduce myself. But the idea of having to repeat and explain my name seemed like more needless aggravation, and Logan was probably just passing through town, so I pretended not to notice him waiting for my name. I pulled out my phone to check messages.

I tipped back the rest of my water just as I saw my self-portrait with the snowman was online and getting comments from my friends. I nearly spat out the water but managed to choke it down.

My Portland friends were saying complimentary things:

What a dapper new boyfriend you have!

Looks like life in Misty Falls is treating you well.

Great to see your beautiful smile!

I hovered my thumb over the button to delete the photo but paused. Yes, it was macabre that I had taken a photo of myself with the snow-covered body, but it was also a great alibi, in case I came under suspicion. I wouldn't have posted the photo online if I were the killer. Or would I?

A new message popped up from my real estate agent, Samantha Sweet, whose use of exclamation points brought her blond perkiness to her online communications.

Samantha: *Thank you so much for meeting with me this morning! Very insightful! I will have some exciting new opportunities for you to look at within two weeks! In the meantime, I have found you the perfect tenant for your rental!*

I wrote back: *Send me the tenant's contact details and I'll set up an interview.*

While I waited for her response, I did some math in my head. I'd been planning to move over to the rental side for a few months while I renovated my side of the duplex, but if I got a tenant in immediately, the cash flow would more than compensate me for having to live with construction mess. This would mean going back to my original plan. Since buying the place, I'd changed my mind a few times, mainly because looking for a tenant had been disheartening. Between the troll-like fellow who showed up in a graphic T-shirt that boasted of his lovemaking prowess, and the pale girl who inquired how many days a week she could have her death metal band over to practice, I worried I'd never find someone I could share a wall with.

Samantha replied: *I've already interviewed the tenant and done a credit check! He's a very busy man, and he's looking at a few places, so we need to move fast! Should I show him the place tonight? He's a lawyer!*

A lawyer? That did warrant some exclamation points. He sounded like someone who wouldn't grow his own smoking herbs or be late with the rent check.

I returned her message: *Go ahead and show him the place.*

She texted back within seconds: *I'm so happy! When I meet him tonight for the in-person showing, I'll try to close the deal on the spot if that's okay with you! He's ready to move in right away. You won't regret this!*

My body tensed at her assurance I wouldn't regret this. It was all part of her sales technique, just the post-deal, feel-good stuff anyone with good training does, but it rubbed me the wrong way. A deal that offers itself up too easily should be thoroughly scrutinized. It's only human nature, a survival instinct, to be wary of anything that appears too good to be true. That was why, in my former career, I would often put an unreasonable clause or two into the first draft of an agreement. It gave the other party something to strike out, so they felt they were in control.

Samantha's offer to get me a tenant seemed too easy, and thus suspicious. But the money would help with cash flow for the upgrades, and, in light of the events of the day, it would be a relief to have one thing in my life taken care of by a professional.

I wrote back: *Go ahead. If you think he's the one, make the deal.*

I put my phone away and glanced over at Logan, who still appealed to my eyes, despite his scruffiness. He'd become engrossed by something on his phone, so he didn't see me scoping him out. His beat-up jacket had holes in the elbows, but it was spotlessly clean. He had the clothing of a working-class man, yet his body language didn't fit. He didn't cross his legs in a feminine manner the way I had, yet he didn't have the space-taking, wide-kneed body language I associated with the transient men employed by the local furniture factory. I wondered if he was on the run or undercover.

He saw something on his phone that excited him. "Yes!" He fist-pumped the air. "I got it."

A minute passed, and in the absence of an explanation, my curiosity grew until finally I asked, "Good news? You got a job?"

He gave me a broad grin, which took his good looks in a boyish direction, transforming him from handsome to downright adorable. "Even better," he said. "I've rented a great place. It's half a duplex in West Creek neighborhood. Is that a good area?"

Keeping my expression politely happy, I said, "Congratulations. Yes, it's a very nice neighborhood."

His chest puffed and he sat up straighter, evidently proud. "It's a steal, too. My cousin's a real estate agent, and she's got a total eccentric as her client."

My body grew numb, and my head got a disembodied, floating feeling. "Eccentric? What do you mean?" Part of me was sickly fascinated, wanting to know exactly what people in town were saying about me. "Never mind," I added. "That's between you and her, not my business."

Logan stretched out his arms along the backs of the empty chairs on either side of him, taking up more space by the minute, as though securing a deal on a rental had been the warm air he needed to inflate to full size. Now his knees widened until one was dangerously close to touching mine.

I reached for a nearby pamphlet and pretended to be fascinated by the life cycle of fleas.

"Maybe you know my new landlady," he said. "If you're from around here."

Without looking up from the flea drawing, I said, "I've been away for about ten years, so I'm not up on local news and gossip. Sorry."

"I think everyone in this town must know about this woman. She's practically famous. She was involved in some technology start-up companies, and she was headed toward becoming very wealthy, like seven figures, but she cracked under the pressure."

I swallowed hard. He wasn't far from the truth.

"And this woman is your new landlady?" I folded the flea brochure slowly. As the numbness in my body receded, I felt waves of shock, anger, defensiveness, and finally acceptance. It wasn't just Samantha Sweet who judged me by my reputation. People in town had talked about me for years, and even if a potential tenant hadn't heard about me through the grapevine, a quick internet search would reveal plenty. Short of changing my name, I would always need to deal with the repercussions of being Stormy Day. I could fight and make everything worse, or I could kill with kindness.

I set the brochure aside and turned to meet Logan's blue eyes. "She might be a wonderful landlady if you give her a chance."

He quirked one dark eyebrow and lifted his phone to show me the screen. "And she might be crazy. My cousin sent me the list of rules for the house. Look. The tenant is responsible for fifty-five percent of the electricity bill. Why not half? Why fifty-five percent?"

I pretended to look, even though I was familiar with the document I'd created. "Maybe the tenant's square footage is fifty-five percent of the house, and she's trying to be fair."

He laughed. "She sounds like one of those uptight Type A ladies. The kind who needs one good night with a real man."

My eyebrows raised so quickly, I nearly gave myself whiplash. "And you think you're the man for the job?"

He shrugged one shoulder. "Maybe she'll knock a few bucks off the rent if I do things right." He leaned toward me, as though asking for a punch in the stomach or at least a verbal response. When he didn't get either, he added, "I bet you the cost of your cat's treatment that after one night on my side of the house, Miss Spinster Type A Landlady will start ripping up my rent checks."

Logan was good at pushing buttons, but he didn't realize I was onto him. Logan was a lawyer and not the studious type who loved poring over contracts. He was a fighter who relished conflict, loved going head-to-head. He knew exactly who I was and was toying with me. Even now, his breathing was twice as rapid as mine, his pupils dilating to make his blue eyes appear black. I allowed myself the delicious pleasure of knowing he considered me a worthy adversary.

I waved my hand across him and said, "They say you ought to dress for the job you want, not the one you have. If you fancy yourself as a skillful rent boy, you ought to dress in a manner that reveals more assets or implies more class." I bit my lip and leaned back dramatically. "Or both."

He was mentally preparing his next missive when our conversation was interrupted by the veterinarian's assistant returning. I jumped to my feet, feeling light as helium from the rush of my exchange with Logan.

Natasha laid some papers on the counter between us. "Jeffrey's all checked in," she said. "His bachelor urges will soon be curbed. You'll still see the external appearance of his furry boy-parts after the surgery, but it's only skin that'll shrivel up because the insides have been scooped out."

Behind me, Logan said, "Ouch." I heard a chair squeak and imagined him crossing his legs in sympathy for the cat.

Natasha collected payment from me, and I filled in the paperwork for the cat's day surgery. I was signing the bottom of the form when the front door opened behind me. Someone came in, noisily stomping snow off heavy boots. It was another man, by the sound of him. He cleared his throat.

I turned to find a man bearing his Italian father's black hair and brown eyes, and his Mexican mother's bronze coloring. I knew his heritage and much more because I'd practically grown up with the guy. Officer Tony Milano had gone straight to the police academy after college and become my father's protégé not long after that. He'd acted like a protective older brother to me and my sister, except for when he hadn't.

"Tony Baloney," I said, using the nickname I knew he hated. "You've got a little something in your hair at the sides. Is that snow? It's really white, or is that gray? My mistake. That's not snow at all."

"Very funny," he said with no sign of mirth. "Get in my car. Now."

Logan, who'd been leafing through a cat magazine, got to his feet, looking concerned. "Is everything okay?"

Tony gave him a withering look. "Go about your business, citizen."

Logan stuck out his chest. "Citizen? I'm an attorney."

Tony snorted derisively. "Not with that beard, you aren't."

He took me by the elbow and firmly escorted me toward the door of the vet clinic. The air around him was cold, his hand like ice on my arm, even through my jacket.

On my way out, I gave Logan a quick wink. "See you around."

Logan said, "Do you need a lawyer? I can come with if you're being taken in for questioning." He held out a business card.

I didn't take the card. It was only Tony, and I could handle him fine on my own. However, as Tony jerked my arm and dragged me toward his car, I wondered if I hadn't misjudged the situation.

CHAPTER 6

CTENOCEPHALIDES FELIS, ALSO KNOWN as the common cat flea, has no wings, so it must use its legs to jump a staggering two hundred times its height to find a new host.

You'd think Officer Tony Milano would have appreciated some fun flea facts to brighten his day, but he did not. He barely acknowledged me as I described how newly-hatched fleas have only seven days to find a home or die. "And they can't exactly peruse the rental ads in the newspaper," I said.

He held open the passenger door of an unmarked police car. "Enough with the fun facts about fleas."

"You admit my facts are fun?"

"Get in the car, and stop talking about fleas. You're making my skin crawl."

I climbed in, buckled my belt, and tried to wait without fidgeting. From the grim set of his mouth to the unwavering edge of his voice, I could tell he was in the darkest of moods. He had good reason to be, considering that morning's events, yet his rigid manner bothered me, the way a scab you're not supposed to touch begs to be picked at, itching the more you try to ignore it. I wanted him to smile. I needed him to smile at me, the urge coming from somewhere deep and primal.

He slid into the driver's side. I immediately picked at his sore mood, saying in an upbeat, singsong tone, "Surprise, Tony Baloney. I'm back in town."

"So it would appear," he said. "I knew you were back. I heard all about it even before this morning."

"Did you hear the juicy rumor I was practically a big-city billionaire before I had a nervous breakdown?"

"What happens outside of this town doesn't concern me," he said, avoiding my question.

I glanced around the vehicle looking for any personal items of Tony's but found none. The vehicle wasn't marked, but had a steel and plastic barrier between us and the empty rear seat. The piercing scent of Pine-Sol wafted up from the back.

Tony hadn't started the engine yet. He checked his hair in the rearview mirror. "Never turn forty, Stormy. Your hair gets scared about the next milestone and turns white."

"I think it might be your two children doing that. Dad always blamed me and my sister for his white hairs."

"Three children," he corrected. "The baby should be sleeping through the night soon."

"Congratulations."

"You didn't know about the newest one, did you?"

I could have answered honestly and said no, but I said, "Adult fleas live four to twenty-five days."

He started the vehicle and steered toward the police station.

I crossed my arms and turned to the window, suddenly feeling younger than I had in a long time. Being around Tony did that to me. My dad started mentoring him when I was sixteen. Tony had been twenty-three, with cropped black hair and big brown eyes, always flexing those muscles he'd started building at the academy. To me, in his tight black T-shirts that showed off his powerful physique, Tony was bigger and better than every cute actor and singer rolled into one. I lived for those nights he came over to see my father because he'd always spend a few minutes chatting with me. I loved how he treated me like an adult, like an equal.

I had dreamed of dating him for ages, but when I finally had a chance at twenty-three, it was pretty much too late. I had my job offer in the city and was leaving the next week. We made the most of those five days, which were extra thrilling because we didn't want my father to find out. When the day came for me to leave, Tony was the one who drove me to the airport. I put on a brave face, but I couldn't wait to get out of the car and away from him, to cry in private. We promised to stay in touch, but then he got his new girlfriend pregnant and got married, and we didn't talk after that. I'd seen him over the last ten years, whenever I came home for the holidays, but only by accident.

"How old is Tony Junior?" I asked. "He must be about nine by now."

Tony grunted in response. After a moment, he said, "We'll have you over for dinner soon, I promise." He tapped the steering wheel in rhythm to a song only he could hear. Tony always drummed his fingers when he was thinking. My father used to give him a hard time over it, saying it was the outward sign of an undisciplined mind.

After a few more minutes, he said, "Why did you run from the crime scene?"

"Obviously because I'm the murderer, Detective Baloney."

"Don't call me that," he barked. "We're not kids anymore."

"Sorry." I crossed my arms tighter.

We drove for a few blocks in silence before he said, "I'm the one who's sorry. I should have come to that party at your dad's house when you got here. I meant to drop by, but I fell asleep on the couch." He stifled a yawn, which drew my attention to the dark circles under his brown eyes.

"You probably needed the sleep, what with having a new baby. I'm sure you've got your hands full."

"You have no idea," he said ominously.

"How did you know I was at the vet clinic? That was some good detective work."

He frowned and kept his eyes on the road. "I came from Warbler Street just now, where the mailman told me you were lugging a pet carrier. There are only two vets in town, so do me a favor and save the flattery for when I close this case."

"Will that be soon? I mean, you guys have a good idea who did it, right?"

"Sure," he said flippantly. "We'll just round up the usual suspects, the ones who are known to kill old geezers and stuff them inside lawn decorations."

I chewed my lip. Tony's sarcasm was not a good sign.

We reached the town's police station, where he pulled into a reserved parking spot. He turned off the engine and rested his forehead in his hands as though he had a terrible headache.

"Tony?" I reached over and put a hand on his shoulder. He wasn't wearing a jacket, and his dark blue uniform shirt was damp from the snow. I wanted to say something reassuring, but what came out was, "Where's your jacket?"

He rubbed his face and glanced back at my hand but didn't shrug it off.

"This is bad," I said. "I'm sorry if my running off from the scene has made things more difficult for you. I'll do whatever I can to help."

He let out a hopeless laugh. "Tell me who killed Murray Michaels, and I'll owe you one."

Brightly, I said, "I'll get right on that." I squeezed his shoulder. "You don't need me, Tony. You're a brilliant detective."

"Am I?" He shook his head and avoided my eyes. "Some citizens reported Mr. Michaels missing five days ago. It was the waitresses from his regular restaurant, concerned that he hadn't been around in a while."

"And you didn't do anything?"

"I went out with a locksmith to check the property. There were no signs of forced entry at his house, and I searched inside, expecting to find the old geezer in bed, or slumped over dead. He wasn't there, and the place appeared to be undisturbed, though it was hard to tell because he was a level one hoarder. The rooms were packed full, but pathways were clear and all the appliances were functional. I figured he must have gone on a trip, maybe a doctor appointment in the city. I told the waitresses he would turn up eventually, but I never expected anything like this."

"He was there at his house the whole time."

Tony let out a heavy-sounding breath. "Hidden in plain sight. In that damn snowman."

I squeezed his shoulder again. "You couldn't have known."

"But you knew, Stormy. You're a better detective than me. You're better than your father, but don't tell him I said that. He and I would both be the laughing stock of the whole town if they knew you were the one who cracked the Donut Heaven case. And you were only eighteen."

"Seventeen."

Groaning, he opened his door and got out of the car. My hand hovered in the air for a moment, where his shoulder had been.

"C'mon, kiddo," he said. "Let's get your statement."

I didn't want to get out of the car, let alone spend my afternoon in an interview room. I got out of the car slowly, closed the door, and leaned against the vehicle feigning exhaustion as I joked, "Can we hook ourselves up to the polygraph and ask each other a bunch of embarrassing questions?"

I watched his dour expression change to amusement. Victory. I could still put a smile on Tony's face, even if it was only a small one.

Two other uniformed officers, a man and a woman, walked slowly past, all eyes on me. The man, who had a thick mustache covering his upper lip, said something to the woman. She studied me with interest. He spoke quietly, but I heard him say,

"That's her, Wiggles. I told you so. Don't skimp on the sugar when you make my cookies."

Tony followed my gaze and barked at the two officers, "You two see something amusing?"

In unison, they said, "No, sir."

"How about my jacket? Did one of you think to bring that back?"

The woman answered, "I'll drive over and get it now."

Tony shook his head and pointed at the man. "Gomez, you go. Wiggles, I want you on this interrogation." He pointed right at me, caught the look of shock on my face, and corrected, "Interview, I mean. Wiggles, you're in charge of Stormy."

Then he barked at me to quit stalling and get my butt into the station.

CHAPTER 7

THE RED BRICK EXTERIOR of the police station hadn't changed since its construction, seventy years earlier. The inside, however, had bravely withstood many rounds of upgrades, including a few since the days I used to come in after school and help my father type reports. I had no clerical training at the time, but could type ninety words a minute without errors. I signed the same privacy agreements as the other secretaries, and my work was good enough that the captain offered to hire me straight out of high school if I chose not to follow through on my college plans. I didn't realize it at the time, but typing those reports and finding out what people were really like was the best education about life I could have gotten. My friends weren't impressed when I warned them away from activities I'd learned were dangerous, such as cramming too many people into a car, but at least we all lived to see graduation.

Tony walked me through the station, glancing around and frowning, as though seeing the interior through judging eyes.

"This old carpet's got to go," he said, referring to the swirling floor covering with the pattern that hid a multitude of sins. "Lots of old things around here have got to go."

The other officer lagged behind us, stopping to say something to a secretary. Tony snapped his fingers impatiently. "Rookie! Look lively."

She jerked to attention and brought up the rear so fast, the toes of her boots kicked the heels of mine. I felt her breath on the back of my neck as we reached an interview room. Tony flicked on the lights and waved us in ahead of him.

He caught the elbow of my coat as I walked by, and slipped me a business card as though he was giving me something secret. It was just his standard card, with a cell phone number written in blue pen. He'd crossed out the line reading In Case of Emergency, Always Call 9-1-1.

And then he was gone.

The woman stood by the door, awaiting his return. The fluorescent tube lights reached their full brightness, draping the windowless room in a sickly gray light.

"He's not coming back," I said. "You're stuck dealing with me."

She gave me a wary look as she made her way to one of the utilitarian plastic and metal chairs next to the equally plain interview room table. Like Tony, she wore a dark blue uniform under the matching winter jacket she shrugged off onto the back of the chair. She looked around fifty, or maybe older, but very fit, with angular facial features that made her cheeks appear hollow and gave the impression of her being thinner than she was. Her movements communicated strength and resiliency. Her eyelids, creped with delicate gathers at the edges, were the only feature that gave away her age. As I took my seat, her wide-set cobalt blue eyes made me feel watched and ignored at the same time.

She hadn't introduced herself but wore a brass nametag: Peggy Wiggles. The four lower-case g's created a distinctive, eye-catching pattern, mimicking the effect of seeing double. The name sounded as cartoonish in my head as it looked on the tag. Was it her real name, or a nametag one of the other officers had gotten her to wear as a prank? They did that sometimes, to initiate people. The brass tag looked new, with a single faint scratch on the diagonal, and not at all like an object kept around for games. It had to be her actual name.

Like I had with the nameless cat, I felt a surge of solidarity with Peggy Wiggles. We oddly-named people had to stick together. I was tempted to point out our commonality but held my tongue. I'd learned the hard way that some people with unusual names don't appreciate having that fact pointed out, and yet others are in complete denial, having never experienced their name through the ears of a stranger.

Her dark, cool blue eyes looked at me, through me, and then past me. The silence in the small room was intruded upon by male laughter coming from elsewhere in the building. "Gomez," she muttered under her breath, rising to close the door to the interview room.

As she returned to her seat, I asked, "Did I hear Tony say you're a rookie?"

She volleyed back, "Were you expecting someone younger?"

I was pretty sure that question didn't have a right answer. "I like your haircut," I said.

Her white-flecked brown hair was cut in the same short style as mine. At my compliment, she reached up and fluffed the back. "I used to wear it long. Only got it cut maybe once a year." She spoke as though answering questions about a case, her voice flat and her face betraying no emotion. She concluded, "Then I went for the buzz at the Academy and decided I like short hair."

"Me, too," I said. "Not the Police Academy part, but I recently went through some major life changes as well."

"Interesting," she said, her passive tone one degree shy of sarcasm. Apparently, the fifty-year-old rookie wasn't as interested as I was in finding points of commonality. She picked up a pen and clicked out the nib. "What led you to believe the body was inside the snowman?"

"Mainly the frozen head sticking out of the top."

She clicked the pen again and set it down on her blank notepad.

I added, "Really, you should ask the cat. He's the one who found it."

I saw her eyebrows move for the first time. "You have a cat?"

"No, it's not my cat. I was running an errand for my father's girlfriend."

Her eyebrows fell, along with her face. She seemed disappointed. I looked more closely at her uniform, spotting what appeared to be pet fur visible on her dark blue collar.

"His name is Jeffrey," I offered.

"Who?"

"The cat," I said. "He didn't have a name until today, but it's Jeffrey Blue."

She wrote the first two letters of his name on her notepad then stopped. She shifted her body, leaning forward with her elbows on the table, as though we were two friends meeting for coffee in a restaurant with a weirdly institutional decor.

"Stormy," she said calmly. "May I call you Stormy? There's no need to be nervous, but if you are feeling upset, I want you to know it's all right. You've had a troubling experience. My name is Peggy Wiggles, and I've been with the Misty Falls Police Department only a short time, but I can assure you, I've come to appreciate this town. I'm going to do everything I can to make sure the person who hurt your neighbor is apprehended and put away forever. Were you very close to Mr. Michaels?"

"What do you mean by close? He was right next door the whole time I was growing up, but he was kind of a misanthrope and not the lovable kind with the witty put-downs. He was the type who would confiscate your toys if they flew over the fence into his backyard."

"My ex was that type. I wouldn't be surprised if someday he winds up in a snowman."

"Really?" I leaned in, eager to hear more about the man I assumed was named Mr. Wiggles. How could you remain humorless with a name like that?

Officer Peggy Wiggles cleared her throat and straightened up, breaking the illusion we were friends at coffee. "Let's start from the beginning, shall we? Your address."

I gave her my address, which led into explaining how my father was the one who lived next door to

Murray Michaels. Her expression changed when she learned my father was Finnegan Day, as though that fact was a key piece of information she'd been seeking. She'd been hired after his retirement, so she hadn't worked with him, but was well aware of his reputation for being a hardworking officer who could have been captain, or even chief, but preferred to keep the exact same job he'd been hired for.

As we talked, I regretted giving her a hard time with my flippant answers at the start of our session. She was only trying to do her job, and couldn't have known how Tony's treatment had put me in a defensive, quippy mood. I meant to say something, to apologize, but she led me through her questions with ruthless efficiency.

She drilled out of me the exact time I'd woken up that morning and then all the events of my day, including my meeting with the real estate agent, picking up takeout coffee, working at my store, the visit from Pam and the resulting cat errand, plus the minute-by-minute details of the cat leading me to the snowman, me taking my picture next to it, and finally my attempts to straighten the snowman's face.

She paused and tapped her pen, flicking her cobalt blue eyes up to meet mine. "You have a photo?"

I pulled out my phone and showed her the picture I'd taken of my face next to the snowman's. "See how his face is a bit crooked? That's unusual, don't you think?"

She agreed the face was crooked and asked me to send a copy to her for the file. She excused herself from the room to get her laptop, leaving me alone long enough to consider going in search of a vending machine. I was rifling through my purse for coins when she returned. I dropped the bag guiltily. A man I'd known for years had been killed, and here I was, thinking about buying a Twix.

She set the laptop between us and brought up the enlarged picture. The goofy grin on my face made me groan and look away. She must have interpreted my horror as being about the case because she gave me a pat on the shoulder and said soothingly, "We're almost done, and you're doing a great job."

"Will the photo help?" I asked. "If there are other snowmen around town with the same face, they could lead you to the killer."

"I'm not sure a snowman's face is as useful as a fingerprint or handwriting sample, but we'll do our best. What's unusual about this snowman is how good it looks, despite being crooked. Almost as if a professional snowman-builder made it."

"If such a thing existed, we'd have this case cracked wide open."

She consulted her notes. "Did you see any other footprints in the snow when you approached the crime scene?"

"I don't remember seeing any, but then again I was focused on chasing the cat."

"How much force did you have to apply to break apart the head?"

"A fair amount. The snowman was constructed to be secure. I had to karate chop the neck to loosen it. Pretty hard."

"One chop?"

"Multiple chops."

"Right hand?"

"Yes. I'm right-handed."

"Amateur karate chop or professional?"

"I've taken some self-defense classes over the years, but I'm no black belt."

"Did the snowman have any scent? Any odor?"

"I don't think so."

"Did it have one of those corn cob pipes? Or a pipe of any kind?" We consulted the photo on the laptop screen, and she answered her own question. "No pipe."

She continued the interview, asking about my last encounter with the decedent, Murray Michaels. I had little to offer besides rumors. He'd shown up at my father's party to complain about the noise, coming in from the porch but not leaving the entryway. He'd not been a topic of conversation at the party before, but after the disruption, the gossip came out as though uncorked from a bottle by his visit. People mentioned how Michaels had become a nuisance to the local retail business owners and how they wouldn't be surprised if he showed up on one of those programs about hoarders, as well as how there was a slim possibility he was involved with a young waitress.

Officer Wiggles noted every detail of the gossip, the idle chatter that had been upgraded to possible evidence in a murder investigation. Once that was done, she looped back to the beginning, asking the same questions but worded differently. I had to admire her technique, which had two benefits: jogging the memory of a witness and providing the opportunity for a guilty party to slip up and contradict herself.

When she asked if I had any questions for her, I did. "Any word yet on the time of death, or the official cause?"

She pressed her lips together. “It’s still early. The coroner has barely gotten him loaded in the van, let alone thawed out. Besides, I couldn’t tell you even if I knew.”

I nodded. “He had marks around his neck. Dark lines, possibly ligature marks. I didn’t see any blood in the snow, so I’m guessing it was strangulation.”

Her metal chair squeaked as she sat back, giving me an appraising look. “How long were you examining the body before the mailman showed up?”

“A few seconds, at the most.” I glanced over at the photo on the computer screen and shuddered as I realized something. “Make sure the pathologist is told about the scarf. If Michaels was strangled, that red scarf could be the murder weapon.”

She nodded slowly. “I was thinking the same thing.”

“Were there any defensive wounds on the body? Tony already told me that on a prior visit to the home, he didn’t see evidence of any struggle.”

She raised one eyebrow. “Tony told you that, did he?”

With that question, the tone of the interview shifted, and the fifty-year-old rookie seemed to be observing me in a new light, not quite as someone on her side of the thin blue line but not as far away as a regular civilian, either.

Testing my theory, I asked, “Do you suppose he was strangled in his sleep?”

“If he’d been married or had a girlfriend, I’d be interviewing her right now and not you.”

That wasn’t much of an answer, but I pressed my luck, rising curiosity making me bold. “Do you have any other suspects? The mail carrier seemed anxious."

She smirked. "Funny. He said the same thing about you. He suggested you as a prime suspect."

"Great." I rolled my eyes. "That's just what my reputation in this town needs."

Her smile left her face as rapidly as it had appeared. "What sort of a reputation do you have, exactly?"

"Nothing to do with snowmen or murders, I assure you." I glanced at the door, willing it to open, and for Tony to tell us to pack up because the crime had been solved already. The door didn't open.

Officer Wiggles went over my details again, until I felt like a sponge that had been squeezed dry.

Based on her tone, I was almost certain she hated me until she set her pen aside and asked who cut my hair.

"Rose," I answered. "And she's great."

"I knew it," she said. "Rose gave us almost the same exact haircut."

"You wear it better than me."

Officer Wiggles chuckled, her voice warming the entire room. "Nonsense. Yours is much cuter, and fewer grays." She pushed her chair back but didn't rise. "Thanks so much for all your help, Stormy."

"Let me know if I can do anything else."

She eyed the closed door, leaning in to say softly, "If you think of anything at all, please let me know. Any time. For example, if you think of something, and you're worried that it might not be useful and you don't want to bother us, I want you to call me anyway."

"I'll let you know if I come up with anything."

She handed me her card and fixed me with her unwavering cobalt eyes. "Anything at all," she said, her voice almost pleading, as though her whole career was riding on closing this case. I took the card, which was damp, most likely from her palms. If she'd been nervous, she'd hidden it well.

As we walked through the station, I searched for Tony, but he wasn't in sight.

We passed the reception desk, where she thanked me again. I reached out to shake her hand, even though she'd been stepping away. She wiped her palm on her hip surreptitiously before the handshake, but it was still damp enough to confirm that underneath her tough exterior, she was nervous.

"You've been a big help," she said.

"I wish I could do more," I said, and I meant it.

As I stepped outside, into the fresh winter air, the sunshine reached through the clouds to brighten the snow-covered world. My mind was already way ahead of me, racing through possibilities and avenues to investigate. I didn't plan to do anything that would interfere with the official investigation, or jeopardize my safety, but I'd helped my father with cases before, and I had a few tricks up my sleeve.

Tony had driven me to the station, so my car was several blocks away, at the vet's clinic. With the afternoon sun low yet bright, the snow clouds were clearing and it was turning into a balmy day, perfect for some window-shopping along Broad Avenue, where local business owners who hadn't yet heard the news about Mr. Michaels might have some insight into how the man had become such a nuisance lately.

CHAPTER 8

IN SPITE OF the town's postcard-perfect appearance, a killer was loose in Misty Falls.

The body was likely headed to the state coroner's facilities the next town over for the pathologist to determine the cause of death. Pinning down the time from the physical evidence would be impossible, due to the freezing that had halted the body's decomposition. We'd been experiencing typical weather for late November, with the temperature hovering around or below freezing for the past few weeks. Tony had visited the residence of Mr. Michaels five days earlier to find no one, whereas I'd seen the man two weeks ago and very much alive. That left a nine-day window that would likely get narrowed once the police checked his phone, bank cards, or even something as simple as the date of the oldest flyer in his untouched mail. Unless they nabbed someone in the next day or two, they would release to the local press the basic details along with a plea for witnesses with information to come forward.

We didn't get many homicides in town. Unlike the law enforcement agencies in larger cities, ours didn't have dedicated homicide detectives. The case would be worked by uniformed officers who were cross-trained to handle almost any type of crime. A capital murder was shocking, yet the fact that a death was involved in a case didn't make the procedure of investigation significantly different from that of a theft or arson. The officers on the case, who I assumed would be Milano and his new rookie, would canvas the neighborhood and friends and family of the victim, and then follow up on leads. If everything went well, they'd have it solved by the time my father returned home.

At the thought of my father, I reached for my phone in a hurry, stopping when I checked the time. He would be out of surgery but not yet awake. Besides, he'd promised he would call as soon as he was alert. I'd tried to accompany him for the operation, but he'd insisted I stay behind to make sure my new gift shop was ready for the busy Christmas shopping season. Now, walking down Broad Avenue, I regretted obeying him. If I'd been in the city that morning, I wouldn't have made the grisly discovery. The body might have remained there, next door, undiscovered until the spring thaw.

Who would do such an awful thing? Who had a motive to wipe out Mr. Michaels? With no wife or girlfriend and no children going after his will or insurance money, that cut out the obvious leads. The killer could be anyone. The entire town of Misty Falls was populated with suspects.

Walking past Masquerade, I lurched to a stop in front of the costume rental store's window display.

The elaborate diorama was a festive winter scene, constructed on a base of white fabric acting as snow.

A female mannequin, wearing a red dress suitable for prom or an equally fancy affair, held a big, white, grinning head in her hands. The headless white body awaited the final touch. The snow-being was evidently a man and not a woman, because he wore a top hat. I fought my gag reflex and reminded myself that for most people, the scene before me was a happy one, the beheading aspect merely a coincidence. The shop owner would certainly change the window display once the news of Mr. Michaels' chilly tomb spread throughout town.

But was the winter diorama really just a coincidence? The display snowman, made of carved white foam, wore a black top hat like the one I'd posed in earlier that day. I used my phone to check the hat in my picture, noting the high, flat top, narrow brim, and the slightly concave curve to the crown. The hat in the window matched the one from the crime scene perfectly. I reached into my pocket and touched the two business cards I'd been given at the police station. Officer Peggy Wiggles had told me to call her with anything, but surely she didn't want to hear about this, the not-so-amazing discovery of a hat at a store that rented costumes and hats.

Without taking my eyes off the top hat in the window, I let my thoughts open themselves, unpacking childhood memories. Snapshots whirled, snippets of interactions with the man who'd lived next door, the man who'd seemed old long before he'd gotten old. I could see him clearly in my mind, confiscating everything from dolls to sticks of chalk. I saw Murray Michaels, his deep frown lines radiating across his entire face, like the rays of a dark sun. He was waving a Frisbee and telling me I should have thrown it more carefully. For someone so obsessed with manners, he'd been incredibly rude. That wasn't shocking, given human nature. Some people become so obsessed with keeping score on the transgressions of others that they forget to observe themselves.

The cranky neighbor wasn't the type to have a snowman on his lawn, let alone such a dapper-looking one. He had never, as far back as I could remember, put up winter lights or any other seasonal decorations. He didn't even give away candy on Halloween. One year, he set a stack of old paperback Westerns on his front step along with a sign telling kids to help themselves. Nobody did.

If he'd purchased the top hat himself, something else must have happened to him this November, before he met his end. Had the message from the many Scrooge-themed movies airing that time of year finally gotten through to him, making his wizened heart grow three sizes? Had he decided to change his ways and discover his fun side, starting with building a snowman? Maybe.

Or, if Mr. Michaels didn't buy a fancy top hat for a holiday display, the killer did. Either way, there weren't many places in town to buy a top hat, so it must have come from the costume and formalwear store before me.

I stood debating my next move, unseen forces pulling me in opposing directions. Indecision wasn't a familiar state for me, but there I was, stuck to the snowy sidewalk as though my legs had been frozen in place. If I kept walking toward the vet clinic and my car, I could be home with my feet up and a hot cup of cocoa in my hands by the time my father called to check in. I'd tell him I'd wisely left the sleuthing to the police, and he'd say something ridiculous to make me laugh. On the other hand, I could just pop into the costume shop for a minute and save the police some time.

A woman and her two daughters crossed the street and started walking toward me. The girls were teenagers, old enough to be independent, yet they both held their mother's hands. The three of them laughed and chatted happily. They wouldn't be smiling tonight, after hearing the day's news. The mother would turn off the radio or the TV and usher the sisters off to bed, assuring them that all would be safe, all would be taken care of by the brave men and women who kept their town safe. But the girls would lie awake in their beds, worrying, watching shadows cross the ceiling, imagining knitted scarves tightening around their throats.

The three walked past me and toward the inset door for Masquerade, merrily discussing costumes.

Something flicked on within me. The flame was small, like the pilot light of a furnace. But when I imagined the killer making one of the members of this innocent family into the next victim, my internal fire flickered up to a medium heat.

My boots didn't move yet, but my body leaned in one direction and then the other. I could do nothing, or I could do something. With people's lives and happiness at stake, how could I do anything less than everything I could?

I followed the trio into the costume shop.

CHAPTER 9

ENTERING MASQUERADE FELT like being swallowed by a whale made of glitter. Within the warm, dim space, racks of costumes covered every vertical surface, taking away the very idea of walls, let alone their angle or color. As my eyes adjusted, details popped into focus, from the flamingo-like feather boas to the shimmering reptilian scales of a display dedicated to sequins.

I spotted the familiar cheerleading supplies and went to them, leaning forward to smell the pompoms as though they were pink chrysanthemums. They smelled of plastic and dust.

"Can I help you with anything?" asked the man working behind the counter. He was so tall and thin; he seemed to be standing sideways even though he wasn't.

"Just browsing." I ducked behind a rotating carousel rack of sequined costume ball masks. I looked high and low for more top hats but couldn't spot any other than the one in the window. If I wanted information, I would need to use that powerful investigative tool, the question. I picked out a glittering purple mask with green feathers and brought it to the counter.

"You're not browsing," the thin man said.

"I'm not?" My heart started pounding. The tall man had long fingers, perfect for strangling. His deep-hooded eyes narrowed behind a pair of rectangle-shaped glasses that accentuated the length of his thin face.

"Looks to me like you found what you were seeking." He offered a thin-lipped smile, flicking his dark, deep-set eyes toward the other customers. His angular chin elevated, he asked, "And how are you lovely ladies? Finding your heart's desire?"

Oblivious to the thunderous pounding of my heart, the woman answered that she was fine and continued to shop, sorting through a rack of ballerina costumes. One of her teen daughters held a phone in her hand and stared at me with round eyes, like a baby owl. Had she gotten the bad news already?

The thin man clicked on a keyboard with skeletal fingers. "Still snowing out there?" he asked.

"The snow's letting up now." I meant to set the feathered mask on the counter, but my body disobeyed; I took a step back, clutching the mask to my chest. The man was familiar, a long-time Misty Falls resident. I knew his name but couldn't think of it because my imagination was too busy picturing his long fingers in action, wrapping a red scarf around people's throats before choking them.

"You can hang onto that if you like," he said, nodding at the mask clutched to my chest like a tiny, glittering shield. "I know the code for those masks by heart." He tapped away at his keyboard as he hummed a tune, the sort of tune that would be a perfect accompaniment for strangling someone.

What was his name? He'd owned the costume shop for years and used to come to the high school often, delivering uniforms. We girls called him something that was both cruel and funny. Creepy Jeepers. We called him Creepy Jeepers because his long-fingered hands moved like spiders, and his real name was something similar.

I set the mask on the counter, glad to have the counter between us, though with the height of him, he could have easily reached those long arms across to strangle me. What was his name? And what had possessed me to go barging around town looking for leads on a murder case? Unlike the police, I had nothing for self-protection snapped to my belt, and the scariest thing inside my purse was an unflattering orange shade of lipstick.

"I'm glad the snow's let up," he said. "It's a balmy day out there. Perfect for building a snowman."

"A snowman?" My mouth got sticky, but the opening was too good for me not to press on with my original goal. "Funny you should mention a snowman. I was just outside admiring your window display. Do you arrange that yourself, or is there someone you hire, and if so, do they use your materials or supply their own?"

His tongue darted out between his thin lips, wetting them. "You ought to know all about that, Miss Day."

Miss Day? The way he pronounced my name, it sounded as though he was saying "mistake." The thought occurred to me that perhaps he was right, and coming into the store seeking clues had been a mistake. The woman shopping with her daughters called out a polite goodbye and left the store, leaving me alone with Creepy Jeepers. At least his real name finally came to me.

"Leo Jenkins," I said. "Remind me. Why would I know all about your window displays?"

He pulled off his rectangular eyeglasses, leaving scarlet indentations on the bridge of his fine nose. He started cleaning the lenses with a handkerchief.

"Pam Bochenek does my window displays," he said. "She's a crafty woman, that Pam. She's living with your father, isn't she?"

"Oh, of course. Yes, she's living with him, temporarily, I think."

"You think?" Eyebrows in the shape of two flattened bugs rode up, bunching the waxy skin of his forehead. "I hope she gives you a discount on her work."

"She offered," I said vaguely. My father's girlfriend had been hounding me to let her create the displays for my gift shop, but I'd done everything myself, claiming I needed the practice. Pam had a strong work ethic, but her taste was a bit off. She couldn't tell the difference between things that were so unusual they were cute, like certain breeds of wrinkly pets, and things that were just ugly, like the orange lipstick she'd gifted me with the week before.

Leo Jenkins said, "In fact, Pam was by here earlier this morning to say hello and chat about this and that." He tilted his rectangular head to the side and donned his equally rectangular glasses. "If you ask me, your new haircut is charming. It really suits your features. You've grown up so much since your cheerleader days."

"Thank you." I ruffled the hair at the back of my head. It would take a while longer to get used to small-town life and everyone knowing everyone else's business, not to mention being around people who remembered me as a cheerleader. Those had been busy days, between my studies and after-school activities. I'd also been in the school band, so I'd seen a lot of Leo Jenkins for the uniforms.

"How long has it been?" I asked. "You've had this store forever, it seems. The last time I saw you must have been fifteen years ago."

He leaned forward in a formal bow, nodding his head down to show me the gleaming, fleshy top of his head. "Back when I had hair up here. The good ol' days, as they say."

"But you're so tall, nobody sees the top of your head, anyway."

He straightened and beamed a wide, skeletal grin at my compliment as he rang up my purchase. I handed over my credit card and became the owner of a purple and green feathered masquerade mask I didn't need.

He asked, "How are things at the gift shop since you took over? I got a postcard from Rhonda. She's enjoying her world tour on that big cruise ship."

"Good for her," I said. "The store must have been a lot of work when she ran it herself. It couldn't have been easy running the place with no computerized inventory system whatsoever."

Jenkins widened his eyes, eager for me to spill juicy details about the former owner of Glorious Gifts, a chatty woman named Rhonda Kennedy—no relation to the famous family. As he waited, I felt a tug of emotion, the compulsion to bond. We had twenty years between us, but now we were the same, both of us store owners. Part of me wanted to befriend Creepy Jeepers, buying gossip credit by sharing Rhonda Kennedy's creative methods for cooking the books to avoid the tax collector, but I bit my tongue. The town already had plenty to talk about when it came to me.

Jenkins tucked my purchase into a bag. He pointed one long thumb in the direction of a corkboard on the back wall behind the counter.

"There's the postcard Rhonda sent me," he said. "Alaska."

The store's whale-belly lighting was brighter near the counter, but I still had to lean in to get a good look. The corkboard contained more than one layer of paper memories, from postcards and business cards to printed-out emails with photos of smiling customers in costumes and formal wear.

Rhonda Kennedy's postcard from Alaska featured icebergs under a full moon. Below the postcard, in the lower right corner of the corkboard, was a straight row of photos of individuals, posed for what appeared to be mug shots. The image on the far right was a picture of Mr. Murray Michaels, chin up in defiance, eyes glowering at something unseen, off to the side of the photographer.

I asked innocently, "What event are those photos from? Gosh. They look like mug shots."

Jenkins shifted a calendar down to cover the row of photos. "I'm afraid that's not for customers to see."

"But I'm not just a customer. I'm a local business owner. That's your Wall of Dishonor, isn't it? Shoplifters?"

"Yes, I'm sorry to say that's exactly what it is." With a robotic stiffness, he turned back toward the corkboard. His long fingers scuttled like the legs of a spider as he lifted the calendar back up to let me have a look. "Keep an eye on these ones if they start spending a suspicious amount of time inside your store."

"The lady with the platinum hair is married into the Koenig family, isn't she? That woman could buy the whole block and have money left over. What's she doing shoplifting?" I pointed to her shame-faced image while keeping my eyes on Mr. Michaels.

"Some do it for the thrill," Jenkins said. "This one's husband always pays for what she takes. I suppose I could let her come and go, but lately she hasn't even been trying to hide what she's doing. I can't let people carry on like that without doing something, without any punishment. It's the principle of the thing."

"I'll keep an eye out for her." I leaned in, squinting theatrically. "I think that's my dad's neighbor over there on the end. What did he steal?"

"This and that."

"Men's clothes? Maybe a hat?"

Eli Jenkins brought his spider fingers to his face and stroked his sharp chin. "He may have helped himself to one of my top hats, but I can't be sure."

"A top hat is kind of a large item to shoplift. Did he simply put it on and walk out? I don't suppose you have cameras in here, do you?"

"No cameras. The hat disappeared on a day I was trying out a new employee, and the girl might not have recognized him from the board." His long fingers curled into a fist, which he shook emphatically. "That was an expensive hat, too. I've half a mind to hold Murray upside down by the ankles and shake him until everything comes loose. He's gone too far."

"Did you report him to the police?"

"Not worth their time," he said. "Have no fear, though. Karma will catch up to the bugger. One of these days he'll snap up something he shouldn't, and he'll be sorry."

I made a non-verbal noise of sympathy. Taking my response as a cue to expand on the theme of vengeance, he let out a torrent of noise, some of it colorful, about shoplifters and the difficulties of maintaining a retail business. I listened, nodding. It wasn't difficult to feel pity for Leo Jenkins, who, from appearances alone, seemed to be going through a rough patch. He'd always been skinny, but fifteen years ago he could have been described as lanky, or even athletic. At my high school, some of the oddball girls seemed to be fond of the costume supplier, especially the girls with the experimental hairstyles and piercings. They also called him Creepy Jeepers but in an affectionate way, and a few cried in disappointment when he got married.

While he ranted, I checked the spider fingers of his left hand to see if the marriage had lasted. His ring finger bore no wedding band, but an indentation sat where one would have been. I noted that a marital breakdown could have caused his bitter mood, while living as a bachelor and cooking for himself could have caused his weight loss.

He finally stopped ranting about shoplifters and removed his glasses again so he could rub the creases around his deep-set eyes. "I apologize for my outburst," he said softly. "I've been under a lot of stress lately."

"Winter is tough," I said with matching softness. "The days are short and cold, but spring will come."

"Spring. Yes. When everything melts." He got a faraway look. "I need to do some spring cleaning."

"You could have a garage sale," I offered. "It always makes my father so happy to see the signs up for garage sales because he enjoys commenting about how people spell the signs wrong and forget the letter B."

Jenkins emitted something akin to a laugh. "How is your father?"

"Exactly the same."

"Good health?" he asked.

"Along with a brand new hip, yes."

"Good," he said with a weak smile. "Too many things change these days. People are under the delusion that all change is an improvement. But what's the word for a change that isn't an improvement?"

"In the corporate world, they say restructuring instead of layoffs."

"Life is full of restructuring." He shook his head ruefully. "The things they shove down our throats these days."

My gaze flitted from his bare ring finger to a pile of paperwork, most likely waybills and invoices.

"True," I said with a sympathetic note as I picked up the little shopping bag and tucked it into my purse along with my wallet. "See you around," I said, hoping otherwise.

He forced out another toothy smile. "Always a pleasure, Stormy Day."

"You, too," I said, finishing with a silent Creepy Jeepers.

He gave me a limp wave as he turned to busy himself with his computer.

I turned to leave, making my way out of the bejeweled whale's belly and back onto the sidewalk, where the plainness of the cloudy sky stretched out overhead like an endless scroll of paper for my thoughts. I glanced around until my eyes stopped at one of the town's landmarks, a circular mirror situated at the corner of Broad Avenue and Bergamot Street. Watching my reflection grow larger, I walked toward the round mirror.

A top hat was nothing to kill someone over. Stealing someone's wife, however, was another story. Because of the ring indentation on his bare finger, I imagined the restructuring Leo Jenkins was having shoved down his throat had something to do with his marriage. Had Mrs. Jenkins been seeing someone new? I wanted to dig deeper for a connection between Leo's wife and Murray Michaels. An affair would explain some of Leo Jenkins' agitation. Then again, if he'd actually killed someone, ranting about the victim to anyone who dropped into the costume store was not the smartest way to let off steam, unless, of course, he was doing so as a smoke screen, to make himself appear innocent by looking too guilty.

The possibilities were endless and utterly, breathlessly exciting. I could barely wait for my father to call so I could tell him everything. In the meantime, I would seek more information by stopping in to see the person who kept her thumb on the pulse of the town. She was on the other side of the round mirror, and I couldn't shake the eerie feeling she'd be expecting me.

CHAPTER 10

EVERY SMALL TOWN has a person whose job makes them an expert on everyone's love life. In Misty Falls, that expert was Ruby Sparkes, the owner of Ruby's Treasure Trove, located at the corner of Broad Avenue and Bergamot Street.

Before entering the store, I checked myself in the building's round mirror, where I couldn't help but smile, despite the day I'd been having. The mirror had that effect on people, and not just because the natural outdoor light was universally flattering. The mirror's circular surface was surrounded by a decorative mosaic made from colored bits of broken tile, dishes, marbles, doll figurines, toy robots, and even a few sturdy firetrucks. Amidst the swirling toys and colors were letters spelling out positive words and phrases, including JOY and LOVE and YOU LOOK SUPER TODAY!

Still smiling at the wall's compliments, I turned the corner onto Bergamot Street, stamped the snow off my boots, opened the glass door, and stepped into Ruby's Treasure Trove.

The store interior was brightly lit by a multitude of spotlights, overhead and within the glass-enclosed cases. A fortune in precious metals and stones stretched out upon sand-colored cloth and pale brown risers, as though a pirate's chest of treasure had busted open at sea and washed up on velvet shores.

Ruby stood behind a jewelry counter with a young blond woman I guessed was her employee, since Ruby had no children. They both greeted me, though no sound came out of the young worker's mouth.

Cheerily, I asked, "How's the delightful Ruby Sparkes today?"

She held one hand to her heart and fluttered her eyelashes. "You remember me!"

"Who could forget the most fun lady in all of Misty Falls?"

Ruby Sparkes tipped back her head and let out a big laugh, not denying my label. Ruby was an energetic woman of sixty-something, with curly hair colored a purple-red shade between auburn and grape soda. She had a friendly voice, a warm smile, and the kind of bosom you want your face crushed into if you're feeling blue. She always wore purple, unless she wore leopard print. Today was a leopard print day, and she looked as fun as ever in a brown-spotted blouse paired with purple slacks.

Ruby came out from behind the counter, beaming and looking as if she might hug me. "Stormy Lou-Anne Day! You've become such an elegant young woman."

"Elegant?" I looked down at my utilitarian ski jacket, casual jeans, and old boots.

"You also look like you need a hug." She grabbed me and pulled my face down to the top of her leopard-spotted bosom. Her hug felt every bit as good as it had when I was a kid. It was a shame my father had no interest in women his own age, let alone older women, or Ruby might have played a bigger role in my life.

She cooed, “I love your short hair. It’s so spunky. Let me look at you.”

From her chest, I said, “You’ll have to let me go first.”

With a burst of laughter, she released me and took a good look at me, from head to toe.

“I haven’t seen you since your grand re-opening of Glorious Gifts,” she said. “I popped in and out before we could speak. I hope you slowed down and ate some of those mini cupcakes I brought. You’re too thin, honey.”

“I ate a few,” I said.

“There’s that lovely smile of yours. You were always such a sweet little girl. I remember when your father used to bring you into the shop every year on your birthday to pick out something special.”

“I still have all those gifts,” I said. “Every single one.”

“Your father always felt so bad he couldn’t pick what you’d like all by himself, but I dare say you enjoyed the shopping trip even more than the trinket, didn’t you?”

I smiled fondly at the memories. “You sure are good at figuring out everyone in this town, Ruby.”

She patted her huge, purple-red curls with a ring-covered hand. “I keep an eye on things.”

The young woman behind the counter knocked over a bottle of cleaning spray with a clatter. “Sorry! Sorry! Sorry, Miss Ruby!” She righted the bottle, knocked it over again, and let out another torrent of apologies.

Ruby said, gently but firmly, "Hayley, less talking about cleaning and more actual cleaning."

The girl, who looked young enough to belong in high school on a weekday, jumped into action, polishing the glass display counters. She paused only to push a strand of honey-colored hair from her sweaty brow.

"Don't mind the new girl," Ruby said to me. "She's as skittish as a baby colt born on a frosty day, but she'll train up fine." In a conspiratorial tone, she added, "If I don't break her first."

Having Ruby speak to me as a peer was new, but I rolled with the change, joking right back, "Don't break her. Christmas is coming. You'll need all hands on deck."

"Let's hope it's a busy one," she said. "What can I do for you today? Picking out something for your equally lovely sister? Will she be home for the holidays?" Without waiting for answers, she led me to a display of earrings. "These delicate ones are perfect for small ears." She pointed to one pair in particular, which were miniature roses.

As usual, Ruby knew exactly what suited someone's taste. The earrings were perfect for my sister, but I needed more time for my secret mission, so I pretended to be unsure. We spent twenty minutes looking over the displays and chatting about business in general before I got my opportunity to inquire about Creepy Jeepers.

Ruby was talking about town spending on Broad Avenue, saying, "And of course, Leo Jenkins didn't see the point of putting up banners on the lantern poles because he didn't want to see the lights changed in the first place."

"How is he doing?" I asked. "I bumped into him on my way here, and he didn't look well. Is there trouble with his wife, that you know of?"

Ruby answered with a brusque, "He's a bit old for you, honey."

I felt my cheeks flush. Asking about someone's marriage didn't come naturally to me, and I'd oversold my concern for the man.

"I'm not asking for myself," I said. "Just worried about the guy, and you always know what everyone's up to. You're so connected, and people open up to you. I bet you could name off which couples are getting engaged next month."

"I do know things," she said cryptically.

"About Creepy Jeepers?" I asked. "I mean, Leo Jenkins."

"Something's up with Jenkins," Ruby said, nodding as her expression grew serious. She glanced over at her employee, who was leaning against the back wall with her eyes closed and her mouth slack, dozing off with a cleaning cloth still in one hand.

I could have made a joke about the employee being broken already, but Ruby seemed to be on the verge of sharing something, and I didn't want to break the spell of whatever magic was happening between us.

She patted her purple-red curls and pursed her lips thoughtfully.

"What is it?" I prompted.

She held up one finger and pulled out a phone, which she consulted with a troubled expression. The phone was small and blue, whereas the one she'd checked three times while showing me earrings had been larger and in a black case.

She glanced up. “You can keep a secret,” she said.

It sounded more like a statement than a question, but I answered anyway. “Yes.”

“May I show you something that must stay between us?”

“Yes,” I answered, perhaps a little too quickly.

A slow smile spread across her face, as though she was about to share some forbidden pleasure with me.

She turned to the sleeping girl and barked, “Hayley, look lively!”

Hayley startled and nearly fell over but recovered and got back to cleaning.

Ruby gave me a knowing look and nodded for me to follow her, behind the jewelry counter and through a door. We were in the stock room, but before I could get my bearings, suddenly I was in her arms again, being crushed against her fragrant and ample bosom. This time she patted my back, as though I was a baby in need of burping.

“You poor dear,” she said as she continued whacking my back in a manner that was surprisingly soothing.

“Poor me?”

“That must have been such a ghastly surprise,” she said. “Finding that sad man’s frozen body.”

My voice muffled against the ruffles of her leopard print blouse, I said, “You heard the news, then.”

“Poor, poor thing, and you’re putting up such a brave front. Don’t worry, honey. I have more of those mini cupcakes. They’re so small; you can’t say no.” She pulled away and looked into my eyes. “Ready for the secret?”

I swung my arm in a chipper gesture of readiness. "Ready as I'll ever be."

"This way, all the way to the back," she said, leading me past stock room shelves stacked with cardboard boxes. We reached another door, where she gave me the eager look again, before opening it and ushering me through.

I found myself smack in the middle of a brightly-lit fancy tea room, with striped yellow wallpaper, prints of flowers in gilded frames on the walls, a lush tapestry carpet on the floor, and sparkling crystal chandeliers overhead.

Most people wouldn't be shocked to find themselves inside a tea room, but I was speechless because I knew Misty Falls didn't have a tea room.

CHAPTER 11

STANDING INSIDE THE impossible room, I understood how Alice must have felt when she jumped down the rabbit hole and floated her way into Wonderland. The window looked out onto the sidewalk of Broad Avenue. I must have walked by it a thousand times. How had I never noticed the adorable little tea room in the back of Ruby's Treasure Trove?

"Sit!" Ruby Sparkes commanded as she plopped me into a chair next to a round bistro table. "I'll be back with your hot tea in two shakes of a lamb's tail."

The nook was big enough for three small tables and comfortable seating for nine people, or a dozen if they were good friends. The window was framed by puffy floral curtains, and the wall before me was richly decorated with silver platters, watercolors of dogs wearing ribbons, antique bundt pans, souvenir baby spoons from around the world, and ceramic busts of cats dressed as people, including a grey feline who resembled Jeffrey, if Jeffrey wore a fisherman's hat.

I turned to the window and watched as Leo Jenkins emerged from his costume store across the street. He appeared to be closing for a late lunch, or closing early for the day, locking the door. He walked to the corner, where a dark-haired lady on a mobility scooter, my employee's grandmother, was talking to a fair-haired young woman who held her hand to her mouth. Jenkins joined in the conversation, and they remained there while the intersection's traffic lights changed and then changed again. I had no way of knowing what they were talking about, but it wasn't difficult to imagine word of the death of Murray Michaels had spread.

The traffic lights changed again, and on the third walk signal, the woman on the scooter rode away. The blonde swayed in place, looking stunned. Jenkins offered his arm and gestured across the street. She hesitated and then timidly took it, and the two of them crossed the street together. Both of them walked directly toward me.

I raised my hand and gave a friendly wave through the window. He looked right at me but didn't return the gesture. He continued, his thin frame, clad in black, cutting a dark line against the view, like the streak of dark ink that sometimes mars a postcard once it's come through the mail.

The girl he'd crossed the street with, a blonde in her early twenties, looked right through me, as though I was a ghost. She let go of his arm and dug around in her purse. She leaned in toward me and applied a coat of too-dark lipstick to her full lips.

I let out a giddy laugh, embarrassed on her behalf because she didn't know I was there but more embarrassed for myself because it had taken me so long to figure out the secret of the window. I flicked the puffy floral curtains to the side to be sure, finding round edges instead of square.

Jenkins and the blonde weren't looking through me; they were looking at themselves, in what they imagined was a regular mirror. I'd never noticed Ruby's secret tea room because it was hidden in plain sight, behind what some people call one-way and others call two-way glass. In all my days enjoying the round reflection, I'd never thought to test it by putting my finger on the surface and measuring the gap in the reflection to see if it was non-existent, the way it was in the observational windows at the police station.

Unaware they were being watched, Jenkins turned to the girl and said something. I couldn't hear him through the glass. He didn't look happy, or sad, or much of anything except hungry. The blonde, however, looked miserable, blinking back tears with red-rimmed eyes. After a stiff nod at him, she continued fixing her makeup, drawing brown eyeliner across the base of pale lashes.

The girl was in her twenties, and other than her dark lipstick and a tiny loop of gold in her pierced nose, she was dressed conservatively, in dark green slacks, a cream blouse, and a brown leather jacket. The pants and blouse seemed familiar, like a uniform, though I couldn't place from where. She was pretty enough to attract attention but not so pretty as to catch trouble. As she studied her face on the other side of the glass, I tried to look away, but the anguish in her eyes drew me in. She rubbed the eyeliner off with her finger and started over, moving slowly, her gaze flicking between her reflection and the spaces over her shoulders, behind her. She seemed to be watching for someone who might be coming after her.

"I wonder what's going on there," said Ruby, startling me at her quiet arrival. She set a tray of tea and miniature cupcakes on the table.

I whispered, "Can they hear us? Or see us?" Jenkins was still there, focused on what seemed to be a broken zipper on his dark jacket.

"Triple-paned," she said. "And nobody can see in during the day. You could sit here naked if you wanted, though I wouldn't recommend it since the crumbs would fall into crevices unmentionable." She picked up a mini cupcake and grinned. "There's a dark shade under the valance, and I pull that down if I'm working back here with the lights on after sunset."

Meanwhile, Jenkins and the blonde were walking away, heading in separate directions.

"Are those two an item?" I asked. "If I'm too young for him, that blonde is all kinds of too young."

Ruby stroked the diamond-encrusted gold chunk of jewelry hanging from her necklace. "Leo's harmless. He's like my old terrier who used to bark at everything but wouldn't know what to do if he caught so much as a mouse." She settled into the seat across the small table from me and poured us both tea. "Leo's wife keeps him on a short leash, just like I did with my Peppy. As far as we know, they're still quite happily in love. God bless 'em."

"He wasn't wearing his wedding band today," I said. "Things change."

Ruby nodded as she stirred the milk into her tea. "He might be getting the ring resized. If it's important to you, we can ask around."

"We? Who do you mean by we?"

"Isn't the view marvelous?" Ruby gushed, ignoring my question. "I could watch all day. I love it when people come out of the bagel shop and stop right here, like clockwork, to check their teeth for poppy seeds."

"You love that?" I chuckled and sipped my tea politely.

"It just makes me laugh how predictable people are. Watch."

She pointed to a dark-haired man exiting the bagel shop next door. Tony Milano, in uniform but still without his jacket, walked toward us. I smiled and waved back as a reflex, even though he couldn't see me. He leaned in and bared his teeth, revealing three dark poppy seeds that he removed with his thumbnail.

Ruby said, "See what I mean?"

I laughed and covered my eyes with my hand. After all the shock and hassle of the morning, it felt good to find something amusing. When I removed my hand, Tony was gone.

A bell rang somewhere nearby. We had a similar bell in the stock room at the gift shop, to let us know a customer had opened or closed the front door.

Ruby pointed to the two-way glass again, at a group of women who were dressed for a yoga class. "What do you think of this trend? Not much left to the imagination." She didn't wait for my opinion before telling me what she thought of the younger generation's fashions. I half-listened, distracted by the sounds from the front of the store, of a woman arguing with Ruby's employee.

I interrupted Ruby's opinions about leggings to ask, "Do you need to check things at the front? For store security?"

She waved one hand at the nearby door. "Not really. Everything of value is locked inside the cases, safe and sound."

"So, you never have any problems with shoplifting?"

"Never," she said emphatically. "Why do you ask?"

"Honestly? I'm curious about Murray Michaels and why someone might put him inside a snowman."

She made a tsk-tsk sound and shook her head. "It's very odd. That killer, whoever it was, is not the saltiest ham in the deli. If it had been me, I would have made it look like an accident or suicide. But nobody gets themselves inside a snowman by accident. What was the killer thinking?"

"They might have been storing the body there, planning to move it before the spring melt." As I spoke, Leo Jenkins' comment about needing to do some spring cleaning echoed in my mind.

"Cold storage," Ruby murmured, shuddering. "Perish the thought. But why?"

I leaned in, even though we were alone in the private tea room. "Rumor is, he was a bit of a kleptomaniac, going around town stealing things for kicks. Jenkins has his mugshot up on his bulletin board at Masquerade, and he also had some creative ideas about inflicting bodily harm. I wonder if Mr. Michaels wasn't killed for taking something he shouldn't have."

She sipped her tea delicately as she leveled her eyes at me. “We knew all about the man’s shoplifting. It was perfectly harmless, more of an irritation than a crime. If Jenkins got excited, it’s because the man’s excitable.”

“So, Murray Michaels hadn’t gotten klepto with other people’s wives?”

She continued sipping. “Honey, some people don’t like coffee, and some people don’t like tea. Murray Michaels was the kind of guy who didn’t like people, not even the softer, fairer sex.” She waved a bejeweled hand. “His loss.”

“Was he ever married?” I asked. “I don’t remember anyone but him living in his house, but maybe he has family from before I was born?”

“Never married,” she answered.

I raised my eyebrows. “Confirmed bachelor?”

“He did make one final push for a wife. Oh, it was ages ago, twenty-five years. He even asked me on a date, but I was in mourning at the time. I told him to try again in a year, but he never did, thank goodness because I do hate to lie.”

I glanced down at my tea, sparing her my eye contact briefly. “You were in mourning? I’m sorry to hear that, Ruby. I didn’t know you were married.”

“I wasn’t,” she said with a laugh. “But when my dear little terrier Peppy went to the other side, I spent a year in dark colors, in a dark mood. Then Peppy came to me in a dream and said he’d noticed I was sad. He wanted to cheer me up, but he had too much business going on up there in heaven, too many things to bark at, so he was sending one of his friends to look after me. A minute later, I woke up in my bed, with a leopard sitting on my chest." She patted the top of her bosom. "I thought I was dead."

I sat up straight and met her eyes. "A leopard?"

She nodded gravely. "Then I woke up again, for real, and it was gone. I didn't think much of the dream again, until a week later, when I saw a beautiful leopard-print blouse on sale and had to buy it. Since that day I haven't spent another moment in mourning, no matter what happens."

I sighed. "Because life's too precious."

She smirked. "Because my heart can't take another well-intentioned visit from one of Peppy's friends."

A banging sound came from the front of the shop. The raised voices had stopped. The shy employee came into the nook and hovered near the door.

"Are we closing early today?" the girl asked. "Out of respect for the, um, gentleman?"

"He wasn't exactly the mayor," Ruby said. "We're all shaken up, but closing early won't help matters much."

The employee wrung her hands as her eyes darted between me and Ruby. "I guess I'll clean the front windows again."

Ruby replied, "Speaking of cleaning, did you jiggle some of the security camera cables when you were dusting the ceiling? Something came unplugged, and we lost an entire day of footage."

"I must have done that," the girl said. "I'm so sorry."

"Don't worry too much. It's just one day of footage we're missing." Ruby turned to me, adding, "Not that a day's worth of people leaning over display cases is anything to be missed, mind you."

"I'll be more careful," the girl answered softly.

"You do that. And I want those front windows so clean they're invisible." Ruby shooed her away with one hand before turning to the window and absentmindedly stroking the wildcat-shaped necklace charm where it lay against her leopard-print blouse.

A sweet vanilla scent wafted up from the table, bringing my attention to the miniature cupcakes. I chose one with yellow icing topped with a candied lemon rind and popped it into my mouth whole. The cake was moist, the lemon tangy and refreshing. My stomach rumbled in appreciation, reminding me I hadn't eaten in several hours. My breakfast had been modest and was now frozen to my father's lawn.

Ruby said, "I'm glad to see you have an appetite. After a shock like you had this morning, you need to keep having something every few hours, even if it's just a nibble. And plenty of fluids." She topped up my cup with more fragrant tea.

I thanked her, and we sat in silence while I made her happy by eating several more miniature cupcakes. She'd been so kind; it was the least I could do.

Her cat charm reminded me of Jeffrey, who was out of surgery by now. I wondered if he would be wearing a cone, and if he would be cross with me for my involvement in the whole ordeal. Then I thought of my father, who still hadn't called to check in. I felt some guilt for having remembered the cat first, but little Jeffrey didn't have a cell phone, so somebody had to look out for him. Finnegan Day was very good at fending for himself.

"How is your father?" Ruby asked.

I nearly dropped my tea cup. Ruby seemed to have a secret two-way mirror into my brain.

"He's missed out on all of today's excitement so far. He picked a fine time to be in the city getting hip surgery."

She asked, "Total replacement, or did he get that other thing some of the younger folks go for?"

"Not resurfacing," I answered. "He liked the idea of the procedure, of simply getting the femur capped, but we both had some concern about the devices, plus his height and age put him outside of the ideal range. He went for the total replacement, and I just found out this morning he gave the surgeon a measuring tape before he went in." While Ruby laughed, I explained how a friend of his had complained of uneven leg length after the same operation. "The physical therapist helped him stretch the muscles, and it turned out the discrepancy was mostly a feeling due to tightness on the one side, but you know my father. He's always doing things to keep other people on their toes."

Ruby wiped away a tear of laughter. "Finnegan never gives you a straight answer if he can have some fun instead." She sighed. "He won't be pleased to come home to a murder right next door, but at least he'll get it solved."

"Solved?" I'd been reaching for another cupcake but stopped. "He's retired now, and he needs to recuperate. With any luck, the case will be wrapped up before he gets back."

"By whom?" She blinked at me.

"By the police, of course. By Tony Milano, probably. He trained with my father, and he knows what he's doing."

Ruby shook her head. "I don't think so, honey. These new cops, they aren't like the older generation. I know your father was never captain or chief, never officially in charge, but you and I both know he always was. Without him keeping an eye on things, we're headed to ruin."

Abruptly, I pushed my chair back to leave. Growing up, I'd learned to avoid discussions with people about whatever opinions they had about the police, whether their opinions involved my father specifically or not.

"Ruby, thank you so much for the pick-me-up. You're very kind, and I am feeling better."

"Stop by anytime," she said sweetly. "I mean it, Stormy. My tea room is always open for a friend in need."

I thanked her again and started making my way out again. Ruby took the tray of chattering dishes toward some unseen kitchen, and I walked through the small stock room and emerged in the showroom. The carpet had been changed recently and was now a deep blue-green, further enhancing the store's beach feel.

Up in the corners of the ceiling were the cameras Ruby had mentioned. Two of them were fakes, dummies for deterrent use only. The model was the same as the one I had at the gift store. A third camera, though, looked real enough, albeit older than the fakes. That camera was aimed at the engagement ring section of the display counter. I scanned the rows until I spotted one that looked the like the ring I'd worn until recently. I pulled away and headed to the door, desperate for fresh air.

The outside world felt even wintrier in comparison to the tropical oasis behind me. Ruby's young employee, Hayley, was also outside, cleaning the big windows with a squeegee and soapy water hot enough to send up billows of steam.

The girl didn't see me at first, but once she did, she squeaked like a mouse. Ruby was right about her being skittish.

"Have you been working here long?" I asked.

She shrugged, eyed me with suspicion, and continued washing the windows.

"Ruby Sparkes is a nice lady," I said. "I'm sure once you learn the ropes, she'll go easier on you."

"Sure," Hayley answered, spitting the word.

I was about to turn and leave, but she tilted her chin up, telegraphing the desire to say something else. I waited calmly, taking the moment to stand up straight. My father always told me people love to talk to a good listener, and there's nothing quite like good posture to show someone you have the self-control to keep your mouth shut and use your ears in a conversation.

After a moment, Hayley said, "You knew him? The guy who got killed and buried in the snow?"

"He was my neighbor when I was growing up. I can't say I knew him well. Did you?"

"Of course not," she said, visibly annoyed in that specific, insulted manner only a teenager can pull off. "I'm not from around here."

"Where are you from?"

Her jaw moved, but no sound came out. She hunched over and tipped the bucket, sending a cascade of hot water across the frosty sidewalk. She grabbed the empty bucket and headed for the door, muttering, “Less talking, more cleaning.”

“Good luck with your training,” I called after her.

I pulled out my phone to see if my father had called yet. I’d missed a number of calls, thanks to it being on silent and being buried deep in my purse. As I scrolled through, the phone buzzed with an incoming call.

The caller identification read MISTY FALLS POLICE.

CHAPTER 12

I ANSWERED MY PHONE, and Tony replied with, "I'm sorry."

"Your new rookie isn't so bad," I said. "It was a bit rude for you to foist me onto her like that, but I know you're busy."

With a gravelly voice that scratched into my ear, he said, "Not about that. This is a personal call."

The surprising intimacy of his voice got me moving. I'd been standing at the corner in front of Ruby's store, but now I started toward the veterinary clinic, walking quickly, with the phone tight against my ear.

"What is it?" I asked.

Again, he said, "I'm sorry."

"Tony, don't be sorry about the other stuff. It was ten years ago. That ship sailed. I'm happy for you and your growing family. Honestly, I am."

"Good," he said, sounding a little confused.

"And I don't need your pity, but just between us, I could use your help with the gossip situation here in town. If you catch people telling lies about the billions of dollars I supposedly walked away from, take out your gun and shoot them."

He didn't respond.

"Not fatally," I said. "Just shoot off a toenail or something. You always were good at target practice."

He didn't laugh. "Stop talking for a minute. I have something to tell you."

I'd neared the vet clinic but didn't want to conclude the conversation inside. I brushed the snow off a bench and took a seat.

"Hit me," I said.

"Have you spoken to Finn recently?"

My blood ran cold as my thoughts raced to the worst possible scenario. Something could have gone wrong during surgery, explaining why he hadn't called.

My voice barely a whisper, I said, "No. Why?"

Silent seconds stretched out painfully. Finally, talking fast, he said, "I have eyewitness reports that your father and Mr. Michaels had a number of altercations, some of them recent."

I leaned back on the cold bench, sighing with relief.

"That's all? Thanks for testing my heart valves, Tony Baloney. For a minute, I thought something had gone wrong with Dad's surgery. I still have to check up on him." With a snort, I added, "And I need to inform him and Pam that they can't tell a girl cat from a boy."

"You're not listening," Tony growled. "Finnegan was overheard threatening to choke Michaels. This happened on multiple occasions."

"Says who?" I asked.

"Witnesses."

"Oh, hell. If those two weren't arguing over whose tree was dropping leaves onto whose lawn, it was about someone's safety lights shining into the other one's window. Those two liked giving each other a hard time."

"A threat is still a threat," Tony said gravely.

"Of course it is, Officer Milano." I pronounced his name icily, transferring the coldness of the bench seat to my voice. "Speaking of threats, I've got a new one. Grab a pen, will you?" I paused, imagining him rolling his eyes. "Ready? Here's the deal. Finnegan Day is going to kick your skinny half-Italian butt halfway to Washington State if he finds out that for even one minute you considered him a suspect."

Tony said flatly, "I'm doing my job."

"Then keep doing your job and investigate this thing properly. Did you know Mr. Michaels was shoplifting all over town?"

He answered cagily, "What have you heard?"

"I've heard he wasn't very popular with the Broad Avenue merchants. You might want to drop into Masquerade and get a look at the mugshot Leo Jenkins has on his corkboard. Don't go now. He's closed early for the day. Oh, and stop in to the Treasure Trove. Ruby's got at least one security camera running in there, so maybe she has footage of him in action. She says she hasn't had shoplifting trouble, but if some of the other merchants have, I bet she'd be able to tell you. Plus she seems to know stuff about people."

"What? Ruby's Treasure Trove? What are you talking about?"

"I'm talking about leads in the case. This is all information I got by canvassing the local businesses, and it didn't take much more than an hour. You could have done it yourself while you were eating your poppy seed bagel. You're welcome, by the way."

He was quiet, but I could see him in my mind, rubbing his temples. "You can't be getting involved in this," he said. "This isn't a donut shop robbery. It's a murder investigation. If you go around asking too many questions, you'll get yourself hurt."

I replied, "Not to mention, I could make you look bad by cracking the case myself."

He snorted. "Right."

I raised my voice. "Fine. Take care of everything. I don't care what you do, as long as you do something, and leave my father out of it."

Before he could respond, I ended the call. My throat felt tight, as though I'd been yelling the entire time, or straining not to. I glanced around to see if anyone had heard me, but the sidewalks were quiet on that street.

The door to the vet's office squeaked open, and an elderly woman with a Pekingese came out, giving me a friendly look as she and the fluffy dog walked my way.

She stopped in front of my bench. "Are you okay, dear? Do you need a ride somewhere? I think you live in my neighborhood. Quite the day we're all having, isn't it? First it was snowing so nicely, but now have you heard about Murray Michaels? Puts a damper on the weather, and I don't think anyone will be making a snowman for a while, at least not until the memory fades. Where are you headed? Are you dressed warmly enough? You should have a hat. Would you like to borrow mine?" She patted the white and gray knitted hat on her own head. The yarn matched her white and gray hair, coming out in curly wisps under the cap.

I smiled and got to my feet. "Thanks for the offer, but I've got my car here, and I'm picking up a cat."

At the mention of a cat, the Pekingese, who was as fluffy as any I'd ever seen, barked sharply. The woman said, "We don't mention the C-A-T word in front of Miss Molly. She's usually a good girl, but some things tend to set her off."

"I know how she feels," I said.

We said goodbye, and the woman gave me a wave with one gloved hand before walking away.

I blinked up at the sky, which was growing darker now that another short winter day in the Pacific Northwest was coming to an end. Standing, I could feel the shakiness in my legs, the adrenaline from talking to Tony. I'd almost forgotten how angry I used to get, all those times I couldn't avoid defending my father. I avoided debates about the role of law enforcement in Misty Falls, and specifically about my father, but that didn't stop trouble from seeking me out.

What was Tony thinking, suggesting my father might have harmed his neighbor?

If anyone knew my father's true character, it was Tony. They'd worked closely together for years. Tony had to know my father was as passionate about justice and fairness as anyone. Sometimes the other cops would rough people up but not my father. He left the judge and jury work to the judge and jury, as it should be. He rarely used force, preferring to get people talking, or better yet, laughing. If he'd said anything to his neighbor about choking, it had to have been a joke.

I shivered. The idea that Finnegan Day could be a suspect was absurd, but Tony must have told me for a reason. What was he up to? He probably expected me to call my father and give him the news.

I looked down at my phone and scrolled through the missed calls and text messages. They were all from Pam, which worried me, until I opened the most recent message.

Pam Bochenek: *I spoke to your father ten minutes ago. He says the surgery went well but he still needs to measure his legs. His biggest complaint is that the coffee at the hospital is terrible. Are you okay? I heard the news. I'm so deeply sorry that it was you who found that mess. It should have been me. How is the cat?*

I composed a message back: *I'm fine. Just picking the cat up now. See you soon.*

My message was short, yet difficult to write. I stumbled, as I had been doing lately, over what to call the house. I wanted to call it home because I'd grown up there, and it had been my home for years, but I didn't live there anymore, whereas Pam did. Simply calling it home felt untrue at best, antagonistic and territorial at worst. Calling it Dad's house didn't feel right either, yet I couldn't bring myself to say it was her house, as in "see you at your house soon." Those words wouldn't come out of my mouth or off my fingertips.

I finished and sent the short message.

What I didn't include was any hint about my father being a suspect. Tony had leaked that information to me for a reason. He wanted me to shake the hornet's nest for him, but he was in for a surprise. I wasn't going to do his bidding.

I dropped my phone into my purse and strode up to the door of the Calico Veterinary Clinic, bracing myself for the place's particular canned-stew aroma.

CHAPTER 13

"HOW'S THE PATIENT?" I asked.

"Who?" Natasha, the veterinary assistant whose hair resembled the vibrant skin of a Red Delicious apple, blinked at me with comically wide eyes.

"The Russian Blue cat," I said. "He came in here for the full spa treatment, if you know what I mean. Did everything go well?"

"Yes, of course. I'll get him for you." She walked backward, keeping her eyes on me.

Natasha must have been talking to the woman with the Pekingese, learning of what I'd discovered that morning. My suspicions were confirmed by the not-quite-hushed-enough tones of her discussing the murder with someone else in the back room.

While Natasha and her coworker debated whether I should get a discount on the neutering simply because they felt sorry for me, I searched for something to read while I waited. There wasn't much for magazines, and since I already knew more than anyone should about the life cycle of fleas, I pulled out my phone.

There was a message from my real estate agent, who either hadn't heard the day's big news or was trying hard to be a professional and not ask.

Samantha Sweet: *Everything's set up for me to show the rental tonight. His name is Logan Sanderson, and he's moved here to work at a law firm. Is there anything specific you'd like me to ask him?*

I looked at the waiting room chair where Logan had been sitting when I met him that morning. My first impression of the tall, bearded man was not favorable. First he'd laughed at me for not knowing Jeffrey was a male, and then he'd made lewd comments about winning the favor of his uptight landlady. Those were two strikes against him. But then, when Tony Milano had come to haul me off to the station, Logan had sprung into action, literally jumping to his feet to offer me assistance. I tried not to be pessimistic about the future, but I could imagine there coming a time, someday, when I might need a lawyer. Having one next door could prove handy.

I wrote back to the real estate agent: *I trust you. If you vouch for this guy, you can make the deal and give him the keys tonight.*

As I tapped the screen to send the message, I knew I'd made the right decision. No tenant or employee or partner comes without flaws, and it's better to know which ones you're dealing with ahead of time.

Natasha returned with a sleepy-eyed Jeffrey, snuggled inside his pet carrier.

"Is it all true?" Natasha asked me.

Because she had the decency to ask me directly, I told her it was, and that Jeffrey was the real hero because he'd led me right to the body.

"Cats know things," she said. "They have special senses for danger, which is why they're so curious."

I added, "And why they need those nine lives."

Natasha frowned. "That's just a myth. They don't come back from the dead." She went on to give me Jeffrey's after-care instructions, warning me to call them if anything alarming happened since the truth was he only had one life.

As I was gathering the pet carrier and supplies to leave, she said, "Such a shame about that Murray fellow, especially seeing as how he'd just reconciled with his family."

I paused and set everything down on the counter. "His family? I didn't think he had any children."

"Well," Natasha said, taking a big breath. "I was talking to Mrs. Catfish, who knows a gentleman who lives near Warbler Street, and he told her that Murray Michaels was excited about getting back in touch with some family members. She seemed to think it was a nephew or a niece."

I asked, "How sure was she?"

"Mrs. Catfish is in her nineties, but she's a sharp one." She leaned over to check on Jeffrey, who appeared to be listening with great interest, his gray ears perky in contrast to his sleepy eyes. "I suppose if there's any money to be had, the family will come out of the woodwork to hear the will."

Right then, Jeffrey decided he'd had enough human conversation. He stuck his gray paw through the door of his cage and caught me with his claws.

"Yes, we're going home," I told him, trying to shake free.

"Be careful," Natasha said. "We're all going to be keeping our eyes open and our doors locked until this thing's settled."

"Definitely lock your doors," I said. "But don't get paranoid about strangers. Most murder victims are killed by someone they know."

Her mouth dropped open, reminding me of how my friends used to react whenever I told them the truth about crime statistics.

Jeffrey dug his claws into my hand deeper, reminding me that my primary obligation was to him. He blinked up at me with jade green eyes that weren't quite focused and curled his paw around my finger as though we were holding hands. My heart melted like a pat of butter on a hot blueberry pancake.

Feeling fuzzy as my parental instincts kicked into overdrive, I thanked Natasha, left with the pet carrier, and got us both loaded into the car with Jeffrey's carrier in the passenger seat. I started the engine, ensured the seat warmers were at maximum, and turned the radio volume down so I could sit quietly for a moment.

Jeffrey let out the most pitiful meow.

"I know, Jeffrey. I know it's cold. Give the heaters a minute."

He tried to stand up inside the pet carrier, but his legs were wobbly. His unfocused eyes seemed to be full of love for me, despite everything. I popped open the hatch at the top of the carrier and gave him some pats. His purr started with a ferocious rumble as he bunted his head against my palm. Just when I thought my heart couldn't melt any more, it did.

"Good drugs?"

He gazed at me, the corners of his shiny dark gray lips turned up in what had to be a kitty smile. He didn't seem concerned about his stitches but had a cone to put around his head in case he did start pulling at them.

"You're such a good boy," I told him. "And now that you've had your little snip-snip, we don't have to worry about any kittens showing up on the doorstep."

Jeffrey grabbed my thumb in his mouth and gave me a sleepy love bite.

"Do you think that's what happened to Mr. Michaels? Some long-lost kid showed up and started shaking him down for cash?"

Jeffrey gnawed and licked my thumb as though it was a delicious breadstick.

"But why kill him?" I asked. "And don't say for the inheritance, it takes ages for wills to get changed, and if the person dies under suspicious circumstances, it's pretty obvious the new beneficiary did something."

Jeffrey fell asleep with my thumb in his mouth. I gently extricated it and reached for my phone as an idea crystallized.

Imagining my thumb as a breadstick had brought to mind the Olive Grove and not because I was hungry for dinner. The waitresses who worked there wore dark green slacks and cream blouses as their uniform, just like the blonde girl who'd applied her makeup in Ruby's two-way mirror. She'd seemed more upset than the typical townsperson about the news, assuming that was what she'd been talking about with Jenkins and the woman on the scooter. I didn't know anything about the blonde, let alone if she was a long-lost relative of Murray Michaels, but I knew someone else who might have more information.

I composed a brief text message to an old friend of mine but paused before sending it. I'd been avoiding Jessica Kelly since my return to Misty Falls. We'd been close, once, but our closeness had been replaced by an uncomfortable wariness, and I couldn't even remember why it was we'd fallen out. Did I really want to contact her for a favor? Was finding out more about the blonde, who might have simply been having a bad day, worth the hassle of blowing on the embers of a relationship that had gone so cold? And what business did I even have, sticking my nose into the investigation?

Then again, what business did Tony have treating my father, a man who did nothing but serve the needs of the town, as a suspect?

My outrage at Tony steamed up inside me. He was going to be sorry he told me to stay clear of this matter. He'd underestimated my abilities and how far I'd go to defend my father. I'd do anything for him.

I hit the send button.

CHAPTER 14

I DROVE TOWARD my father's house one-handed, my right hand in the pet carrier, rubbing Jeffrey's head and chin to keep him from meowing about the inhumanity of being in a cage, inside a moving vehicle.

I parked at the back of the house, next to Pam's car, in the space next to the garage. The sun was already setting, and judging by the brightness of the windows next door, the crime scene technicians were collecting evidence to be tested. They would have their work cut out for them because Murray Michaels had been what some people call a packrat. His garbage can was never overflowing on pickup day because the man didn't throw out anything, not even broken items. Whenever some type of pest appeared in my father's house, from pantry moths to mice, Mr. Michaels would be blamed.

"Pam!" I called out as I came in through the back door. "I'm home. I mean I'm here."

The floor creaked in an adjoining room.

I called out, "How are you doing? Did Tony's crack team of investigators already interview you?"

Her voice came weakly. "Yes. It was just awful."

I kicked off my snowy boots, moved some other coats so I could use my regular hook, and brought the pet carrier through to the living room. The television was on but muted, and Pam wasn't in the room.

"Pam? Are you hiding? Don't jump out from a closet at me."

Her voice came again, "I just want to forget all about today."

"Do you know they're treating Dad as a suspect?"

Without hesitation, she answered, "Your father did threaten the man."

I stopped in the kitchen. The cat carrier was getting heavy. Jeffrey meowed for me to let him out.

Did Pam actually think my father did something to Mr. Michaels? Where in the house was she hiding? She was smart to hide from me, if she was going to say things like that.

"Stormy, I know your father didn't do it," she called out, as though she'd read my mind. "They've got nothing on him. He's innocent… of that crime."

"Of course he's innocent. They're being ridiculous." I looked around the kitchen, at the mess from a recent meal. Pam had apparently experienced technical difficulties using my father's vintage electric can opener; a red trail of tomato soup stretched across the counter.

Her disembodied voice said, "I'm glad you're here, but I'm not sure if I want to talk about the awfulness next door."

"Okay." I used my free hand to clean up the soup with some paper towel. "We'll talk about something else."

Jeffrey meowed with conversation topic suggestions ranging from releasing him to feeding him.

Someone sniffed behind me, in the dining room that didn't get much use. The lights were off, but Pam was in there, sitting in the dark. She was probably shaken up, and my father wasn't in town to calm her down. It was up to me to be supportive in her time of crisis. Was this the terrible thing that was fated to bring us closer? Would she ask me to be a bridesmaid at some as-yet-unplanned Bochenek-Day wedding? Was this our tender moment? I swallowed hard against the bile rising in my throat.

She sniffed again, and though her sniff smacked of theatricality, I did feel for her. Pam was the chief architect of most of her own trouble, but she still suffered. I didn't want to be her friend, but my father cared for Pam, and I loved him, so I would make yet another effort at being nice to her.

I went to the doorway and asked softly, "Are you having one of your migraines?"

"Just a regular headache," she answered. "I could use some cheering up. Tell me one of your little jokes."

The only joke that popped into my head was a dirty limerick, so I said, "Your little Russian Blue cat got a sex change. He's a boy now, and he has a proper name."

Pam's curly-haired head didn't move. "What? Is that a joke?"

"It's the truth. Jeffrey Blue was very brave at the vet's office, and he hasn't touched his stitches."

After a long stretch of silence, she answered, "Bring the cat in, but please don't switch on the overhead lights."

I came in, set the carrier on the table, opened the lattice door, and gently lifted Jeffrey out. When I brought him to my chest, he snuggled against me. Cuddling him in my arms like a baby, I swayed from side to side in the dark dining room. I hoped that comforting her cat was buying me some points.

After a moment, Pam started talking. "That poor man," she said. "One day, he's minding his own business, and the next day, he's a snowman. It could happen to any of us."

"But it probably won't," I said. "Most murder victims are killed by someone they know, someone with motivation and opportunity."

Breathlessly, she said, "It could have been one of those thrill killers. An honest-to-goodness serial killer. Wouldn't that be something?"

Jeffrey squirmed as I squeezed him too tightly. My first instinct was to argue with Pam, to tell her how thankfully rare thrill killers were, but setting her straight would likely lead to an argument. Any disagreement with Pam's Official View of the World resulted in acrimony. So, I chose to agree.

"Yes, a serial killer would really be something," I said. "It would put Misty Falls on the map but not in a good way."

"I'll say." She sounded almost excited.

"Pam, can I get you something for your headache? Or something to eat? Did you get any of that innocent tomato soup into a bowl?"

She took a gasping breath. “What if this serial killer comes for me next? What if he’s going house by house?”

“That wouldn’t be very practical,” I said. “He’d only be able to get two before the pattern was obvious to anyone with eyes, and they’d nab him at the third house.”

“He’d still get two of us,” she said with a sigh. “But I guess you know better than me. I’m no expert. I don’t care for those ghastly TV shows your father watches. I can’t even go into the room when they’re on. Too much sex and violence. Anyway, that’s what I told the police today.”

“They asked about what Dad watches on TV?”

She made a non-verbal noise.

“What else?” I asked. “Did they say anything about Dad having arguments with Mr. Michaels?”

“They’re simply being thorough,” she said. “It certainly doesn’t mean your father did anything. I didn’t say he did. Exactly what are you accusing him of?”

“Nothing.” My tone was sharp. Jeffrey squirmed in my arms. Softer, I said, “Take it easy, Pam. Nobody’s accusing anybody of anything. I’m sure they’ll have this figured out before Dad gets home.”

“He will not be pleased,” she said with a snort. “This whole thing will be a nightmare that never ends.”

“Maybe not,” I said. “I’m trying to help with the investigation.”

She replied, “Are you sure that’s wise? Wouldn’t it be dangerous?”

"I'm looking into a rumor about Mr. Michaels getting back in contact with estranged family members."

"You must have heard wrong," she said icily. "Murray didn't have any family."

"Maybe he did." I went on to explain what I'd learned at the veterinarian's that afternoon, finishing with, "But it might not be true at all. Plenty of gossip flies around this town without fact-checking."

Pam pushed her chair back and stood. "I'm tired and ready for bed."

"But it's barely dinner time. And don't you want to see your cat? He's happy to be home again."

"I can't sleep in this house tonight. I'll pack a bag and go to my friend Denise's house."

"Were you planning to take Jeffrey with you? He won't like getting jostled around again. He should recover here in his own house."

"Why do you keep calling her Jeffrey?"

"I told you, Pam. She's a boy. He's a boy."

She snorted. "Sounds to me like you two have quite the bond." She came around the table and reached for him. He gave her a sleepy hiss that made her step back.

"Sorry," I said on his behalf.

She turned on her heel and left the room, muttering under her breath about ungratefulness.

Jeffrey relaxed, melting in my arms.

I rubbed his chin and whispered, "She's had a tough day. Be patient with her. She's okay sometimes. We shared a bottle of wine at the paint-your-ceramics place once, and we had quite a nice evening." I kissed his shining, dark nose. "Try giving her some wine. Everyone's more tolerable after a glass or two. You can have yourself a bowl of catnip. Do you like catnip?"

Five minutes later, I was still petting Jeffrey in the dark dining room and saying increasingly ridiculous things about catnip parties and such.

Pam came thumping by with a wheeled suitcase. She stopped at the arched doorway, an imposing shadowy figure.

"Your hair looks different," I said. "Did you get a new perm today?"

She patted her hair. "Yes. I was at the salon this afternoon."

"Was that before or after your doctor appointment?"

She reached into the room and flicked on the overhead lights, blinding me with the chandelier.

"The doctor was last week," her shadowy form said. "I'm all done with the doctors."

"That's good news," I said. She'd not disclosed to me what the appointments had been for, but I was genuinely relieved to hear the positive news that she'd been cleared.

"You'll stay here with the cat," she said. It was a command, not a question.

"Sure," I said.

"If you need me, my friend Denise's phone number is on the fridge," she said, and then she was gone.

Once we were alone again, I resumed talking to my new buddy, Jeffrey. "Did you see that? She's always so dramatic. Everything's life or death with Pam Bochenek. Heaven forbid you get yourself a haircut without checking in with her. She's probably mad at you because you changed into a boy without her permission."

Jeffrey kept on purring.

The refrigerator in the adjoining kitchen clicked off, and the house echoed with emptiness around me.

Something creaked. The dining room was now bright, and with the curtains open, I felt exposed to the world. Something creaked again, and my body tensed.

I jumped up and went to make sure Pam had locked the back door. It was deadbolted, but given the age of the old wooden frame, it wouldn't take much to kick down the door if someone wanted in.

I nuzzled my chin against Jeffrey's head as I walked through the house, checking all the doors and windows. When I got to the front room's window, I peered out into the wintery darkness. Next door, the crime scene technicians were loading up their vehicles, done for the day. I squinted, but couldn't distinguish anything interesting.

They started up their engines, washing the snow with a red glow from their tail lights as they pulled away.

Now it was just me, Jeffrey, and the terrifying serial killer from Pam's overactive imagination.

CHAPTER 15

LATE AT NIGHT, when the house is making noises and your imagination's creating images for every creak, serial killers don't seem so rare.

Alone in my father's empty house, I tried not to imagine a crazed killer going house to house.

I took Jeffrey to the kitchen, found his food, and put out some canned dinner for him before foraging in the fridge for myself, settling on a roast beef sandwich. I sat at the kitchen table, facing the back door, and took out my phone.

I called my father's cell phone and got his voicemail. I left a message, my voice as neutral as I could make it.

Jessica Kelly had replied to my text, which had been a vague let's-get-together-soon message. She was inviting me to come out that night for drinks with some other people. She didn't specify with whom, so I filled in the blanks with my least favorite people from high school days. I wanted to pick Jessica's brain about coworkers at the Olive Grove, but the stress of the day made me pessimistic. I'd rather have a dental work than sit in a local bar while people yelled intrusive questions over loud music.

I turned to the Russian Blue cat who was eyeballing my roast beef. “Jeffrey, you need me to stay with you, right?”

He blinked innocently. He was recovering well from the day’s surgery, but surely the little man was too weak to be left alone, fending off the neighborhood’s serial killer with nothing more than his claws and good looks.

I dug through my sandwich for a chunk of beef with no mustard. He licked his glossy black lips in anticipation.

“The vet did say to keep an eye on you tonight, in case you need the Cone of Shame. What do you say to a sleepover party? We can watch old movies in the guest room.”

He didn’t take his green eyes off my sandwich.

I gave him a chunk of beef to work on while I sent a message back to Jessica: *I have to stay in and look after my father’s cat tonight. He’s a bit shaken up.*

A few minutes later, she wrote back: *The cat? You are so cute! I heard about everything. I’m very sorry for your loss. I remember your neighbor and how he tried to give out cowboy books instead of candy. He was a real hoot. I just found out he owned a share in my apartment building. It’s a small world in a small town like ours!*

I wrote back: *Murray Michaels was your landlord?*

My message went through, but her status showed that she was away, so I didn’t expect an immediate answer.

The cat and I finished our roast beef sandwich before retiring for our sleepover.

The guest room was on the top floor, along with a powder room, another bedroom, and my father's study, which had originally been two rooms. He'd knocked out the dividing wall between the two bedrooms at the front of the house not long after I'd vacated one of them. His contractor had been a friend from the fire department who liked putting his muscles to good use during off-duty hours.

I took Jeffrey into the study and showed him where I'd hung my posters when half the room had been my domain. He blinked appreciatively at the view of the neighborhood and the charming circular window in the attic of the house across the street.

We settled into the guest room as best we could while we waited for the electric baseboards to take away the chill. I closed the curtains, blocking out the view of the crime scene next door, which helped make the room cozier. I turned the TV on with the volume muted before I put in another call to my father. The call went to a message saying the mailbox was full.

I looked up the number for the hospital. The receptionist took my name and put me through to his floor.

A woman answered, "This is Dora. You're calling to check on Finn?"

"Yes, I am, though I'm guessing he's doing just fine if you're on a first-name basis."

She giggled. "He's been telling us stories about his glory days."

"How did the surgery go?"

"Great! He'll be as right as rain in no time. The surgeon was able to do the minimally invasive procedure as planned, with the two smaller incisions, and it went very well because your father is an ideal candidate. You'll have to make sure Finn does his exercises, but also that he doesn't strain himself."

"I'll try," I said, thinking of the strain he'd be under as a murder suspect. "May I speak to him?"

"He's sleeping now, and we do prefer not to wake someone when they're resting."

"Hmm." My eyes went to the flickering TV screen, showing an old movie with a killer nurse glancing around nervously as she jabbed a syringe into a patient's arm. The older male patient fluttered his eyelashes before slumping his head to the side.

"He's doing very well," said the woman on the phone.

"Are you sure he's asleep? I'd love to hear his voice."

"I'll let him know you called. He'll be glad to hear of all the people who've been checking up on him. His friend Tony sounded very concerned."

My throat tightened. "Tony called?"

She paused as something clattered, wheeling by, and then Dora said, "I'm sorry, but I should be going. I hope to meet you soon."

"You probably won't see me, since he's got a ride home arranged." I kept my eyes on the TV, watching as the killer nurse hid away her evidence. "Unless you think I should drive out there? I'll probably do that. I'll drop in very soon, unexpected."

Dora didn't answer. In the background, a woman complained about a vending machine and its hateful brown excuse for coffee.

"When are visiting hours?" I asked.

The woman hurriedly answered, "Don't you worry about Finn." She said a quick goodbye and ended the call.

Being told not to worry had the opposite effect. I looked up the hospital's visiting hours and considered driving out the next morning.

I would need a good night's sleep no matter what, so I settled back on the bed, grabbed the remote, and switched the channel to something less creepy. It took a while to find a show that wasn't about people being murdered, but I found one about a guy helping real people and cats with lifestyle disagreements. The first featured cat preferred to lurk behind the toaster and hiss at people, whereas his owners wanted their kitty to not act like a kitchen gargoyle. By the time the episode ended, with everyone enjoying healthy play time together, I was sniffing back tears.

Jeffrey curled in next to me, twitching his ears when the cats on the screen meowed.

The channel was running a marathon of the show. After a few episodes, I stripped down to my T-shirt and slipped under the covers, which triggered play time. Jeffrey chased the lump of my toes under the covers as though they were monsters.

When I'd had enough of the emotional roller coaster of the cat program, I switched to a late night talk show. My eyelids were heavy. I drifted in and out of exhausted sleep.

Suddenly, Jeffrey let out a yowl that was five times as terrifying as anything we'd seen on the cat program.

"What is it?" I looked around the room. "Where are you?"

He howled again. I opened the swaying curtains to find him growling on the windowsill. I turned off the TV and the bedside lamp so I could see outside. I searched the snowy ground, expecting to see a nocturnal rodent going about its business in the bushes. There was nothing down there, but movement in the window next door caught my eye.

Something bright was flickering in Mr. Michaels' house. Was it just the reflection of a nearby vehicle? I held still, becoming increasingly aware of the pounding of my heart. His curtains were partly open, and from where I was on the second floor, I had a good view of the incandescence of a flashlight skimming the floor and furnishings.

Someone had crossed the crime scene tape and broken into the house.

They were hunting around, searching for something.

Or destroying evidence.

CHAPTER 16

JEFFREY KEPT WATCH on the windowsill, fascinated by the flashing circle of light in the house next door while I stumbled around the bed in the dark in search of my clothes. I pulled on my jeans and retrieved the two business cards from my pocket. Tony had asked me to contact him directly instead of calling 9-1-1, so I did.

He answered groggily, "Now what?"

"Flashlight," I said, waving my hand excitedly.

He replied, "Are you drunk?"

I took a deep breath and tried again. "There's someone inside Murray Michaels' house right now, and it's not the crime scene techs. I saw them leave hours ago. Plus the techs don't use flashlights."

He swore. "How do you know? Did Finn rush back from Portland?"

"I'm at Dad's house with Jeffrey."

"Who's Jeffrey?" he demanded.

"Are you going to send someone to catch this guy, or am I going to have to go over there and do it myself?"

He spoke to someone else, and the sirens came on. I'd feared he was home in bed, but he was in his vehicle, and on the way. Relieved, I slumped on the edge of the bed. Something in the house creaked. I jumped up, a wordless shriek in my throat.

"Still there?" he asked. "Try to relax."

"I can't relax. I'm going downstairs to check the house."

"Fine, but don't you dare go next door," he said. "Stay right where you are and don't move an inch. We're on the way. It's just going to take some time."

"How long? If you're too slow, you'll miss him. He might even be gone already." I could hear the other officer, a female, talking on the radio to dispatch, her voice hopeful about another car being near Warbler Street. Tony swore again.

"I'll go stand on the porch with all the lights off," I said. "I'll be careful."

Tony growled, "I don't like the sound of that. Do you at least have a gun?"

"A gun?" I nearly laughed. My father's revolver was a mere five yards away, locked in the safe in his den. Even if I could open the safe with my trembling hands, I wasn't trained. I was more likely to miss anything I shot at, inadvertently supplying the Crazed Snowman Strangler with another weapon to add to his arsenal. That was the last thing I wanted to do.

"Stay there," he said forcefully. "We aren't far." After a pause, he added, "But if you could station yourself near a window with a good view, I can't say that wouldn't be helpful."

"Done." I ended the call and clambered down the stairs, navigating the familiar steps easily, even in the dark.

I went to the kitchen, which had the only window on the lower floor facing the Michaels residence. I watched, barely able to breathe, as a shadowy figure searched the kitchen next door, yanking open cabinets and drawers. The figure was dressed in black and wearing a dark hat. With only the refracted glow of the flashlight, I couldn't tell if it was male or female, let alone age or identity. Whoever it was, they were definitely looking for something. Was this an estranged family member, looking for a revised will? Or the key for a safety deposit box? Or the combination to a safe?

Or was it just some opportunistic burglar, looting a house they knew to be empty?

I watched for what felt like an eternity. I checked my phone, finding that seven minutes had passed since I'd ended the call with Tony. Seven minutes. The town wasn't that big, and there wouldn't be any traffic at midnight, but he could easily be another ten minutes if he'd been at the station when I called.

Somebody had to get a look at whoever was in the house. The only parties nearby were me and the cat, and I doubted the cat's testimony would hold up in court.

I walked purposefully to the back porch, my pulse rushing in my ears. I pulled on my boots, talking to myself in a whisper. "I'm going to be very careful. I'm only going to get close enough to the window to get a look inside. That's all. Just looking. Very carefully."

As I visualized my plan, I saw one problem. The motion-sensitive security lights along the side of my father's house would light me up like a Christmas tree. It wouldn't be a problem if I flicked off the switch, though, so I did.

On my way outside, the back door creaked extra-loud, just to scare me. I pulled it shut behind me and walked down the back steps. It was brighter in the yard than it had been inside the house, thanks to the diffused glow of the streetlamps, and I felt exposed. The cold night air made me more aware of the sweat gathering at the nape of my neck.

I kept close to the wall of the house and inched my way toward the space between the homes, wincing at the sounds my feet made. For additional security, my father had installed noisy gravel instead of lawn against the side of the house. Luckily, all those hours I'd spent playing outdoor Hide and Seek had given me the ability to walk over the snow-dusted gravel with minimal noise. The secret was to put your foot down slowly and flatly, not heel to toe.

Murray Michaels' house seemed to hold its breath as I approached. There was no movement visible in the kitchen. The home seemed as empty as debris on the moon. My heart sunk over missing my chance.

A glimmer of light, like the first spark of a fire, came from an adjacent room. My heart jumped with hope. I approached the window, standing on my tiptoes. The person in black had moved on from the kitchen, and I couldn't see more than a flickering glow from elsewhere in the home, but if the person came back through the room, I'd be in a prime viewing position.

A breeze played with the back of my hair, sending a chill down my spine as it rattled a few dry leaves clinging to nearby trees.

Something crunched; it was the sound of gravel underfoot. A hand clamped over my mouth while an arm snaked around my waist. I reacted without thinking, biting my assailant's thumb.

"Stormy, it's me, Tony," he said in my ear.

I bit him harder. He let me go, and I whirled to face him. His face contorted with pain, shock, and anger. He shook his hand and ducked down, out of the line of sight of the window. I ducked down to join him.

He managed to sound like he was yelling, even at a whisper. "I thought you were going to stay inside your house."

"I thought you were going to get here quickly and catch the bad guy."

"Stay right here and I will." He didn't move, except to shake his bitten hand.

I whispered back, "What are you waiting for? Get out your gun and go shoot this guy."

He shook his head. "You're the worst."

A nearby door creaked. I pushed Tony toward the back of the house, where it seemed the sound had come from.

"He's getting away," I said. "Go, go."

We both ran along the side of the house, no longer concerned about gravel sounds.

At the back of the Michaels residence, a tall, dark-clad figured emerged from the back door.

"Stop where you are!" Tony yelled.

The dark-clad figure seemed to consider this for a second and then flew down the few back steps, crossed the snowy backyard, and leaped over the side fence as easily as an Olympic hurdles jumper.

Tony reached for his sidearm holster, undid a latch, but didn't draw the gun. He ran after the suspect, his dark boots punching the fresh snow tracks, and jumped over the fence with a grunt and what sounded like a hard landing. He yelled again for the suspect to stop and identified himself as police.

I hastily tied the laces on my boots and joined in the chase.

CHAPTER 17

THE SUSPECT HAD long legs that covered ground quickly as he darted down the alley, but he lacked the upper body strength to scale the tall fence he attempted.

Tony was closing in on the dark figure and might have caught up sooner if he hadn't wasted precious energy yelling at me to stay back.

"Pretend I'm not even here," I said between puffs.

He muttered something about using the taser on me.

"Good idea," I said. "Use the taser! Get him!"

The suspect, upon hearing my suggestion regarding the taser, found the upper body strength to get over the tall fence.

Tony tried to follow, but what he had on the perp in upper body strength, he lacked in height.

Meanwhile, I unlatched the rusty hook-and-eye hardware, pushed open the tall fence's gate, and whistled to get Tony's attention. Instead of thanking me, he told me again to go home as he rushed through the opening.

The suspect was halfway across the yard when he slipped on some ice.

The guy's long arms were still windmilling when Tony took him down bodily, like a panther pulling down a stumbling gazelle.

Within seconds, the black-clad suspect was face-down in the snow, next to a colorful children's playhouse.

I parked my hands at my waist and caught my breath as Tony put the cuffs on the suspect and recited his rights. I mouthed along with the words I knew by heart.

The suspect's dark cap had slipped off, letting the home's security lights bounce off his bald head. Tony got him to his feet. Leo Jenkins, the costume shop owner, spat snow out of his mouth and gave me a bewildered look.

"I didn't do it," Jenkins said. One lens of his square glasses was shattered. A dark spot of blood ran down his cheek like a teardrop.

Tony said, "Didn't do it, huh? I feel like I've heard this before."

Jenkins stammered, "I s-s-swear I didn't do anything that any regular person wouldn't have done."

Tony said, "Regular people don't break into houses in the middle of the night."

Jenkins looked right at me. "Stormy. You've got to believe me. Help me."

I held my hands up. "Tell it to your lawyer." Despite his pleading, I tried to remain cool and dispassionate. Claiming innocence was exactly what any guilty person would do. But Jenkins did look awfully pathetic with his thin shoulders slumping under his broken glasses and cut face.

Tony spoke to a woman on his radio. A moment later, a car pulled up and stopped in the alley. Officer Peggy Wiggles met us at the gate. She gave me a stiff nod before helping Tony load their suspect into the back of the police cruiser. The two spoke in tones too low for me to hear over the running engine of the car.

Tony slid into the driver's seat while she walked toward me. "I'll walk you back to your house," she said.

"Do you need me to give you another statement?"

"Tell me on the way," she said. "Take your time."

We started walking back toward my father's house. "I saw someone breaking in, called Tony, and he caught Leo Jenkins. Not much of a statement, but there you have it."

"Is there more?" she asked.

There was plenty more, including me urging Officer Tony Milano to utilize the various weapons on his belt and disobeying his orders to stay back. Those details didn't paint either of us in a flattering light.

"That's the gist of it," I said.

"Good," she said. "Looks like we got our guy, so you can sleep easy tonight."

"Thanks," I said." "And luckily my father didn't have to get dragged into any of this. You guys totally dodged a bullet."

She looked confused. "We dodged a bullet?"

"I guess you started after he retired, so you don't know him, but trust me. Finnegan Day would not have been amused by being considered a suspect."

"Most people wouldn't find that amusing," she agreed.

We approached the back of Mr. Michaels' home. Another two cruisers were pulling up nearby, sirens off but lights flashing, casting blue and red streaks through snowy yards. Lights flicked on in nearby houses as neighbors assembled to talk from porch to porch.

I blew air on my hands and rubbed my bare arms. It wasn't the coldest November night, and I hadn't pulled on a jacket in my rush to catch the burglar. The sweat from my adrenaline rush was evaporating, chilling me.

We reached the back door of my father's house.

"Would you like to come in?" I asked Officer Wiggles. "I could get you a glass of water, hot tea, or a cup of coffee. You must be tired, going into your third shift by now."

"I'm fine," she said, peering into the back porch through the window in the door. "You don't live here with your father, do you? I thought you had a place in the West Creek area."

"I'm here with Jeffrey. He's upstairs waiting for me."

"Is Jeffrey your boyfriend?"

"Sorta," I lied.

She gave me a suspicious look. "And he sent you running outside after a burglar? What kind of a guy does that?"

"A feminist," I said.

"Oh." She looked surprised but not displeased.

Tony cleared his throat behind us, on the walkway.

Officer Wiggles said, "Suspect locked up tight?"

Tony replied, "He can cool down in the back seat while we check the house." Tony turned to me with a curious look. "Your father didn't mention you were seeing someone."

I pretended to be surprised my father hadn't mentioned my feminist boyfriend with long gray whiskers.

"It's been a whirlwind," I said, which wasn't untrue. I'd barely met the cat before today, and we were already having a sleepover.

"Let me know if you need anything," Tony said. "For example, a background check."

"He's had all his shots," I said.

Tony frowned at his rookie partner, who shrugged.

"Thanks again," I said, pulling open the door. "I'd better get in before Jeffrey calls 9-1-1 to report me missing from the warm bed upstairs."

"Lock your doors," Tony said.

I assured him I would.

Back inside the kitchen, I flicked on the light and found Jeffrey sitting by his empty food dish.

"We're official now," I told him. "Tony knows all about us. I understand you wanted to keep things hush-hush for a while, but you can't keep a secret for long in a small town."

He rubbed against my shins in a show of affection that was more honest and touching than flowers and chocolates.

I got him more food and sat cross-legged on the floor while he ate, his slurping and crunching noises quietly comforting.

"Take your time," I told him.

I wasn't eager to go upstairs and close my eyes, for fear of what I'd dream. I'd hoped to feel some relief over a suspect being arrested, but I didn't feel relieved. If anything, remembering Leo Jenkins' gaunt face, with his broken glasses and the blood running down his cheek, I felt worse than ever.

He'd cried out that he was innocent, and he'd looked into my eyes as he pleaded for help. The girls at the high school had called him Creepy Jeepers because he was odd, and he definitely was unusual, but he'd never struck me as evil.

What if he wasn't the person who killed Murray Michaels? The killer would still be around. Maybe watching the house.

I got up and double-checked the locks on the doors.

CHAPTER 18

AFTER CHECKING ALL the doors and windows three times, I did manage to doze off. It wasn't restful sleep because I kept waking up at every tiny sound, which was a relief from my nightmares of Leo Jenkins being tortured. In my dreams, he suffered countless injuries while he pleaded for mercy, maintaining his claim of innocence.

Morning came, and the nightmares faded.

The room was bright when somebody started licking my eyebrows. I checked the guest room's clock. It was well past the time I usually got up, but I didn't want to face the world.

Jeffrey's raspy tongue became more like gritty sandpaper with each loving lick.

"Five more minutes," I groaned, pushing him away.

Jeffrey gave me about twenty seconds' reprieve and then started exfoliating my forehead again.

"Easy there, champ," I said. "You're going to lick my eyebrows right off, and then what will people say? Pam will tell me I look like a permanently-startled woodchuck."

He yawned to let me know that whatever Pam thought about my appearance, it was not important enough to warrant further discussion. He was right.

"How are your little man parts?" I turned him around to check the surgery site. To my relief, I found he hadn't been applying the same intense eyebrow-cleaning to his stitches.

As thanks for my nursing efforts, he gave me a disgusted look and swished his tail. "Everything's fine back there," I reported. The only thing unusual about his recovery was his sociability. The veterinarian's assistant had warned me he would likely hide for days.

"You're doing great," I told him. "I, however, am going to stay in this bed until further notice."

I rolled over and went back to sleep, back to the nightmares. Leo Jenkins was making snowmen, rolling balls of snow across a field while an unseen tormentor cracked a whip and shouted orders. The orders sounded like bells.

I woke up to the chorus of half a dozen phones ringing. I rolled over and picked up the guest room extension.

"Day residence," I answered.

"There you are," boomed my father's voice, with its gentle Irish brogue. "Pam said you volunteered to babysit the cat, and I thought for a minute she had relocated her sense of humor, but there you are. What did you do to get Tony so worked up?" He chuckled. "You've got to let me know, so I can try it myself."

"Nothing bad," I said defensively. "I helped him catch Leo Jenkins, who was breaking in next door."

There was a pause, a rare moment where I'd caught my father off guard and rendered him speechless.

"Good for you," he said at last. "I'm alone in my room at the moment, so be quick and tell me everything."

I sat up in bed and propped a pillow behind my back. "In a minute. How's your new hip? How's your pain level? You sound good. I should drive out to see you today."

"Don't bother," he said. "The coffee's terrible, and the company's worse. These pain meds make me nod off mid-sentence. It's too long a drive for the small pleasure of watching your old man snore. I'll be home soon enough. What's this about you getting the cat mixed up with another cat?"

"No mix-up. Your cat is a boy and always was. I did check the collar tag, so don't try to make me worry. His name is Jeffrey."

"All right. That's easy to remember. Are you going to tell me your side of what happened yesterday? You can leave out the part about whatever horror was done to the poor cat at the clinic."

I walked him through the previous day's morning, glossing over my meeting with the real estate agent, and then on to Pam stopping by the gift shop with the pet carrier and my subsequent frosty discovery. I admitted to my cowardice, running off when the husky mail carrier started making accusations. My father chuckled at this but agreed I'd been wise to trust my instincts. He was very quiet when I described my trip to the police station and interview with Officer Peggy Wiggles, commenting only that she sounded like a good addition to the force, a "balancing energy."

He got downright excited when I told him about dropping into Masquerade to ask about top hats. When I got to visiting Ruby Sparkes, I felt bad censoring myself, but I left out the details of her secret mirror window, admitting only that we'd had tea.

"Ruby has connections," he said. "She's a good contact for you, if you continue this line of work."

"You mean running a gift shop?"

"Among other things," he said. "How did you notice someone breaking in next door? Did you have the house under surveillance?"

I explained that I'd had my best cat on the job, and he'd alerted me. Then I'd called Tony, stationed myself outside to keep watch, and finally helped him catch the suspect by chasing "at a safe distance" before helpfully opening the gate in a neighbor's fence. "I didn't do much," I said. "I just unlatched a gate."

"Don't sell yourself short," he said. "You kept a cool head and used the smarts you inherited. I'm very proud of you."

I whispered, "Thanks." I knew how lucky I was, having heard my father say he was proud of me countless times over the years. Some kids wait an entire lifetime and don't get it. Finnegan Day was tough on people, but he always gave credit where it was due.

He burped. "Whoops. That'll be the coffee, coming back for a second roundhouse kick to the taste buds."

"That's it," I said with finality. "I'm driving over, and I'll bring you some decent coffee. It's either that or stay inside your house until the food runs out. You still have all those pickled beets?"

"You don't have plans?" he asked.

"My employee can run the store without me. Dad, I need out of this town. If I show my face anywhere, people are all over me. It was humiliating before, and now it's going to be worse. I need to get away, drive away, just get in the car and go."

"No," he said sharply. "You need to get back on the horse. Remember how we saw that thing on TV about brains, about things firing together and wiring together? I've seen it happen after a shooting. People get spooked, and they can't do the regular things they used to."

I remembered the documentary. "Neurons that fire together, wire together," I said.

"Right. Neurons. Some folks will say you need time off, and sure, you do need rest, but if that horse bucks you off, you need to climb right back on." He paused, waiting for a response.

"Sure," I said. "Get right back on the horse. I just need a horse."

"The horse is a metaphor," he said.

A metaphor? I laughed. "Hello? Who is this, and what have you done to Finnegan Day?"

"Gotta go," he said. "Dora is here to do unspeakable things to me."

I asked him what these unspeakable things entailed, but he'd already hung up.

Jeffrey watched me with great interest as I crawled out of bed and dressed in the same jeans, T-shirt, and cat-fur-covered cardigan sweater I'd worn the day before.

I went downstairs to the kitchen, rustled up some food for both of us, and used my phone to catch up on messages.

My employee, Brianna, had sent a flurry of notes, all following a pattern. She'd ask me where some item was, and in another message time-stamped five minutes later, she'd tell me she'd found the item. There'd be a third message apologizing for the first two. She would be fine running the store without me that day. If anything, my absence would encourage her to become more self-sufficient.

I thought over what my father had said about getting back on the horse. For Brianna, dealing with various retail crises was her horse. What was mine?

I heard the thumping of boots on the front steps. Was facing the husky mail carrier my horse? I ran to the front door.

He must not have been expecting a wild-haired woman to yank open the front door. The poor man dropped his satchel of mail on the porch, and, by the look on his face, peed a little.

"Sorry for jumping out at you," I said. "If you haven't already heard, I thought you'd want to know the police caught the guy. Oh, and I'm sorry about ditching you at the crime scene yesterday. That wasn't very nice of me, but look at how tiny I am compared to you."

His mouth opened, but no sound came out.

"Sorry!" I said again. "It's just that you're a big guy. Not big in a bad way. You look strong. Do you work out? What can you bench? I bet it's a lot."

He stammered, "Wha-wha-what?"

"You look like you could bench-press a lot more than me. I went for a personal training session once, and you know what I lifted? The bar. With no weights on it. Just the bar. And I was sore the next day."

He blinked. "Did they really catch the guy who killed Mr. Michaels?"

"I hope so. I can't say who, unfortunately. I'm not going to start any more rumors."

"It was someone local?"

I nodded. "He broke into the house last night. It was pretty stupid to come back, but my guess is he was worried about evidence."

"That's such a relief." The shorts-wearing man knelt to gather his dropped mail, his bare knees pink against the snow.

I asked him, "Have you been looking over your shoulder all morning, wondering if the killer was someone you deliver mail to?"

"I've been jumpier than a baby squirrel sitting on a barrel of pecans." He stood, digging around in his satchel, pulling out a good-sized carrot.

I took a step back. His carrot looked like the one that had formed the snowman's nose, nearly a foot long, thick and unpeeled.

"You must love carrots," I said.

"Not really."

He kept crunching away as he thumbed through envelopes from his satchel. Another bite later, he thrust my father's mail directly at me.

"There you go," he said. "Mail's delivered and a killer's been caught. All's well that ends well. The town can sleep easy tonight."

"Totally." I nodded in agreement.

He took another bite of his giant carrot, stomped down the porch steps, and carried on his way, whistling a carefree tune. He seemed to sense my eyes on him, turning to look over his shoulder and give me a cheery wave.

What was he so happy about? Was it simply relief that a killer had been caught, or relief that he'd gotten away with something? Walking around chomping on giant carrots was no crime, but it seemed distasteful, given recent events.

Jeffrey wound his way around my legs, drawing a figure eight with his body. We both stood in the doorway, but he didn't seem interested in leaving the warm house. A black-capped bird flew down from a nearby tree and perched on the porch railing, but even that didn't entice Jeffrey outside.

I crouched down and stroked his smooth gray fur. With each pet, my paranoia over the mail carrier eased up. I did have to get back out into the world before I drove myself crazy.

The bird, a cheeky little chickadee, hopped closer along the porch railing. Jeffrey watched, yawning.

"You're so mellow," I said to him. "Don't you want to get back on your horse? You can patrol the street, chasing birds and meowing at girls."

He sat on my foot and gave me a sweet, slow blink, telling me I was all the woman he needed.

We went back inside, where I gave serious consideration to my mission for the day. Looking around for paper, I found Pam's sketchbook and spent a few minutes flipping through her sketches of store windows and houses. When I came across a page of wedding dress sketches, I made a gagging sound and put the book back where I'd found it, on the coffee table.

Jeffrey jumped up and sniffed the sketchbook, his tail swishing back and forth in gray question marks.

"Can you manage without me for a few hours?" I asked.

He knocked a crumpled ball of paper to the floor and chased it out of the room. Yes, he'd be fine. I found some junk mail and jotted down a dozen things I could do that day. Because I wanted to make my father happy, I pulled on my coat and boots and bravely headed out to get back on my metaphorical horse.

CHAPTER 19

MY EMPLOYEE, BRIANNA, greeted me cheerfully when I walked into Glorious Gifts. When she looked up from the display rack of tableware accessories and saw it was me, she said, “Oh, it’s just you.” With a devilish look on her round face, she said, “Never mind.”

I clutched my free hand to my chest, feigning hurt feelings. “I don’t warrant a good morning?”

“My boss prefers for me to save the charm for the paying customers.”

“She sounds like a real tyrant.” I raised the tray of hot beverages I’d been hiding behind my back. “A mean boss like yours wouldn’t bring you a hot mocha, would she?”

Brianna clapped her hands and jumped up and down on the spot girlishly.

We gathered behind the counter to pull the lids off our drinks and dip in the biscotti I’d also picked up. Brianna was twenty-one, but with her large eyes, round face, and tiny nose and mouth, she resembled the innocent-looking dolls we sold. She was quite petite, so if she didn’t wear makeup, she could pass for about fourteen. It was hard for me to reconcile the fresh face in front of me with the person who ran the gift shop as well as she did.

She didn't ask me about the events of the previous day, but I could tell by the way she kept watching me, she knew what I'd been through. I'd been happy to relay all the details to my father over the phone, but thinking about going through it again and again, answering people's questions, made me feel like hiding under the counter. If Brianna could pretend nothing was out of the ordinary, I could do the same.

"Did you call everyone with special orders?" I asked.

"Yes, Boss." Brianna bobbed her head, her straight brown hair swinging around her doll-like face.

"Did you sort out the recycling?"

She grinned. "Yes, Boss."

"Order more cash register rolls?"

"Yes, Boss."

"Grow five inches so you can dust the top shelves without a ladder?"

She stood on her tiptoes. "Working on it."

"Did you get that tattoo you were talking about?"

"Not yet." Her big eyes widened. "Wanna come with me?"

"Let me get back to you on that." I crouched down and started moving bags so I could reach the lockbox and the safe. "I'd better do a bank run for the deposit and get some coins, since you've made me look bad by doing your job and most of mine. If you need me, I'll be in the office for a few minutes, running reports."

"Sounds great." She took her mocha and returned to her task, organizing a new display of tablewares.

A minute later, the door jingled. Brianna called out, "Good morning, sir!"

I was kneeling behind the counter refilling the lockbox with rolls of coins, so I didn't see who'd come in, but he said hello back to her with a deep voice that sent a ripple up my spine.

"Is it still morning?" she asked with a giggle. "Sometimes I say that all day, even after it's past lunch time. There should be another greeting that you can say all the time."

"Hello," the man said.

"Hello, yourself," she said.

"I mean you can say hello all day long, morning or evening."

She snorted in response. Brianna was an agreeable, joke-loving girl, an aspiring cartoonist with her own web comic, but this man was eliciting far more than her typical friendly patter.

"Are these for curtains?" the man asked.

"Those are technically napkin rings, but you could use them for anything you like. I think you could use them with a curtain rod, if you got the right hardware. Is that something you're looking for? A curtain rod? We mostly carry gift items, but we can do special orders." The way she was carrying on, I half expected her to offer to sew him some curtains out of our best tea towels.

I straightened up enough to peer over the top of the counter. The customer was a handsome, dark-haired man in a gray suit paired with a trenchcoat-style jacket.

If my brain were able to make cartoon sound effects, it would have made one now, perhaps the AWOOGA of a jalopy honking.

This dapper-looking customer was Logan Sanderson, my new tenant who didn't know he was my tenant. He'd recently trimmed his mountain man beard to a refined and fashionable length and looked nothing like the sloppily dressed drifter I'd seen the day before.

"Why do napkins need these beaded twirly things?" he asked Brianna. "Do napkins have a habit of getting all unruly?"

"Napkins have been known to misbehave." She twirled a lock of brown hair around her finger.

He continued, "Then I'll need these for future dinner parties. If the napkins are bare-naked, everyone will know I'm a dumb bachelor who doesn't know anything."

"You don't look dumb to me. Aren't you that new lawyer guy?"

"That's me, the new lawyer guy. Let me know if you require any legal services. Do you find yourself getting into trouble a lot, here in the bustling metropolis that is Misty Falls?"

"We're not that boring!" she squealed. "We had a real murder. Technically, they think the murder happened two weeks ago, but the body was frozen inside a snowman."

"I did hear about that." He continued browsing, moving over to the cloth napkins and tablecloths.

"My boss found the body," she said.

"Your boss?"

Brianna clamped her hand over her mouth. "Actually, forget I said anything about that. I shouldn't talk about other people's business, and my poor boss didn't deserve to get caught in the middle of anything."

"I heard that my new landlady was the one who found the body, so I guess you and I have something in common."

She glanced over at the hall to the office, presumably looking for me. I ducked the top of my head below the counter quickly to avoid detection.

"Your landlady is my boss?" she hazarded.

He chuckled. "And we both live under her iron rule. Does she put up bossy signs around here, too? There's one in the basement laundry room, about not leaving wet clothes in the washing machine because it makes the whole house smell of mildew."

Still in my hiding spot behind the counter, my jaw dropped open with indignation. The bossy sign in the laundry room had been there when I bought the place. Sure, I agreed with it, which was why I hadn't taken it down, but it wasn't an unreasonable request.

"I can't complain," Brianna said through giggles. Then she got louder, presumably for my benefit. "Stormy is a terrific boss. I'm extremely grateful to be working here. Yes, Stormy is very nice, and totally cool for a lady in her mid-thirties."

I thought my jaw couldn't drop open more, but it did. Mid-thirties? Thirty-three was early thirties, barely thirty, not mid-thirties.

"So, she's my age," he mused. "From the stories and the signs, I imagined someone much older. Do you know where she is? I've been keeping an eye out for her at the duplex, so I can properly introduce myself, but she hasn't been around."

"I'll get her for you. I think she's in the office."

I heard footfalls as they walked together to the back of the store.

"Not if she's busy," Logan said. "I don't want to disturb her."

"It's no trouble. I think she takes naps in the office when she's here." She let out a laugh. "I'm kidding about that, by the way. Stormy is not the kind of lady who takes a nap. You'd need to give her warm milk and sleeping pills to get her to slow down."

Brianna walked past the counter, not noticing me where I crouched. She creaked open the door of the office and called my name.

I didn't respond because that would give me away. She would see me upon her return unless I hid better.

The space under the counter was a hodgepodge assembly of cabinets and scrap wood. There was a curtain to hide the mess, but we always kept the curtain open for easy access. Still crouching, I inched my way back, huddled up, and squished myself into the cupboard. I pulled the curtain across, but it got stuck and wouldn't close all the way.

"Stormy?" she called again into my office. The door clicked shut. "You might catch her at the bank," she told Logan.

She walked past me again, not looking down to see me huddled below the store's counter, half hidden by a curtain.

"She must have slipped out the back," she said apologetically and then abruptly cried, "Oh, no!"

"What's wrong?" he asked.

"She left her coffee behind, and she barely had a few sips. Such a shame."

He made a *hmm* sound.

Brianna asked him, "Do you want to leave a note for her?"

"No, but I will buy some cloth napkins and the beaded things that keep them from becoming unruly. Can you help me pick out a good combination? I'm colorblind."

"Aww, you poor thing," she said.

"It's just blues and greens that are hard to tell apart. That's why I always wear brown suits and brown ties."

"Um. Your suit and tie are gray, sir. A moody sort of gray."

He chuckled. "I know that. I was testing you." Something rustled. "I'll take these ones if you think they're okay."

"Excellent choice, sir. I'll ring these right up."

As she returned to the counter, I nudged a few inches further into the cupboard, next to the computer and extra rolls of receipt paper. I should have stood up as soon as they'd started talking about me, but now it was beyond awkward.

Brianna clicked away and gave him the total, adding, "That's with the family discount, since technically you live with the store's owner."

"Watch yourself," he said dramatically. "That's how rumors get started."

She laughed. "You'll like Stormy," she said. "Just don't make her mad, and you'll be fine. She really is funny, and smart, and generous, and kind."

My cheeks flushed. The cupboard was getting very warm.

Objects clattered on the counter above my head, and a bag rustled. They finished the transaction, and the door chimed as he left.

Once Brianna was distracted with another customer, I opened the curtain, crept out from under the counter, and slipped away through the back door.

CHAPTER 20

FOR THE SECOND TIME that morning, I walked into the House of Bean for coffee. My first vanilla latte was back at Glorious Gifts, barely touched. I couldn't have taken it with me, or Brianna would have known I'd overheard her conversation with Logan.

I approached the coffee shop's counter with rising dread. The little bundle of evil known as Chad was working the cash register. He was my least-favorite barista, the one who insisted on using official House of Bean menu terminology.

"Good morning," I said.

The young man replied with an aggressively cheerful, "Good morning to you, ma'am!"

I dug in my purse for my wallet, avoiding eye contact. "Vanilla latte, please. Large."

"Sorry," he said in a sing-song tone that was anything but apologetic. "We don't have those. May I interest you in a Teenie Weenie Beanie Steamer?"

I glanced up with a blank expression, playing dumb. "But isn't that just a latte with vanilla syrup?"

Evil Chad's eyes narrowed to their most evil setting. "Our Teenie Weenie Beanie Steamer is a delicious blend of steamed milk, hot espresso, and two pumps of our signature vanilla bean flavor."

We faced off in silence.

Evil Chad didn't know who he was up against. I would quit drinking their specialty coffees before I ordered a Teenie Weenie Beanie Steamer.

There was nobody waiting in line behind me, and I wasn't in any rush, so I took the opportunity to share some helpful tips with the young man. What followed was less of a discussion than an informative lecture. After about five minutes of my persuasive, reasonable, somewhat loud words, he bowed his head slightly, as though acknowledging that perhaps when a customer ordered something that he knew darn well was something they offered, albeit with their own silly name on the menu board, he could just make them their coffee without further humiliation.

Evil Chad took my money wordlessly and made my drink, letting his grumpy expression speak volumes.

"Careful you don't burn yourself," he said, handing it over. "It's very hot."

"Can I have a sleeve?"

He tossed a cardboard sleeve on the counter. "Yes you may," he said. "You may have a sleeve for your Teenie Weenie Beanie Steamer, Mountain-Sized."

"Thanks, Chad," I said brightly. "I appreciate your commitment to excellence."

On my way out of House of Bean, a dark figure, lean as an exclamation mark, caught my eye. I turned my head just as the shape disappeared around the corner. I could have sworn it was Creepy Jeepers, but it had to be my overactive imagination because Leo Jenkins had been arrested.

CHAPTER 21

RESIDENTS JOKINGLY REFER to the Fox and Hound as the Lost and Found, on account of the many scarves and mittens left behind in the darkened booths, as well as the spontaneous relationships that are "found" right around last call. With its many interconnected rooms and well-worn upholstery, the place was a far cry from the nightclubs in bigger cities, but in a small town like Misty Falls, it was the closest thing to a "scene."

After a full day of normal activities, I drove to the corner of town, parked at the pub, and went in to meet an old friend, Jessica Kelly.

It was eight o'clock when I walked in. The Fox and Hound pub was about a third full, and my entrance did not go unnoticed. Many heads turned my way; I checked behind me to see if someone far more interesting had followed me in, but I was on my own.

I self-consciously wove my way around the tables, scanning for Jessica's bright red hair. I walked slowly, dreading this reunion, though I couldn't remember exactly why I'd been avoiding her since my return to town. I'd only sent her a message because I was playing detective, but now that the police had made an arrest, I didn't need to ask about her coworkers. When she'd messaged back, suggesting drinks tonight at the Fox and Hound, I'd felt so guilty for my selfish intentions, I'd said yes, and now here I was, out in public, with everyone staring at me. I climbed the stairs to an upper level, spotting her near one of the pub's three cozy fireplaces, alone at a round table for three.

She saw me and jumped up, squealing my name. We hugged, and I got a mouth full of her red hair. She squeezed me so hard I had to gasp for air. "So good to see you," she said, finally releasing me.

I felt many eyes on us as I took a seat at the table. "Small-town life is so different," I said. "In the city, nobody even looks up when you walk into a place."

Jessica grinned at me over her drink, a glass mug of something amber, speared with a cinnamon stick.

"I'm sure guys were always checking you out," she said. "Even if you were too busy to notice." She leaned to the side to look under the table at my boots. "Wowzers. Nice dress, bracelet, tights, and new boots, too. Stormy, did you go to Blue Enchantment and buy everything off the window mannequin?"

"Is it that obvious?"

"Only because I've been dreaming about doing the same thing. But on my salary, I have to hope the good stuff is still around for seasonal clearance sales."

I turned quickly toward the glowing logs in the fireplace so she wouldn't see my reaction. I remembered why Jessica and I lost touch. She'd talked about money every time I saw her, mostly about how she didn't have any whereas I did.

Her comments about my spending always put me on the defensive, which wasn't fair. I worked hard, and didn't deserve to feel bad for having a nice car. Other people didn't see the long hours I put into my career, the sacrifices I made. I missed our high school's ten-year reunion because I was overseas on business, having the most miserable time of my life. The trip to Hong Kong had been years ago, and while I couldn't recall details about the business, I remembered vividly how lonely I'd been in my hotel room, looking at the online photos of everyone who'd made it to the reunion.

If Jessica had ever needed a loan, I would have given it to her, but she refused both charity and debt. I'd try taking her for dinner at nice places as a way of sharing, but she was too proud to let me pay. It killed me to see her digging through the change in her purse for her share of a bill. I eventually resorted to fibbing, secretly intercepting the waitress so I could pay the bill before telling Jessica the restaurant had comped our meal because a dish had been too spicy.

"Earth to Stormy." She waved a pale hand in front of my face. "What are you thinking about?"

I considered telling her the truth, all at once, like ripping off a bandage. If we were going to be friends, I didn't want money coming between us.

"Just remembering that one time in Portland, when we went to the Japanese steakhouse," I said. "Actually, I've been meaning to tell you something about that night."

Her blue eyes widened. "The steak house? That was the best night ever! Seriously, it was the best night of my life, better than prom."

"Really?" I shifted my chair away from the fire.

"And you're so smart, the way you always get those freebies for us." She used her cinnamon stick as a straw to finish the last of her mulled cider. "You know what? I ordered a hot chocolate, but Dharma brought me this cider, and I drank it anyway. I'm such a dummy." She waved for me to lean in over the table and said, "Can you coach me in your ways, oh wise one? How do I charm my way to a free refill?"

I was still reeling from the news that our trip to the steak house had been better than prom for her, but even if I hadn't been so stunned, I didn't have the first clue how to get free stuff in a restaurant.

"Do you want the hot chocolate you ordered, or another cider?"

She licked her lips. "The cider was really good."

I pushed my chair back. "That's an easy one," I lied. "Which one is our waitress?"

Jessica pointed out an older woman with pure white hair. She must have been in her sixties, but by the way she balanced pitchers of beer and a platter of buffalo wings for another table, I could tell she was the type of granny who dragged the other grannies out for tango lessons.

When I intercepted the woman near the bar, she apologized for not checking on our table yet. I gave her my credit card to run a tab. I finished my instructions by saying, "And if my friend asks, could you imply that the next round is on the house?"

"Let me guess," the white-haired waitress said with a knowing smile. "Your friend's poor and you're rich?"

"I'm not rich."

"Your car tells another story," she said. "I was outside to checking that the sidewalks were salted when I saw you pull up."

My cheeks warming, I admitted the priciest car in the parking lot was mine.

"Then you're not rich after all," she said. "Rich people don't drive flashy cars. They drive old ones, so people won't know."

"I should trade my car for something more practical."

"You could trade it for my old van." She winked. "Just kidding. I wouldn't trade my van for anything. The old gal's hitting her prime, and we ladies need to stick together, you know? Men and everything else may come and go, but friendship is forever."

I murmured a half-hearted agreement and returned to the table.

Jessica had her eyes closed and was swaying to the blues song playing over the pub's speakers.

"Good song," I said.

She startled and held her hand to her heart. "I'm the worst," she said. "I've been babbling about steak dinners and hot ciders, and I haven't even asked how you're doing. You look great. Do you want to talk about everything that happened yesterday, or would you rather I didn't pry?"

"Thanks for asking," I said. "Yesterday was—"

I cut myself off when the waitress arrived with two fresh hot ciders. "On the house," she said with a smile.

After the waitress left, I finished, "Yesterday is in the past. Let's leave it there. We've got better things to catch up on. We can talk about boys, like we used to."

I picked up my mug, but she put her hand on my arm, stopping me from taking a sip. Her expression got very serious; I braced myself for something upsetting.

"You should do a toast," she said. "One of those fabulous Irish toasts your family does. Would that be okay?" Before I could respond, she was shaking her head, saying, "No, I'm being silly. Never mind. It's just the two of us, and you're only here tonight because you feel sorry for me, weird little Jessica Kelly who never left Misty Falls or even tried to make something of her life." She turned toward the fireplace, the orange glow of the gas flames catching in the tears she blinked away.

I pushed my chair back and stood.

Still facing the fire, she said, darkly, "We'll save that toast for your going-away party when you get to leave again."

I grabbed my mug and raised it. People were watching, but I didn't care.

Jessica turned to me, tilting her head in confusion.

"You gotta stand," I said.

She got to her feet and held up her mug with a shaking hand.

In a pale imitation of my father's brogue, I intoned, "There are good ships, and there are wood ships, the ships that sail the sea. But the best ships are friendships, and may they always be."

We clinked glasses and took a sip. The mulled hot cider was perfect.

The next hour passed quickly as we talked about old friends, our wacky families, and next month's plans for Christmas and New Year's Eve.

"You should come here to the Fox and Hound," she said. "It's the best place in town because they do a masquerade party. It's fabulous. You should come with me, and you'll meet my friends Marcy and Marvin."

I coughed and shifted uncomfortably in my chair. "If the costume shop is closed due to the owner being behind bars, that might put a wet blanket on everyone's masquerade plans."

"Behind bars?" She looked confused. "I hear Creepy Jeepers made some sort of deal, and he won't even serve time for the break-in."

"But what about the murder?"

She tipped her head to the side. "I'm guessing by the look on your face, you didn't hear the news. He was out of town at the time the police figured the you-know-what happened."

I folded my hands in my lap looked down, making my face neutral, acutely aware of the sensation I was being watched.

Jessica jumped up, waving her hand and calling to someone. She asked if I would mind if someone joined our small table, and I mumbled something, barely able to hear my words over the buzzing in my head.

The third chair pulled out, and slender legs in tight jeans came into view.

CHAPTER 22

JESSICA SAID TO THE NEWCOMER, "This is Stormy Day. She's basically my best friend, so you might be seeing a lot of her."

"Yes," I agreed, looking up with a pleasant smile for the newcomer. "You must be… Marcy?"

"Not even close," she said. "My name is Harper, like the author, Harper Lee."

I shook her hand and repeated, "Harper Lee." Her fingers were very cold.

"Minus the Lee," she said. "Just Harper." She turned to Jessica and complimented her lipstick as well as her hair, worn down and unbraided for a change from how she had to wear it at work.

Harper wore the same too-dark lipstick she'd applied in front of me the day before when she'd fixed her makeup in the one-way mirror at Ruby's. She'd been standing next to Mr. Jenkins, the man who'd broken into the victim's house, but was apparently not being charged in the mysterious death. Was Harper connected somehow? She'd seemed rattled by the news yesterday, but then again, who wouldn't be? I was still reeling from Jessica's bombshell about Creepy Jeepers. When I'd seen the skinny guy outside House of Bean, it must have been him after all. I would do well to trust my instincts more, and right now they were telling me something wasn't quite right with Harper.

I watched her with interest. She scanned the pub again and again, twisting the jewelry in her nose piercing with fingernails that had been bitten to the quick.

Jessica continued the introductions, telling me she worked with Harper and telling the blonde, "Stormy's father is a cop."

"A retired police officer," I said, watching Harper for any signs of discomfort. She sat up straighter and blinked repeatedly.

Jessica said to her, "Don't worry. Stormy's not a stick-in-the-mud just because her dad's a cop. In fact, she's the one you want to get in trouble with because she can talk her way out of anything."

"Cool," Harper said with a head bob. "What kind of trouble?" She tucked a lock of blond hair behind her ear with one hand while she twisted the jewelry in her nose piercing with the other.

Jessica answered on my behalf. "In high school, Stormy used to go after the bullies. She'd teach them a lesson."

I held my hands up. "Guilty as charged. I dumped mashed potatoes and gravy on a few guys in the cafeteria, and now I have a reputation for being nuts."

Harper gave me a sly smile. "Cool. All the best people are crazy."

"I'm not crazy," I said. "I can get a little emotional about things."

"She's passionate," Jessica said with a knowing smirk. "For example, if Stormy wants a vanilla latte, that's what she wants, and not something with a silly name. Once she picks a battle, she'll die on that hill."

I crossed my arms and gave her a pretend-scathing look. "What did you hear?"

She gave me an innocent expression.

Our snowy-haired waitress appeared with three ciders. We hadn't ordered another round yet, as I still had most of my original cider remaining.

"On the house," she said.

"Dharma, no way," Jessica said, rummaging in her purse. "I'll get this round."

The waitress winked at me before saying, "The bearded gentleman at the bar has already paid."

All three of us turned at once to see who she meant. There were three men with beards sitting around the bar, but only one looked back at us with a smile and a wave. Logan Sanderson. He'd changed out of the gray suit he'd worn into my store earlier that day, but he looked every bit as suave in a casual denim shirt.

"What's he drinking?" I asked the waitress.

"Whiskey," she said.

I asked her to list their top-shelf whiskeys and returned his gesture by sending over a glass of twenty-one-year-old Bushmills that my father would have approved of.

After the waitress had left, Jessica wanted to chip in on the drink. I practically had to arm wrestle her to get her to put her purse away.

Harper asked me, "Is that guy a friend of yours? He's cute."

"Cute?" I pretended I hadn't noticed.

Jessica said, "Great. I get you to come out one time, and now some handsome guy is going to steal you away from me."

Laughing, I said, "That's highly unlikely. Never mind me. What's new in your love life? Have you got the usual crew of admirers wanting to find out how fiery a genuine redhead can be?"

"You're so bad." She slapped my knee playfully. "I've really missed having you around to keep me on my toes," she said with a sigh. "Things haven't been so great in the dating department, though. Maybe your friend at the bar has some friends he can introduce me to. How do you know him, anyway?"

"Stop trying to change the subject. What's happening with your skateboard guy?"

"Oh," she said, and soon the details were flowing.

While Jessica filled me in, I replied just enough to keep the conversation going while I observed Harper. Whenever someone walked in the door of the pub, she didn't just glance up casually to see who it was, the way the other people in the pub did. She would stop talking and freeze, like a prey animal looking out for the big, bad wolf. Was she watching the door for the cops, or for someone else? What was her story?

When the conversation came around to her, I asked, "Where did you say you were from, Harper?"

"Here and there. Nowhere interesting." She leaned in and settled her chin on her palm, pretending to be at ease, but leaning to one side if I moved my head enough to block her view of the entrance.

"And what brought you here? Did you move here just to fulfill your lifelong dream of working at the Olive Grove?"

Jessica reached across the table and flicked my arm. "What's next, Stormy? Asking the poor girl what her five-year plan is? Gosh. Lighten up." Jessica explained to Harper, "Stormy owns that cute little gift shop. She's looking for someone else to work part-time so she has more time to…"

Jessica trailed off, looking perplexed. "Stormy, what exactly will you do on your days off? Besides hang out with me. Do you have any hobbies?"

I crossed my arms, unhappy with the way the conversation had turned. "Fine," I admitted. "I'm a recovering workaholic. Maybe I'll take some arts and crafts classes at the community center. I might try yoga, or meditation."

Jessica laughed, leaning forward as she shook, dropping her wavy red hair around her face like a modesty curtain. She kept laughing until she was wiping the corners of her eyes.

Harper bobbed her head, a forced smile on her lips, her eyes on the door.

Jessica wiped her eyes and said, "I might be down to my last twenty dollars, but I'd pay good money to see you in a meditation class. You can't sit still for five minutes, let alone an hour."

"I could if I wanted to."

"Do you want to?"

I frowned at my cider. "Not really," I admitted.

They both laughed and began talking about various exercise classes they'd tried.

As we emptied our mugs of mulled cider, I warmed up to Harper. I wondered if my suspicion of her had any logical basis or was part of some reluctance to meet new people. Making friends was hard. You had to take a risk and feel insecure.

Compared to me, Harper was so young. I kept glancing over at Logan to see if he was looking at her, but he seemed focused on the game playing on the TV.

Jessica reached over and wrenched away the napkin I'd been twisting in my hands. "It's dead now," she said. "You strangled that napkin expertly." To Harper, she said, "You can tell when she's stressed about something because her hands won't stop moving. If there's paper around, she'll start making lists."

"Cool," Harper said. "That must have been scary when you found that man in the snow. Did you know he was one of our regular customers? He came for the early senior's dinner a few times a week."

"He came by himself?" I asked.

Jessica answered, "Table for one, and he brought one of his cowboy novels to read." Her brows knitted together. "He seemed happy enough. He'd talk to the waitresses, and most of the girls didn't like him much because he didn't tip, but he never did anything awful. I can't see why someone would kill him."

I asked, "Did you mention he was your landlord or something like that?"

"I heard he was an investor in the holding company that owns our apartment building. Harper lives in my building, too." She snapped her fingers. "Wait. That's how I know. Harper, he was talking to you about where you lived, and he said he was basically your landlord, so he wondered if he could get a discount." She smiled. "He was funny like that. We never caught him, but I think he took things from the table. Spoons and salt shakers."

Harper jumped to his defense. "He only took one salt shaker. He wasn't that bad. I worked in this other restaurant before, and we had this one family who'd clean us out, everything from ketchup to sugar packets and the big rolls of toilet paper in the bathroom."

Jessica asked, "What restaurant? I thought you didn't have any experience waiting tables before."

Harper's cheeks reddened. "Oh, I was just the cashier, and it was only for a few weeks." She took a sip of her drink and looked at me. "Poor Mr. Michaels. I hope it was painless. You saw his face, right? How did he look?"

I considered my response. The muscles of the face contort with rigor mortis, and it's only in extreme situations, such as a painful death from strychnine poisoning, that facial expression gives any hint of the deceased's emotional state on passing. The peaceful expressions seen on loved ones at open casket services are the result of the good work done by caring embalmers and funeral cosmetologists.

Harper was leaning in, looking both sad and hopeful, giving the impression she cared about how Murray Michaels had felt as he passed into his next adventure. She didn't want to hear forensic science. With her sweet expression and the flickering light from the fireplace making her pale hair a golden halo, she looked like an angel who'd come to watch over the man's final days, refilling his coffee cup and looking the other way while he snagged silverware. She didn't look at all like someone who'd snuff out his life. I felt slightly guilty for even considering a suspect.

"Well?" Haper bit her lower lip. "Did he look scared?"

"He looked peaceful," I said. "Very peaceful, considering."

"Good," she said softly. "May he rest in peace."

CHAPTER 23

IT WAS MIDNIGHT when I got home. I'd avoided bumping into my tenant at the house so far, but by the look of the bright windows on his side of the duplex, he'd beaten me home from the Fox and Hound.

I bypassed the driveway and pulled up along the sidewalk, where I could catch a glimpse into his place. The curtains were wide open, showing off his living room furniture, which was all modern and enviably stylish. His color blindness hadn't hampered his decorating efforts. While there were some unpacked cardboard boxes stacked in the corner, he had, in less than twenty-four hours, made his side of the duplex look more like a home than my side.

"What a jerk," I muttered with equal parts indignation and amusement.

My car was still running.

The mature thing to do would have been to get out of my car, walk over to his door, knock politely, and properly introduce myself. There would be an awkward transition when he realized he'd made crude remarks about his landlady to his landlady, but we could get over that. We could be friends. He could tell me where he bought his very attractive standing lamp.

My eyes wandered from the lamp to the framed prints on the wall to a man's bare chest. I let out a girlish squeal. Logan was shirtless, walking around the brightly-lit living room half naked. He brought a laundry basket full of clothes to the sofa and began folding clothes.

I couldn't tear my eyes away. He flexed and stretched, his appealing torso completely changing my feelings about laundry. When he was done folding and placing everything in neat stacks, he nestled everything back into the laundry basket and disappeared down the hallway.

Now what? If I knocked on his door now, would he answer shirtless? Or was he down to his underwear by now? Or naked?

I didn't have to knock on his door tonight. I could go straight to my side and put off the introductions until tomorrow. So why couldn't I shut off the car's engine and get out?

I was spooked. The bubbly feelings I got from seeing Logan with his shirt off terrified me. After breaking off my engagement, I'd planned to take a long break from anything romantic. I thought it would be easy to ignore the flirtations of men, that I'd feel numb, closed off from so much fighting and acrimony in that department. But I didn't feel cold and dead inside after all. Some naive part of me felt as girlish and optimistic as I'd been as a teenager, before I'd ever known heartbreak. Naivety was a vulnerability, the exact opposite of being numb.

Now fate had practically dropped into my lap this handsome, single lawyer. It was too good to be true. Like a big chunk of cheese resting on a ten-cent mousetrap. I knew a trap when I saw one.

The only thing worse than having a girlish crush on a guy was dating him, losing him, and having to live next door while he carried on with other women. That exact scenario had never happened to me before, but I was able to imagine it with such perfect clarity, I wondered if it hadn't happened to me in a previous life.

I reached over to my purse to grab my phone. Jessica had made me promise to call her again soon. She wouldn't be expecting me to do so within an hour, but she'd laugh at my predicament and probably have some words of encouragement. Her own relationships were disasters, but she gave sage advice to others. I had a feeling she'd tell me to go for it, go knock on Logan's door, even if he was shirtless. She'd cheer me on, the way she always had in high school whenever I got uncertain about something. It was because of her that I learned how much fun could be had when I stepped outside of my comfort zone.

If Logan was indeed a trap, she'd tell me to step right in and enjoy the ride.

Instead of my phone, I accidentally pulled out a cloth satchel of something crunchy. It was the parting gift of catnip the Calico Veterinary Clinic had sent me off with, as a pick-me-up for Jeffrey during his recovery. At the thought of his sweet face, my heart filled with a different type of longing. All plans to call Jessica for girlish encouragement evaporated. I wasn't a teenager anymore. I had responsibilities.

The little guy was at my father's house. I'd assumed Pam would be back and taking care of him, but what if she wasn't? I hadn't spoken to her since the day before.

The cloth satchel smelled faintly of mint but mostly like my father's wool socks.

I put the car in drive and steered away from the curb.

CHAPTER 24

I WOKE UP to more unwanted eyebrow licking.

"Jeffrey, you're insatiable," I said.

I rolled onto my back, and he settled on my chest, his chin hovering over my chin.

"Why are you in my room?" I asked him. "Don't you want to sleep on Dad's bed with Pam? She's your real owner. Not me. I'm only here because I'm too chicken to return to my duplex and… make nice with my tenant." Jeffrey twitched one ear. "Plus I was worried about you."

He began to purr, a loud rumble that expressed his loyal devotion to me, the amazing person who had fed him twice as much canned food as he was supposed to get for each meal.

"You do love me," I said.

His purr got even louder, in agreement. And also to let me know it was time for breakfast. Now, please.

I got out of bed and went down to the main floor bathroom for a shower, as the upstairs bathroom was only a powder room. I passed through the kitchen to give Pam a quick good morning.

She looked up from the pots she was banging in the sink. "The woodchuck is awake!" she exclaimed. "Can you see your shadow? Will it be an early spring?"

"You're thinking of the groundhog," I said.

She blinked. "No. Your hair reminds me of a woodchuck." She looked down at my legs, bare from the knee down below my sleep shirt. "Is that what you're wearing today? I have some leggings you could borrow. It's still winter outside, last time I checked."

I glanced longingly at the coffeemaker, which was running but not finished brewing. "Shower first," I said. "Then coffee. Then I swear I'll be a better audience for your jokes."

"You people and your coffee." She rolled her eyes. "Shower fast and you can have some french toast."

I thanked her for the offer I couldn't refuse and hustled off to the bathroom.

While I showered, Jeffrey sat on the counter and howled, deeply concerned that I was getting wet. I had to leave the shower curtain partly open so he could see that I was okay. After the terrifying (according to Jeffrey) shower, I got dressed in some of the new casual clothes I'd picked up the day before. The brown cords and emerald green blouse looked smart and chic and were a different look for me.

When I'd lived in Portland, I'd alternated between ultra-conservative gray business suits at work and comfortable jeans and polar fleece on the weekends. I didn't have much in the dressy casual range, but thanks to my new favorite boutique, that was about to change.

I found her in the kitchen, making enough french toast to feed five of us. Jeffrey made happy warbles as I put some food out on his plate.

"You're spoiling the cat," she said.

"He's still growing, Pam. I would hold back on the canned food if he was getting chubby, but he's perfect. Lots of good muscle. Right, Jeffrey?"

She kept frying french toast at the stove, her back to me.

"I didn't mean with the food," she said. "I mean the way you talk to her."

"Not her. Him."

"Whatever. I heard you in the guest room, carrying on with him. If you talk to the cat like he's a person, there's not going to be any room in your life for a real man." She sighed. "It's bad enough you went and practically shaved your head."

I turned to Jeffrey, who had gobbled his wet food and moved on to the bowl of dry kibble Pam had set out for him.

"Jeffrey, you tell Pam there's nothing wrong with this haircut. Modern men aren't afraid of a woman with some style. Tell her about the handsome lawyer who bought me a drink last night."

"Lawyer?" Pam coughed. "When did you meet with a lawyer? Why?"

"He was at the Lost and Found. I mean the Fox and Hound."

"But why? Why was he there?"

"To drink beer and watch sports on TV, same as half the other guys there." I hovered near her shoulder. "Do you need a hand with anything?"

"Sit," she commanded. "Eat."

I helped myself to coffee and french toast, taking both to the kitchen table.

"This is great," I said. "For the last few years, breakfast has been something I cram down my throat while I stand over the sink."

"Hmm." She didn't turn around. "The corporate lifestyle. Busy, busy."

"I'm not complaining," I said. "But it could have been better. I wanted to have dinner parties, but my fiancé wasn't social. He was competitive, actually. We had another couple over to play board games, and he put them into bankruptcy."

"Hmm."

"Not real bankruptcy. Just inside the game." I could smell something burning. "Pam, are you burning something?"

With her back still to me, she said quietly, "I suppose it's a good thing the two of you didn't get married or have children to fight over."

"Sure," I said. People kept saying that to me, along with how good it was we didn't have children. It never made me feel like any less of a failure, but I'd learned it was easier not to disagree.

"What about him?" she asked. "Is he having a fresh start?"

I snorted. "Probably."

"Younger women?"

"Honestly, I don't know," I said. I told her how I'd blocked him on my social media accounts so I wouldn't have to be informed of his every move. Unfortunately, we still had some friends and business contacts in common, so I did see him in group photos, often with his arm around one or more young women. When we were a couple, he avoided loud music and crowds, but now that he was single, he sure popped up at a lot of parties for someone who hated to go out.

Girls flocked to him, of course. They didn't care he was the kind of guy who screamed when he saw a harmless little spider under a plastic cup. They wanted to get on board with someone who had both family money and a future that promised fat bonuses.

"Men!" Pam exclaimed angrily. "Always one eye roving around for something better and younger!"

I was surprised by how upset she'd gotten. As far as I knew, her previous marriage ended five years prior when her husband passed away. She'd been with my father for less than a year, and I didn't think there'd been anyone else in between.

"Pam? Is something bothering you? Has Finnegan done something? You know he's always been friendly to people. That's just his way. He's very friendly."

By now, the kitchen was full of the unmistakable smell of burning food. She still hadn't flipped over the french toast, and by now it had to be blackened.

"Friendly," she said with distaste. "Of course you'd take his side. You people stick together."

"What people?" I asked lightly. "Do you mean the Irish?"

Instead of answering, she started cursing under her breath. I hadn't spent enough time with her to know if she was genuinely outraged, or if this was her weird, funny side coming out. I'd seen her rant about my father before, and it usually sputtered out after a few minutes of running its course.

The smoke detector let out a warning chirp. It would go off any second unless I did something. I reached carefully over Pam to flick on the fan in the range hood and then opened the window over the sink. I looked across into Mr. Michaels' kitchen and felt my stomach knot instantly. It was hard to forget about what had happened next door when the crime scene was your kitchen view. I'd talked to Pam for a few minutes the night before, about how Leo Jenkins was no longer in police custody. She hadn't seemed worried, saying at least she knew who to look out for, but then she'd suddenly remembered seeing another man lurking around the neighborhood a few weeks earlier. I'd tried to get more details to pass on to Tony, but she'd been tired.

"Pam, do you remember anything else about that guy?"

She snapped, "I can't keep track of everyone all the time."

I sighed. "Last night, you told me you saw someone skulking around the neighborhood, knocking on Mr. Michaels' door. Do you remember if he was old or young?"

"Heck if I know," she said before moving on to words more flavorful than heck.

I gently took her by the shoulder and gave her a shake. "Easy now. Shh," I said. "The window's open now, and we don't want the whole block to find out what a filthy truck driver mouth you have."

She turned her head and looked at me blankly, as though she'd just awoken in a strange location. I'd been smiling, somewhat amused by her colorful ranting, but now that I saw how dazed out she was, it wasn't as funny anymore.

"Are you feeling okay?" I asked. "Did you take your blood pressure medication yet? Or is it thyroid pills?"

"Fools," she said. "They're just silly, old fools. We all are."

I turned off the stove burner and took the spatula from her hand.

"Let me finish up here, Pam."

"I've ruined everything," she said.

"There's plenty of french toast already. You've made enough to feed an army."

She blinked rapidly and turned away from me. "I need a nap. I didn't sleep well last night, and you woke me up when you got in late from the bar." She gave me an accusatory look. "Why are you staying here? You don't think I need looking after, do you?"

"Go have your nap," I said gently. "I'll clean up here. Don't be so hard on yourself, okay? Dad will be back soon, and everything will be back to normal."

She muttered, "I doubt that very much," and left the kitchen.

I tidied up and sat down to eat my french toast. To Pam's credit, the ones she didn't burn were delicious.

CHAPTER 25

WITH A STOMACH full of breakfast, I left Pam to her nap and showed myself out. When I'd arrived the night before, I'd found her vehicle crookedly blocking both spots at the back of the house, so I'd parked in the front. I left through the front door, and as I locked up, my eye was caught by a yellow envelope resting between a snow-covered plant pot and the porch railing. I reached down and retrieved not one, but four envelopes, all yellow and the same size.

I would have put them in the mailbox for Pam to retrieve, but they weren't addressed to my father's house. They were for the deceased man, Murray Michaels. They must have fallen there the day before, when I'd startled the carrot-crunching mail carrier. He'd dropped his bag, scattering its contents on the porch.

Now what was I supposed to do with these? They weren't just junk mail. By the look of the portion visible through the clear address window, these were checks. The return address was from a company called R&F Brokers. The moisture from the snow had made the envelopes soft. As I turned the envelopes over in my hands, the flap on one came loose. With a barely-perceptible nudge of my thumb, it flipped right open.

My breath caught in my throat. I looked up and down the street, self-conscious of my mail tampering. Opening someone else's mail was a serious offense, but I really wanted to see what the checks were for. Was this what Mr. Jenkins had been searching for when he broke in?

I gave the envelope a gentle shake. The check fell out into my hand. The check was from R&F Brokers, the same as the return address, and the dollar amount was for only $43.77. My heart sank as I double-checked the puny figure. So much for cracking the case wide open. People killed over relatively small sums of money, but $43.77 was too small. The memo line held only an alpha-numeric code.

I shook the other envelopes until their checks "accidentally" fell out as well. The others would have bought a few rounds at the Fox and Hound but not much more. I slid the checks back into their envelopes and went to my car.

I'd planned to work on some orders and data entry at the store, but it could wait. I glanced over at the envelopes on the passenger seat, noting that the address of R&F Brokers wasn't far from the hospital where my father was recovering. I entertained the notion of going to R&F myself and finding out what Murray Michaels had been pawning and how frequently, but then I quickly dismissed the idea. As intrigued as I was, getting myself further involved in the investigation would be rash.

I drove to the police station with the intention of hand-delivering the checks to Tony, but once I'd parked, my body felt as heavy as cement. The station had once been a friendly place for me, but most of the people I knew had all retired. For the first time in my life, I viewed the red brick building as intimidating.

The front door opened, and the instant I saw it was Tony Milano, I knew my dread about entering the building was actually dread about seeing him. I heard my father's voice in my head, telling me to jump back in the saddle. Considering some of the moments I'd shared with Tony during our brief fling, my father's advice took on a comically inappropriate tone.

I jumped out of the car and waved at him. "Tony Baloney!"

Shaking his head, he walked over toward me. "Stormy, I can only do what the law allows. If you want someone shot, get your own gun." He stopped in front of me and stuffed his hands in his jacket pockets. "On second thought, stay away from weapons. Someone with your temper shouldn't own anything more deadly than one of those gardening fork things, and even that's questionable."

"How about a crossbow? I just bought one. It's in the trunk with my dynamite and my nunchakus."

He ruffled the white hairs at his temples and fixed me with his dark brown eyes. "What are you doing here?"

"Helping with the Michaels case."

"We don't need any help," he said, spitting the word help with distaste. "Pam Bochenek gave us a description of the guy she saw skulking around the place a few weeks ago. The guy was big, dark hair, bearded, and looked like a drifter. Sounds a lot like your friend from the vet clinic. The one who calls himself a lawyer."

"Do you mean Logan Sanderson? He's not your guy."

Tony straightened up and scratched about two days' worth of stubble on his chin as he looked down his nose at me. "And how do you know that? Are you his alibi?"

"Never mind about Logan. Why'd you let Creepy Jeepers go?"

"Creepy Jeepers?" Tony's mouth threatened to betray him with a grin, but he fought it. "You mean Leo Jenkins? He was out of town during the week-long window that Michaels disappeared. We could charge him for the break-in, but in light of the fact he was looking for some items that the man had stolen from him in the first place, I don't know. We might look the other way."

"What items?" I asked. "What was Jenkins looking for?"

"He didn't have anything on him, but he claimed he was looking for a pair of cufflinks and a bag of none-of-your-business." He looked me up and down as he stepped back. "You'll read about it in the paper with everyone else once we get this business cleaned up." He started walking away, calling back over his shoulder, "Stay out of trouble."

CHAPTER 26

PORTLAND, OREGON, is not exactly New York City, but I'd forgotten how busy city traffic was. Cars zoomed by, changing lanes without signaling, the drivers distracted by their phones, speeding toward congested intersections like red blood cells toward a wound. By comparison, in Misty Falls the traffic jams lasted all of a minute, and nobody dared honk since they probably knew the person in front of them.

When I got to the hospital, I did something I hadn't done in ages; I paid for parking. Sure, it was tricky to order a grande vanilla latte in Misty Falls, but you never paid a cent for parking.

I stretched my arms and back as I walked into the hospital. I found my father's floor without incident, but when I got to his room, he was sleeping. I took a seat on the hard-backed chair near his side, expecting him to open his eyes at any moment. The room had another bed, but it was unoccupied. The window had a view of a small city park with green grass. Unlike our town, which was further inland and much higher in elevation, Portland hadn't received any snow yet that winter, and would get no more than four or five days of frozen precipitation, at the most.

After ten minutes of the pleasure of watching Finnegan Day sleep, a dark-haired woman in pale green scrubs came in.

She saw me and said sweetly, "You're as lovely as I imagined. Which one are you, the sunshine or the rain?"

I got up to shake her hand. "My reputation has preceded me. You could say I'm the rain. Stormy Day."

The woman was forty-something, with flawless dark skin, a high forehead, and chin-length curly hair. She had an energetic presence and quick eyes, darting around to check everything in the room. She reminded me of my dental hygienist in Portland, who was from Jamaica, but it must have been because of their similar bone structure, for she had no accent. Her handshake was firm enough to make me wonder if mine was weak.

"Your father is quite the man," she said breathlessly, as though talking about meeting her favorite actor. "He says I should move to Misty Falls now that my son's off to college."

"Oh, did he?"

Finnegan Day continued sleeping peacefully, unaware of my accusatory glare. My father loved his town, but he didn't go around recruiting random people into moving there. His interest in this woman had to be personal. And here I'd thought those days were behind him.

The woman said, "I have to admit I'm curious. He's been telling me about your town ever since we met." She walked around the bed, tucking the blankets in along his sides.

I checked her name tag, and everything clicked into place. Dora Jones. We'd spoken on the phone when I called to check on him, and she'd been so friendly.

This was the woman who had helped with my father's physical assessments. The way Pam had gone on about Dora being bossy, I'd thought she'd just been complaining for the sake of complaining. Suddenly, it all made sense. No wonder Pam felt threatened. No wonder she'd burned the heck out of the french toast. She knew he was here at the hospital, being cared for by a compassionate woman with big, amber-brown eyes and a lithe body that made hospital scrubs look flattering.

Dora finished tucking him in and said, "How about you? Are you glad to be living back in your hometown again? Hanging out with your old friends?"

"Somewhat," I said. "It sounds like you've been spending a lot of time with my father. You two must talk a lot while you do whatever it is you do. Exactly what is that, Dora? Are you a physical therapist?"

She made the face people make when someone gets the title of their occupation wrong. "I'm an orthopedic nurse," she said, enunciating each syllable carefully. "I've been with your father through everything, including the surgery."

"Did you get to use the power tools?"

She squinted for a few tense seconds before laughing. "You've got your father's sense of humor." She wagged her finger at me. "Power tools. You really had me going." She patted my sleeping father's arm. "We'll have to tell him when he wakes up."

We both turned and watched him sleep.

Gazing at him tenderly, Dora said, "Poor ducky. He's been living with a lot of pain."

I chuckled. "He does live with Pam Bochenek."

Dora's expression contorted, her smooth brow wrinkling. "It's a shame he took that tumble, or he might have delayed the surgery for years."

"That tumble?"

Dora turned to give me a knowing look, sisterly warmth in her eyes.

"Sometimes I wonder if someone pushed him," Dora said icily. "Your father claims he slipped in the bath, but the injuries weren't consistent with the fall he described."

"Right," I said, pretending I knew what she was talking about. "And what do you think happened?"

She glanced around, shifting her weight from one foot to the other, looking as though she wanted to say something but needed more prodding to overstep her boundaries as an orthopedic nurse. What did she know? My father hadn't mentioned a fall, let alone being pushed. My head got fuzzy as the edges of the room darkened.

"Was it his neighbor?" I asked. "A man named Murray? Is that who pushed him?"

"Who?" Dora didn't show any recognition of the name Murray.

"Dora, if you know something, please tell me."

She appeared to struggle with a desire to flee the room but finally said, "I don't think she meant to push him down the stairs." She waved one hand dismissively. "He was probably saying something sassy, like he always does, and she gave him a shove, and down the steps he went."

"Are you saying Pam pushed my father down the stairs? Do you mean the ones inside his house?"

She took two steps backward, toward the hallway, shaking her corkscrew curls. "I'm not saying anything, dear." She forced her mouth into a disconcerting smile. "But you might want to ask him about his fall."

"Dad," I said, shaking his shoulder. "Stop pretending to be asleep." His nostrils flared, and the rhythm of his breathing broke, but he didn't wake up. I shook his shoulder again.

"He won't be out much longer," Dora said, talking quickly and edging toward the door. "Would you like to borrow a book from the floor's library? I could get you a real coffee from the staff lounge. Don't use the vending machine in the hall if you know what's good for you."

I looked once more at my father, who was smiling, enjoying whatever dream he was in.

"What do you say to that coffee?" Dora asked. She stood in the doorway with her palms pressed together in a prayer-like gesture. She wore three rings on her fingers, but her wedding ring finger was bare. She was a single mother with a full-grown son, and I knew she was just my father's type because his type was any female who found him charming.

"Thanks for the kind offer," I said. "I've got an errand here in the city. If he wakes up, tell him I need to speak with him, and he'd better not go anywhere."

"Don't you worry," Dora said. "I won't let him get away."

CHAPTER 27

NO MATTER HOW DARK things get, life has a way of getting better when you do a good deed for someone else.

Though I was worried about my father's hip, his situation with Pam, the prospect of my new tenant being wanted for questioning, plus a killer on the loose back in Misty Falls, I could do some good during my visit to Portland. I got into my car and punched the address for R&F Brokers into the navigation system. If Mr. Jenkins had broken in looking for stolen cufflinks, they likely had some sentimental value, and it would be a good deed for me to retrieve them. I had to assume Tony had checked his alibi for the time during which Mr. Michaels had disappeared and that the man was innocent. The good deed would also assuage some of my guilt for continuing to call him Creepy Jeepers in my head.

R&F Brokers was, as I suspected, a pawn shop. An assortment of tough-looking guys were leaving when I arrived. Despite the chilly winter weather, the men wore no jackets, all the better to show off their arm tattoos and thick gold chains.

They gave me an appreciative look when I stepped out of my car. I was wearing my new lace-up boots, wool jacket, brown cords, and emerald green blouse. One of the bigger guys gave me a chin-lift gesture as he walked by, letting me know he liked what he saw. I smiled to myself, happy my new clothes had been a good investment.

I walked into the pawn shop and immediately started sneezing from the dust. A young woman of about twenty, with a shaved head and multiple piercings, sat behind the main counter on a stool, oblivious to me as she thumbed her phone screen. I sneezed again, and she didn't even glance my way, let alone greet me.

I told her, "Your customers wouldn't sneeze so much if someone ran a damp cloth over these display cases."

She looked up at me as though I was a fussy older person who stuck her nose in everyone's business. I realized, with horror, that I wasn't so different from Pam, who'd said the same thing to my employee three days earlier.

The girl with the buzz cut gave me a dull stare. "Sure," she said. "I'll get right on that. Anything else?"

"I'm looking for some cufflinks. They're possibly vintage."

"What are cufflinks?" She stared at me steadily, her expression unchanging.

Instead of explaining, I reached into my purse and pulled out the yellow envelopes. "These checks are from here, right?"

She shrugged. "Looks like it. What's wrong, lady? Did your kid pawn your stuff for drug money?"

"My kid?" She'd basically handed me a premise far better than the one I'd had in mind. I stood on the precipice for several seconds before taking the plunge, casting my eyes down so she wouldn't see my discomfort over lying. "He used to be such a good boy," I said.

"Sorry about that," she said, hints of genuine sympathy in her tone. "That's a real bummer when they steal from you, but I can't cash those checks, and if the goods are sold, they're long gone."

The dust was making my eyes water. I sniffed and rubbed my eye. "I'll never be able to replace those cufflinks."

"Don't cry," she said. "I can look up the lot number from one of those checks and cross-reference it to see if anything's still here, if you want."

I sniffed convincingly. "Thank you so much."

"I'll have to look it up on the computer, but yeah, whatever." She took one of the checks and started tapping away at a computer terminal that looked older than she was. Her movements stirred up more dust, making me sneeze. With each sneeze, she gave me a suspicious look, as though I was doing it on purpose to make her feel bad about not dusting. I busied myself by looking around at some of the musical instruments on display. An accordion caught my eye, and I wondered what stories the old squeezebox had to tell.

The employee called out to let me know she'd found something. I met her at the counter, where she showed me a tray with four small items. There was a pair of cufflinks, a jeweled money clip, a man's gold wedding band, and a panther broach.

"You're amazing," I told her. "I really appreciate your help. I only need the cufflinks. How much?"

She pointed to the check on the counter between us. "I might be able to do a straight exchange for the check since it's been less than four weeks."

I guiltily took back the check. "I appreciate the offer, but I'll pay for the cufflinks with my credit card. I need these checks for evidence."

"Evidence, huh?" She whistled. "Your kid is in some serious, deep trouble." A phone rang loudly, and she excused herself to answer the call.

While she had her back turned, I used my phone to snap pictures of the other three items. According to the dollar amount of the check, none of these objects seemed valuable enough to murder someone over, but I would pass the information along to Tony, or, better yet, Officer Wiggles, who'd probably be more appreciative of my help. The panther resembled the charm I'd seen Ruby wearing.

While I was paying for the cufflinks, another customer came in, the door movement setting off a trio of bells and alarms. The employee finished her phone call, shot me an apologetic look, and went to greet the other customer. It was a female who asked if the shop's owner was in that day.

"Never this early," the girl answered. "He's more of a night owl."

"Can I leave a note?"

The employee sighed but fetched a pad of paper and pen over to the other customer. I was busy trying to take some decent photos, which was difficult given the low light, and only paying attention to the other interaction peripherally. As the customer was saying goodbye, I glanced over.

I was surprised to see a familiar face. The other customer was Harper, the blonde who worked with Jessica.

"Harper," I said in a friendly tone.

She didn't look over, even though I was only a dozen feet away. Had she not heard me over the '80s-era rock ballad playing on the shop's dusty speakers?

I tried again. "Hi there, Harper."

She handed the paper to the employee, turned, and walked out of the shop without acknowledging me.

The employee rubbed her shaved head and gave me a sheepish look as she came over to finish ringing up the cufflinks. "I guess your friend didn't want to talk to you," she said.

"We've only met once," I said. "Maybe it wasn't who I thought it was." I looked at the folded sheet of paper in the employee's hand. "What name did she give you?"

The girl looked even more uncomfortable. "Ma'am, this is a pawn shop. It's not the public library."

"I understand. Could you maybe blink once if she left her name as Harper?"

The girl stared at me. She had beautiful eyes, one green and one blue. Neither one blinked.

After a moment, she clicked some keys, an old printer spat out a receipt, and she handed it over with a plain paper bag containing the cufflinks.

I thanked her and hurried out of the store, scanning the parking lot for the girl. People were coming and going, visiting other shops in the strip mall, but none of them looked like the blonde I could have sworn was Harper.

Then I spotted a flash of golden hair as a girl stepped into the driver's side of an older-model green Ford Torino. I whipped out my phone and took a photo of the license plate as she drove away.

CHAPTER 28

TRAFFIC WAS BAD, and the trip back to the hospital took twice as long as the reverse direction. I got stuck behind a truck advertising soy sauce, the bottle photographed next to delicious Chinese food. By the time I got to the hospital, I was hungry enough to eat a whole order of the Golden Wok's sweet and sour chicken balls.

I took the elevator up to my father's floor and walked down to his room. He was awake, but he wasn't alone.

Sitting next to the bed was Officer Tony Milano, who looked as thrilled to see me now as he had been several hours earlier, outside the police station.

I asked, "What's going on?"

My father was sitting up in bed, awake and alert. He almost looked like his usual self, except for the hospital gown and a scruffy jawline in need of a shave.

"Business as usual," my father said calmly. "The Misty Falls police department is trying to pin a case on me."

"Not again," I said.

He shrugged. “It’s been a few years. I suppose this is their way of letting me know that just because I’ve been put out to pasture, I haven’t been forgotten.”

I walked around the bed, to the opposite side of where Tony sat. The other bed was still empty, so it was only the three of us in the room. The sun had pierced the Portland Mist and was brightening the pale lavender wall across from the beds.

I glared at Tony. “You’re not actually going after my father for this one, are you? Don’t you have more important things to do?”

“More important than catching a murderer?” Tony’s dark eyebrows raised. “I’m doing my job.”

“It’s okay,” my father said to me. “In a small town, you can’t skip investigating the people you know, or you’ll have to skip everyone. I’d come after me too, if I were him. After all, I’m the dummy who uttered death threats, on multiple occasions.”

I crossed my arms. “No, you didn’t.”

“Old Murray knew I was joking,” he said. “Everyone did. But threats are threats. He was a notorious kleptomaniac, did you know that?”

I glanced over at Tony, who nodded. “We’re getting a clearer picture of the situation every day.”

“He took an extension cord,” my father said. “It was brand new, perfect condition. I told him I’d be happy to loan him anything he wanted, and he didn’t have to take things and lie about it. He swore he hadn’t seen my extension cord, so I told him if I found it inside his house, I was going to wrap it around his neck.” He shifted to arrange the pillow behind his back. “In hindsight, that wasn’t a very gentlemanly way to deal with a situation, but the pain made me cranky some days."

"Did he return the cord?" Tony asked.

"It appeared one day on my porch, as if by magic."

"Good," Tony said. "That's good to hear."

While Tony jotted notes on his notepad, I asked, "Dad, did things ever get physical? Did Murray ever push you?"

His gray-flecked eyebrows raised. "What have you heard?"

"Your orthopedic nurse told me you hurt your hip because of a tumble. Why didn't you tell me you fell?"

He dismissed the notion with a wave of one hand. "This hip's been bothering me for years. I did give it a bump recently, when I slipped on the wet floor, but it was nothing."

Watching him very closely, I said, "I heard you slipped in the tub. Now you're saying it was the floor. Which one is it?"

"Same thing," he said. "One foot on each." He turned to Tony. "Murray was nowhere near the bathroom."

Tony said, "I believe you."

"What about Pam?" I asked. "Was she there when you fell?"

"Not that it's any of your business, young lady, but no," he said vehemently. His Irish accent became more pronounced, as it always did when he was either being charming or getting agitated. "Pam was not there when I stepped out of the tub and slipped on some water and fell."

Tony said, "At your age, you need to be careful. I can get you some stick-ons to put inside the tub. We have them for the kids. Little yellow ducks."

My father sat up straighter in the bed and told Tony what he could do with his little yellow ducks.

Tony patiently flipped through the pages of his small notepad. Once my father's rant was over, he said, "You were heard promising to 'choke some sense' into Mr. Michaels. Was that in reference to the electrical cord incident?"

"Could have been anything. The man was in need of some sense."

I patted my father's hand. "Dad, you don't have to answer these questions now. We can talk to a lawyer."

Consulting his notepad, Tony asked, "How long ago did your relationship become contentious?"

My father scratched the gray scruff on his chin. "We started off on the wrong foot, right from the beginning, when he moved in over twenty years ago. He kept asking me what the girls' real names were."

I interrupted, "Did he really?"

He chuckled. "He thought I called you two Sunny and Stormy just to irritate him."

"I never knew about that."

"He suggested the whole family see a psychiatrist."

I smirked. "Now that's funny."

My father grinned. "It was right after the Halloween that your imaginary friend, Johnny Green, or whatever his name was, egged Murray's house. In hindsight, I probably should have taken you somewhere to get your brain fixed."

I rolled my eyes. “Oh, Dad. I couldn’t have actually believed in imaginary friends.”

Tony cleared his throat. “As much fun as this is, catching up on old times, can Finn and I have a few minutes of privacy?”

I patted my father’s arm. “I’ll wait outside of the room. I still need to talk to Tony about something.”

Tony said, “Don’t lurk around the hallway. I’ll meet you down in the cafeteria when I’m done here. I’ll even buy you lunch.”

“I’m not hungry,” I lied.

“Yes, you are,” my father said. “I can hear your stomach rumbling. I’ve already had my lunch. You go have yours, and we’ll talk after.”

I hesitated by his side. “Dad, just give Tony straight yes and no answers. Your pupils look awfully dilated right now. If you feel confused at all, it’s probably because of the pain meds. Promise you’ll call for me if you need me.”

He pointed to the door and gave me his I’m-Your-Father look, which hadn’t lost any of its power.

CHAPTER 29

THE HOSPITAL CAFETERIA had closed the hot lunch buffet and didn't have dinner ready yet, so I chose a sandwich from the cooler, paired with a bowl of vegetable soup. I ate quickly, pausing only to set the four yellow envelopes on the table and write down the blonde's license plate number on the back of my receipt. Minimizing my time with Tony would save us both aggravation.

He arrived in the cafeteria as I was finishing. When he spotted me, he gave me an unexpectedly warm smile that was the exact opposite of the expression he'd given me twice that day. I actually glanced over my shoulder to see if someone better was sitting behind me.

He got his lunch and joined me without saying a word. He used a cafeteria butter knife to methodically cut his ham and cheese sandwich into quarters and then eighths.

"That's cute," I commented.

He frowned at his sandwich as though confounded. "Did I just cut this sandwich into quarters?"

"Technically, those are eighths."

He sighed and rubbed his temples. “Tony Junior will only eat sandwiches cut like this. I must have been on autopilot. This is what kids and lack of sleep will do to you.” He gestured to my empty dishes. “Good job cleaning your plate. I’ll buy you dessert. They just put out a fresh tray of Jell-O.” He handed me a twenty. “Get me one, too.”

I left him to his sandwich and returned with two bowls of colorful gelatin cubes.

Between mouthfuls, I said, “I haven’t had Jell-O in years.”

“If you don’t like the red cubes, I’ll eat them for you.”

I curled my arm around my bowl protectively. “Nice try. Those are the best ones.”

After a few minutes of comfortable silence, I asked, “Do you guys still have the quote board?”

He looked surprised and then amused. The board was a running gag at the police station. They’d use it to whenever, during the course of their work, one officer said something that would get a person fired from a corporate job. Taken out of context, the quotes were even more shocking and thus funny. They didn’t keep the board to disrespect their work or the victims of crime but to break the darkest moments with a laugh, to keep their sanity.

“Officially, there’s no quote board,” he said with a wink.

“Your new rookie seems sharp,” I said. “How are things going with Officer Peggy Wiggles?”

His mouth kept smiling, but the crinkles left his eyes. “Super. She’s great.”

“Except?”

His brown eyes seemed to grow darker. "Never mind about Wiggles."

"How about the case? Did you get anything useful from my father?"

He turned to the cafeteria window. "Yes. Plenty."

"You're wasting your time," I said. "He's just messing with you because he's bored."

"In a small town, you can't skip investigating the people you know, or you'll have to skip everyone."

"How about strangers?" I asked. "Have you tried rounding up all the new residents and checking their records?"

"I know you're joking, but it's not a bad idea. What do you know about this Logan Sanderson guy? I should show his picture to Pam, to see if she recognizes him from skulking around the neighborhood."

I rolled my eyes. "He's a lawyer, not some itinerant thrill-killer."

He clenched his jaw, flexing his cheek muscles several times. "Stormy, you've got to be careful. Go to work, go home, and don't go poking around. Let me handle this."

"Too late." I pushed the envelopes and license plate number over to him. "The mailman dropped these on my porch, and the moisture from the snow made the flaps accidentally come open."

He let out a long sigh as he dug into the envelopes. "Save us both the hassle and tell me everything."

"Do I have immunity for the mail tampering?"

"Full immunity," he said. "Spill it."

I explained how I'd stopped into the pawn shop to look for Leo Jenkins' cufflinks as a good deed, but then Harper had shown up and not responded to her name. I gave him the license plate number and suggested he look into the girl. As I gave my instructions to the uniformed man, I was keenly aware of how flimsy my logic was. My suspicion of Harper was little more than a gut feeling.

To my surprise, he got his phone and called in the license plate number without protest.

"Thanks for humoring me," I said after he was done.

"What's your theory?" he asked. "And don't tell me you don't have a theory. I know you, Stormy. You always have a theory or two."

I explained how I'd heard gossip about Michaels at the veterinary clinic, about him reuniting with family, and then how Harper had been defensive about his activities as a regular at the Olive Grove. I concluded, "She might be a long-lost relative, either a niece or a daughter. Maybe she killed him, or had him killed, to get at his money. If she's lying about her name, that's got to be a sign she's up to something."

He tilted his head to the side. "That's an interesting theory. It would make sense if Michaels actually had any money. We've looked into his financials, among other things. He had multiple mortgages on his residence and had partnered in a number of investments, none of them profitable. There's no will, but it won't matter. After his debts are cleared, there won't be enough to pay for his final bachelor pad." Tony paused dramatically. "By which I mean his pine box."

"The girl might not have known about all the debt," I said.

The cafeteria darkened. We both turned to the window as dark clouds overtook the low-hanging sun.

"So much for his legacy," Tony said ominously. "A man lives and works and dies and nothing changes."

CHAPTER 30

I BUMPED INTO my father's orthopedic nurse in the elevator. Dora kept catching my eye, as though she wanted to chat, but we were accompanied the whole way up by visitors and hospital staff.

When we got to my father's room, he groggily called out, "Sunny?"

Dora bustled past me, first into the room and to his side.

"Finn, it's your other daughter," Dora said, fluffing his pillow.

"The one who brings the storm clouds," he said, pointing to the gray window. His voice sounded thick, sleepy. "This weather is no coincidence. Soon there'll be thunder and lightning. Don't make my Stormy mad, whatever you do. The sky listens to her."

"Good grief, Dad. What sort of drugs are you on?"

He bobbed his head from side to side as though he was five champagne toasts into a wedding reception. "This and that. Dora here takes care of me. Pink pills and blue pills."

I raised my eyebrows. "Blue pills?"

Dora looked mortified. "Not any blue pills," she said hurriedly. "I swear, Stormy. Not the blue pills. Your father and I are just friends."

"Good friends," my father said.

I collapsed into a visitor chair next to his bed and dropped my face into my palms. "Dad, what have you done now?"

Dora said, "I'll leave you two some privacy."

Through gritted teeth, I said, "That would be great, Dora."

Once we were alone, my father said, "It's not what you think."

"So, you're not chasing after your physical therapist?"

"She's an orthopedic nurse," he said. "And I can't exactly chase her until the new hip's working, can I?"

I gave him a behave-yourself look, not that it ever did any good.

"What are your thoughts on swords?" he asked. "Specifically, I'm thinking of getting a cane-sword, since I'll need a cane for walking anyway."

"What about Pam?" I asked.

He snorted. "She's the last person who should be walking around with a sword. That's why we have laws against concealed weapons."

I rubbed my temples the way Tony had been rubbing his at lunch. "I mean, what about your relationship with her? Didn't she let her apartment go when she moved in with you?"

"Our living arrangements were always supposed to be temporary," he said. "She can get herself another apartment."

"Does she know?" I asked. "Have you two officially broken up?"

"Officially," he scoffed. "You make us sound like teen lovebirds." He shook his head. "For your information, Pam and I have broken up. It all went down a few weeks ago. Please don't think any less of Dora. She had nothing to do with it. She's a fine woman."

"Why didn't you tell me?"

He avoided my gaze, his attention flitting around the room. With every second of silence, the unanswered question seemed to weigh heavier on him, causing his body to sink deeper into the hospital bed. He looked at me, and suddenly I saw myself through his eyes. Stormy. Angry. Disapproving. Demanding answers he didn't have.

And he was just a person in a green patient gown, recovering from major surgery two days earlier. There was a bag attached to the side of his bed, collecting his fluids. I looked away quickly.

"Relationships are tough," I said. "I'm not upset that you don't want to be with Pam. I can't say I blame you. And it's not as though I told you about every event or sea change in my love life. But I would have appreciated a heads-up, so I knew what I was dealing with at the house."

He answered quickly, "She doesn't want people to know yet. She's embarrassed. I say we let her have her dignity, let her find a new place and move out, and she can tell everyone it was her choice. It's the least I can do. She was sweet to me, for a while, and I can't say I don't have a soft spot for her, despite everything."

"Sure," I said because I did understand. Pam hadn't told anyone about the breakup for the same reason I'd avoided telling the truth about my own relationship, which had been over long before I moved out. I couldn't admit my failure to others because then I'd have to endure their pity. Denial was also a factor. By ignoring the problem, there was always the slim chance it would get better on its own.

"I'm surprised Pam's still at the house," he said. "I thought while I was here at the hospital, she'd finally pack up the cat and the rest of her stuff."

Horrified, I exclaimed, "Not Jeffrey!"

He looked confused. "Who's Jeffrey? Tony implied you were dating someone, but I told him you weren't. Have you made me a liar?"

"Jeffrey is your cat. Didn't I tell you already? He wasn't a girl, after all."

He chuckled. "Life is full of surprises."

CHAPTER 31

ARMED WITH A CUP of vending machine coffee that was, surprisingly enough, not the worst coffee I'd ever had, I started driving back to Misty Falls. With the dark ribbon of highway in front of me, I enjoyed that unique feeling of stability that only speedy forward movement gave.

So what if my father had just nuked another relationship? It was his life.

And so what if there was a killer on the loose in town? It had barely been a couple of days since the discovery of the body. I could trust Tony and the rest of the force to catch the guilty party. I had my own life to live. As of that moment, I would focus solely on my own business.

Hypnotized by the road, I didn't notice blue and red lights flashing behind me until the siren came on with a startling whoop. I checked my speed guiltily, huffing in annoyance when I found I'd been barely over the speed limit. I pulled over, rolled down my window, and started digging for my wallet.

The passenger door opened. Officer Tony Milano slid into the passenger seat.

I called him a few choice names and berated him for giving me a fright. He stared straight ahead until I was done and then asked what else I knew about the blonde.

"Just that she works at the Olive Grove," I said. "Why? What did you find when you ran her plates?"

He turned and gave me a look so serious, chills ran down my spine. "Stay away from her."

"Tony, you've got to give me something concrete. I can keep quiet. You know that. Is she involved with the Michaels case, or is it something else?"

He took his time answering, and his words came out with care. "The young woman is a person of interest in an ongoing investigation."

"Is her real name Harper?"

He shook his head. "No."

"Okay." I rubbed my hands together. "Whoever this chick is, she's friends with my friend Jessica. The three of us had drinks last night at the Fox and Hound. She didn't open up much, but give me time. I'll get some wine and takeout food and have the girls over to my place. It's easy these days to record people, too. I'll just run the memo app on my phone."

"No, you won't," Tony said gruffly. "If you see that girl, you'll turn around and run the other way. And then, once you're a safe distance, you'll call me."

His extreme seriousness made me snicker.

"This isn't funny," he said, which only made me snicker harder.

He pushed the car door open but remained seated until I stopped laughing.

"I'll definitely call you if I see her," I promised. "I won't invite her back to my house to murder me."

"Don't invite anyone into your house," he said. "Not until this thing's settled. Just go to work, go home, and lock your doors. Stay there and stay safe."

"I'm thirty-three years old," I said. "I haven't had a curfew in almost twenty years."

"This isn't a curfew," he said. "It's more of a suggestion." He stepped out of the car, leaning down to add, "For your own good, please listen to me for a change."

He shut the door on my colorful response.

CHAPTER 32

I GOT BACK TO MISTY FALLS after sunset, jittery from all the caffeine I'd consumed and famished for dinner.

Jessica had called while I was on the road, asking about the investigation. She knew my father was retired but figured I would still get news before everyone else. I didn't let on that her coworker was a person of interest, but the new information made me uneasy. Harper not only worked with Jessica but also lived in the same building. I wanted to warn my friend, but Tony's "suggestions" reverberated in my head.

Disobeying his orders, I invited Jessica to hang out at my house that night. She sounded excited about seeing my new place but declined due to a giant backlog of laundry in need of washing. We settled on the plan of me going over to her place and helping with the laundry.

I picked up some pizza before heading straight to her place.

Jessica rented a top-floor corner unit in a three-story walk-up called Katrina Court. The building was in need of maintenance, as I'd reported to the real estate agent who'd suggested it as an investment. At least it was only decrepit enough to make the rent cheap yet not so bad that I feared for Jessica's safety. One of the units on the lower floor used flags as curtains, but at least they were colorful, international flags.

She buzzed me in, and when I got to her apartment, she was running around in what appeared to be pajamas, her phone to her ear.

"Hang on, Mom," she said into the phone. "I'm listening, I swear, but Stormy's here, and my timer's going off. I need to grab my clothes and toss them in the dryer so I don't get a rude note from the building manager."

I set the pizza box on the stove and swiped her keys from the counter, along with a handful of quarters. "I'll take care of your clothes," I said.

She held her hand over the bottom of her phone. "How will you know which loads are mine?"

"Don't you worry about that," I said with a wink.

I was still smiling when I located the subterranean laundry room and the two washers full of what I'd accurately predicted would be mostly pink loads. Jessica had always defied the advice that redheads shouldn't wear pink.

The load of mostly green towels that had been tumbling in one of the building's three dryers came to a stop with a buzz. In the silence, the cool, cement-lined room became as still as a crypt. I glanced at the dark corners as I fed quarters into the hungry machines. The murkiness in the far corner was playing tricks on my eyes. Between me and the darkness, a bare bulb hung over a counter-height table that I guessed residents used for folding laundry. Its plywood surface had been wrapped loosely with a plastic shower curtain. The sight of the shower curtain on the table turned my stomach.

Plastic shower curtains are not the only things used by killers to wrap body parts, but if there were a list of preferred household materials, shower curtains, which are sturdier than painters' drop cloths, would be in the top ten.

I finished loading Jessica's pink clothes into the dryer and fled the dank basement.

Up in the apartment, she was finishing the call with her mother when I walked back in.

"Parents," she said, shaking her head. "You'd hope that at their age, they'd have the whole dating thing figured out, but they're just as confused as anyone."

"Tell me about it," I said. "My father's up to his old tricks. What's going on with your mother?"

"She really likes the head chef at Accio Bistro, but now he's making special desserts for Sandra Gomez, who's not even officially divorced yet."

"Sandra Gomez? Gary's wife?" I asked. "I'm sorry to hear that, on all accounts." Gary Gomez was a police officer and friend of my father.

We got some plates and started eating pizza while Jessica filled me in on her mother's recent foray into dating.

After a while, we moved on to my father and the Pam situation.

Jessica looked stunned, her blue eyes wide. She twirled a strand of red hair nervously. "And Pam's still at your father's house?"

"Still there. Hasn't said a word about the breakup, but by the way she was burning the french toast this morning, she's not exactly coping. What if she won't move out? He'll need to evict her."

"I can't imagine," she said. "You poor thing."

"I'll probably stay there again tonight. That sweet little kitty needs somebody sane to look after him, plus I'm not ready to deal with the whole tenant thing."

"You're crazy." She gave me a sidelong look as she adjusted her seat on the sofa, pulling her knees up to hug them girlishly. "I haven't officially met the guy, but from what I saw of him last night, I didn't have any objections."

"It's complicated. Logan doesn't know I'm his landlady. We met at the veterinarian's office, and he said his landlady was a Type A hotshot from the big city who needed a man to take her to bed and, you know, set things right in her world."

She reached across me for another slice of pizza. "But isn't that exactly who you are and exactly what you need?"

I gave her upper arm a playful flick. "Nice."

"There's nothing wrong with this guy that we know of," she said. "If you don't like his beard, I'm sure he'd shave it off. Tell him it's a condition of the lease agreement."

"I can't date my tenant. It's too much pressure, and if it doesn't work out, I'll have to see him constantly."

She gave me a knowing look. "Misty Falls is pretty small. That's going to happen no matter who you date."

"Good point," I mused.

I helped myself to another slice of pizza, even though I knew the pepperoni would give me heartburn later.

She said, "What do I owe you for my half of the pizza?"

I glanced at the stack of mail on the coffee table, all of it unopened and looking an awful lot like bills.

"The pizza was free," I said brightly. "They made the wrong toppings for another customer, so I took this one rather than have them throw it out."

Jessica clapped her hands. "You have the best luck."

We turned on the TV and selected an action-comedy movie about a female spy going undercover. The story was getting tense when both of our phones started ringing. Jessica had another call from her mother, and my alert was for the dryer loads being nearly finished. For the second time, I told Jessica to help her mother in her time of crisis while I took care of the laundry.

On the basement level, I walked as the dual dryer loads buzzed and tumbled to a stop. I pulled open the first dryer and started folding the larger items immediately so they didn't wrinkle.

Someone opened the door behind me and came into the laundry room. I was in such bliss folding the hot clothes into tidy squares; I didn't even turn to see who it was.

A female said, icily, "You again."

I turned to find a horrifying sight. Harper. Not that Harper was her real name. Her blond hair was pulled up in a tight bun and pierced with two sharp-looking sticks. The person that Tony had pulled me over on the highway to warn me about stood no more than twelve feet away, a cruel look on her face.

We were alone in a concrete, windowless basement, and the only exit was behind her.

She had no laundry.

She did, however, have a hammer in her hand.

"Hi there," I squeaked.

She gripped the hammer tightly. "I see you're following me."

CHAPTER 33

ALMOST ANYTHING, when used creatively, can become a weapon.

As I faced off against an attacker with a hammer, I scanned the vicinity for something to arm myself with. There was only a warehouse-sized jug of liquid detergent and a box of dryer sheets. I grabbed the jug and held it between us as a shield.

"People know I'm down here," I said evenly. "You won't get away with this."

Her mouth dropped open, and her eyes bulged. "Get away with what?" She raised the hammer by an inch.

"I saw you today," I said. "I saw you in Portland, at the pawn shop. I said your name, but you didn't turn around because your name's not really Harper."

She took one step toward me, her pale eyes narrowing to slits. "Who told you that? Who told you my name's not Harper?"

"Officer Tony Milano is looking for you, right now. He'll be here any minute to arrest you."

"No," she breathed.

I gripped the jug of detergent tighter. "Yes," I said. "Now put down your hammer and step back."

"What?" She gave me a dumbfounded look but didn't set down the hammer.

Suddenly, she lurched forward.

I did what seemed both necessary and prudent at the moment; I chucked the nearly-full, warehouse-sized jug of detergent at her.

The jug struck her in the stomach. She released the hammer, arms flailing. The hammer soared through the air and landed inside an open washing machine with a loud clang. As the metallic echoes faded, she stumbled backward.

Eyes bulging, she gasped, "Can't. Breathe. Help."

As she crumpled to the ground, I got the feeling I'd made a terrible mistake. She looked so small and fragile on the gray concrete floor. She kept gasping, making an awful wheezing sound.

I started toward the door but stopped at the light switches. One light was off. I flicked the switch up. A lamp in the far corner of the room came on, illuminating a pegboard wall of tools, which was full except for the space marked off by the outline of a hammer. The girl had come to the basement to return a tool, not to make me the next victim.

I went to the gasping girl, got down on my knees, and patted her back. She shrank away from my touch.

"You're okay," I said soothingly. "I just knocked the air out of your lungs. Try to calm yourself, and the breath will come to you."

She kept wheezing. Her bun had come undone, and her golden hair fanned out on the grimy floor. I stayed by her side, apologizing and telling her how I'd had the wind knocked out of my lungs a few times. The last time had been when I was playing touch football and someone decided to turn the touch into tackle. Having your diaphragm spasm like that can be frightening.

I kept patting her back, saying, “Easy now. Let it all out, pause, and then you’ll be able to breathe again.”

Between gasps, she asked, “What did I ever do to you?”

“Nothing,” I said. “I’m so sorry I hit you with that jug, Harper, or whatever your name is. I overreacted when I saw you with that hammer.”

She said, “I’ll tell you my name if you really need to know.”

“Catch your breath first,” I said gently.

While I waited for her to breathe normally, I read the sign posted for Katrina Court residents who wished to borrow tools:

1. All tools must be signed out using the sign-up sheet.

2. Tools not returned within 36 hours will be considered stolen and replacement value charged to the borrower’s apartment.

3. No auto body work beyond oil changes may be performed in the underground parking lot.

After a few minutes, the girl I’d assaulted with a bulk-warehouse-sized jug of laundry detergent was breathing normally, sitting upright, and sobbing on my shoulder.

“You were at the same pawn shop Murray Michaels used,” I explained. “Was he more than just a regular restaurant customer to you?”

“I didn’t kill him,” she said. “He was my friend. Honestly, I wouldn’t ever hurt him. I only went by his house a few times because I was curious.”

"Did you see something at his house?"

She sniffed and pulled away from my shoulder.

"I didn't go inside," she said. "One time, after he disappeared, some people saw me outside the house and asked who I was. It was an older man, and a little old lady, walking a small dog."

"What did they look like?"

She wiped the tears from her eyes. "Like regular, normal people."

"Do you remember the breed of dog?"

She sniffed. "I think it was brown. I told the couple I was his daughter. I forgot this was such a small town, where everybody knows everybody. The guy said Murray didn't have a daughter, and they were going to call the police because I looked like I was casing the place, so I told her about how he and my mother used to date, and I thought I was his daughter, but didn't know for sure." She shook her head. "I'm so stupid."

I considered what she'd told me. "You're not stupid for telling the truth," I said. "When you talk to the police, just be honest."

Her body tensed, and she used her feet to push herself away from me.

"Why did you throw that thing at me?" She inched toward the room's only exit.

I held out my palms to show her I was unarmed. "When you accused me of following you, I took it the wrong way. I guess you were talking about how you just saw me yesterday, at the pub, and again, today."

She nodded. "It was a stupid joke." She buried her face in her palms. "I'll never fit in here, will I?"

I wanted to reassure the crying girl that she would fit in fine, but I wasn't exactly one to talk.

"Everything is so messed up," she groaned.

Her tears were getting to me, but I hadn't forgotten Tony's warning. This girl was hiding something, or hiding from someone.

I asked, "Why are you here? Why Misty Falls?"

She lifted her face from her hands. "I moved here so my sister and I could get a fresh start. My mother always said good things about the town. She only lived here for a year or two. She's gone now, but I wanted to see if it was as nice as she said."

"And Mr. Michaels was your father?"

"I don't have proof, but I thought I could save up for one of those DNA tests. I wasn't sure if I wanted to know. I wanted to meet him first and see what he was like." She wrinkled her nose. "He wasn't perfect, was he?"

"He had his good qualities," I said. "I grew up in the house next door, so I knew him a long time."

She looked up at me with red-rimmed, hopeful eyes. "Was he a good man?"

"He didn't deserve what happened to him, if that's what you mean."

She held her arms across her chest in a protective posture. "But what was he like?"

I paused to consider how to best frame what I knew about the deceased man, to leave his living descendant with the best of him.

"He loved books," I said. "He tried to get the neighborhood kids interested in reading."

The corners of her mouth twitched up. "That's nice," she said. "What else?"

I remembered running a lemonade stand on the sidewalk and Mr. Murray asking questions. My sister and I thought he was going to be his usual ornery self and make us move so we weren't in front of his house, but he didn't. He brought us a calculator and paper and showed us why we weren't charging enough to cover our expenses. He helped us make a new sign and then guilted several neighbors into buying lemonade from us.

I told Harper the whole story, including more details as they came to me. By the end, her eyes were dried and she was smiling.

"That's a cute story," she said.

"I never realized it before now, but when he showed me how to figure out a profit margin, something clicked in my head. Mr. Michaels was the first person to get me interested in business."

"He was a good man," she said.

Now that I was looking for it, I could see the family resemblance. There was something in the tilt of her nose and the cool blue of her eyes.

"You do look a bit like him," I said.

She gave me a weak smile. "My father, the town's kleptomaniac." She looked off into the distance. "Could be worse, though. I've got a fifteen-year-old half-sister who moved here with me, mainly to get away from her father and other jerks."

"Sorry to hear that." I got to my feet, dusted myself off, and helped her up. She groaned and rubbed her solar plexus, where I'd hit her with the jug. "And sorry again for knocking you down," I said.

She went to the door and stopped, her back to me. "It's always darkest before the dawn," she said softly.

I replied, "Can I ask you one more thing? Why were you at the pawn shop today?"

"One time at the restaurant, I said something about selling some jewelry. Mr. Michaels recommended that particular shop. He said the owner was an old friend." She gave me a sad look over her shoulder. "The jewelry is junk, but I wanted to talk to the owner, to get some closure or something."

"Did Mr. Michaels know who you were?" I asked.

She held my gaze. "One time he told me I reminded him of someone special."

"That's something," I said.

She gave me a wistful smile. "I like to think he's smiling down on me now and that he's glad we met."

"That's a really nice image."

She pulled open the door and slipped out, leaving me alone in the laundry room. I leaned into the washing machine, picked up the fallen hammer, and returned it to the tool box, as per the posted sign.

The door opened again, so I armed myself and whipped around.

"Just me," she said, holding her arms up in a defensive position.

"Sorry." I put the laundry detergent down.

She said, "I wanted to let you know I'm going to call the police and try to help them with the case. I don't know if it will do any good, but I'll tell them which people Murray used to complain about when he was having his lunch."

"Was my father one of those people? His name is Finnegan Day."

Recognition flashed across her face. "I'll leave your father out," she said. "But I will tell the police about all the fights he had with the owner of that costume shop."

"Great idea," I said, not letting on that it wouldn't do much good, as Leo Jenkins had been cleared as a suspect.

CHAPTER 34

"WOW. YOU FOLDED EVERYTHING," Jessica said when I returned with the laundry. "Is that what took you so long? I thought you'd gotten lost."

"I love folding hot laundry," I said, which was true.

We got back to watching our spy movie, and for the rest of the evening, I didn't mention how I'd hurled a year's worth of liquid detergent at her neighbor. If Harper was on the run from someone or something, it wasn't my secret to share.

By ten o'clock, we'd run low on pizza and girl talk, so I thanked Jessica for the fun evening and drove home.

At the duplex, Logan's side was brightly lit.

I sat in my idling car and watched as he walked by the living room window, shirtless. He walked up to the window and glanced left and right, first at the snow-covered lawn and then at the cloudless night sky. He stretched, rubbing his nice-looking stomach.

During the drive home, I'd been thinking about the spies in the movie we'd watched. Even while bullets were flying, the man and woman kept flirting with each other, their romance progressing. Some of the scenes had been so corny, but Jessica and I had both swooned, enjoying every minute of it.

Now that I was single again, the romance aspects of movies meant more to me. The romantic gestures weren't just unbelievable things I'd roll my eyes at. The corny moments now seemed like hopeful possibilities, actual things that could happen to me. My former fiancé would never have looked into my eyes and said the perfect line, let alone swept me up into his arms with perfect time, but now my future was wide open.

And Logan's curtains were wide open. Why? And why was he always walking around with no shirt? Was he putting on a show on purpose?

Another car drove down the street, slowing as it passed my vehicle. I leaned over and pretended to be digging through my purse. The other car stopped next to my car. I straightened up and turned to look out the driver's side.

Officer Peggy Wiggles waved back and signaled for me to lower my window.

She called over, "Do you normally park on the street? I would imagine you'd park up there, on the driveway."

"I like to mix it up," I said. "How about you? Any breaks in the case?"

"You know I shouldn't discuss that with you." She glanced down at a screen that glowed blue on her face.

"Are you going to a call in this area?" I asked.

"No," she answered without looking up. "Just checking on your residence, as per Milano's request."

"I saw Tony today," I said. "We had lunch."

She looked curious but didn't press for details. I told her anyway, including my new information about the girl I was still calling Harper.

"You guys should run a DNA test," I said. "Harper would probably want to know for sure, and it would back up her story."

"I'll pass that along to Officer Milano," she said, glancing past me at the house. "Would you like me to walk you to your front door and check the residence?"

"Am I in danger?" I asked.

She took her time before answering, "It never hurts to be careful."

"Officer Wiggles, is there anything in particular I should be careful about? Have you got any new suspects, or information from the coroner?"

"Sleeping pills," she said. "Stormy, please keep this under your hat. The toxicology report suggests that somebody drugged Murray Michaels then strangled him. I'm only telling you this so you can be aware of what you're eating or drinking."

I took a deep breath as the news washed over me like a bucket of ice water.

"If he was drugged first, it was pre-meditated," I said. "That's cold."

She guffawed. "Very cold."

She had her arm sticking out of the window and patted the side of the cruiser with a metallic whack.

"Well, have a good night," she said cheerily.

"You, too. Be careful out there."

"I have a gun," she said, and she drove off.

After she left, I sat in my car for a long time, thinking about how Murray Michaels had lived his life. Someone had despised him enough to plan his murder. Things might have turned out different for him if he'd made more of an effort to connect with people.

Along with my memory of him helping me with the lemonade stand came more memories, each coaxing out another, like the string of silk scarves coming from a magician's top hat.

Mr. Michaels had confiscated toys for crossing over his property line, but he'd also made a show of generosity once a year, returning the items in a cardboard box left on the porch, no note or explanation. When it snowed, he'd shovel the walkway in front of his house, skip ours, but then shovel in front of the homes of some of the widows on the street.

Sure, he'd argued with my father over the years, but only because he loved a good debate. Talking was his entertainment, but it had to be deeper than small talk. He wasn't content to stand around and muse about the weather when there was business, politics, and even religion.

If he hadn't gotten himself killed, we might have had some lively discussions now that I was back in town. He'd always seemed a bit of an outsider, like me.

It was easy to be friendly to people who were kind and polite all the time, but most people had flaws. He couldn't see past the flaws of others, so they wouldn't look past his.

I wondered, if I could work on myself in general, work on building bridges with people who weren't so perfect and easy to love, would that help me in life? I didn't want to end up cranky and alone, my death unnoticed for weeks. And I didn't want to start another romantic relationship only to hit the same obstacles again.

So, with the best of intentions in my heart, combined with some cowardice about facing my shirtless tenant, I put the car in gear and drove to my father's house to offer emotional support to Pam.

Or to let her make fun of my hair.

Whatever would make her feel better.

CHAPTER 35

FOR THE THIRD morning in a row, I awoke to a raspy tongue on my forehead.

"Jeffrey, don't take this the wrong way, but I think we should start seeing other people."

He gave me an offended look, which only got worse when I turned him around to check his surgery site. He scampered off with the remainder of his dignity, his long gray tail swooshing in question marks.

I got dressed, brushed my teeth in the upstairs powder room, and went down to see what Pam was burning in the kitchen. We hadn't spoken the night before. She'd turned off the TV and gone to bed as soon as I'd arrived, leaving a still-hot cup of tea on the coffee table in her haste. I didn't take it too personally. She'd probably heard about my trip to Portland and suspected I knew about the breakup.

Pam let out a shriek when I walked into the kitchen. She held her hand over her heart. "I forgot you were here," she said. "I heard the floor creak, and I thought for sure it was a big man with a beard, coming to strangle me."

"Not on my watch," I said with dramatic flair. "I'll protect you, Pam."

She stared at me for several seconds before letting out the first genuine-sounding laugh I'd ever heard pass through her lips.

"Good one," she said. "Coffee's on."

I was already helping myself. "Dad looks good," I said. "I made the drive to see him yesterday. He says they might even spring him as soon as tomorrow."

"Tomorrow? I'd better get ready." She continued with what she'd been doing, which was rinsing off dark leaves of curly kale before adding them to a light-colored mixture already in the blender.

"Do you mean ready with a nice dinner?" I had to choose my words carefully, or she'd know that I knew about the breakup. Part of me wanted to get the messy emotional stuff over with quickly and then offer to help her pack. In the bright light of the morning, my soft-hearted feelings from the night before seemed sappy and foolish. By the way she was looking at my hair, I imagined she was busy thinking up new insults. Why did I think being nice to her would do me good?

She turned on the blender, ignoring my question. I regretted promising my father that I'd go easy on her.

I took a seat at the table and looked around the kitchen, mentally noting which items were unfamiliar and could be tossed into a cardboard box as soon as I got the go-ahead. Pam finished blending the green smoothie and offered me half. The brackish concoction looked like the exact opposite of something I'd want half of.

"No, thanks," I said. "I'm trying to cut back on pond scum."

She joined me at the table, giving me a stern look as she sipped the green drink and licked her lips dramatically. “I’m not surprised you don’t have a taste for healthy foods,” she said. “Growing up the way you did, with no woman in the house, you might as well have been raised by wolves.”

I sipped my coffee and licked my lips, mimicking her. “We did have that wolf we called Nanny.”

“It’s a miracle you made it to adulthood.”

I crossed my arms. “Who are you calling an adult?”

She rolled her eyes. “And that hair of yours! Tell me you didn’t pay good money for that accident.”

“Pam, how can you even say that? Get a mirror. You and I have the exact same haircut.”

She shook her head. “It’s not the same. Mine is tapered, and I have normal hair. Yours is curly, or wavy, or kinky, or something. It’s not normal.”

I looked away. “It must have been all the wolf milk I was nursed on, while my father was out working to support his family.”

“He didn’t have to do it alone,” she said. “I knew him back then, and he could have had anyone. He should have gotten married and made a proper home for you two girls, but he didn’t put your needs ahead of his own, his own selfish desires.”

Through gritted teeth, I said, “We turned out just fine, thank you.”

She gave me a patronizing look. “Is that so?”

The phone rang, and she jumped up to get it. Through the rushing in my ears, I heard her repeat a doctor’s name. I listened, wondering if it was news about my father. She lowered her voice and left the kitchen with the cordless phone.

Once I'd simmered down and finished my coffee, I followed her into the living room, where she was pacing at the window and giving brief yes and no answers on the phone. I picked up her sketchpad from a side table, and wrote out a question: *Is that about Dad?*

She glanced at the note, shook her head, and snatched the sketchpad out of my hands. Still murmuring brief answers, she left for the main floor bathroom and closed the door behind her. I listened, curious about her phone call, but her voice was too low.

Jeffrey wove his way around my legs before jumping on the living room's window sill. He flicked his tail and then turned to watch the little winter birds forage for frozen berries in the front hedge. His tail swished as he chattered at the delicious-looking birds as if they were the cat equivalent of french fries and ketchup.

I sat on the couch for a moment and watched him watching the birds. Time passed. Watching Jeffrey felt very restful, the exact opposite of trying to have a conversation with Pam.

She seemed to be finished her phone call but hadn't emerged from the bathroom yet.

I tapped on the door. "Pam, is everything okay in there?"

She answered, "Did you want to use the shower?"

"No, thanks. I guess I'll be on my way. I've got some errands to do."

"Errands?" she echoed. "Where are you going?"

"It's kind of a long story," I said to the closed door. "I bought back some old cufflinks from a pawn shop where Murray Michaels was selling things he'd picked up. They belong to Leo Jenkins, so I'm going to do a good deed and return them to him today."

She cracked open the door and looked me up and down. "That's awfully kind of you," she said. "How did you know where to find the cufflinks?"

I waggled my eyebrows. "I have my ways."

"What else was he selling? Did you happen to see a scarab-shaped broach?"

"Just a panther," I said.

She sniffed with annoyance. "Never mind. I probably lost it in the street when I was getting out of my car. You remember my scarab. I always wore it on my wool jacket."

"Do you mean the dung beetle? That was pretty cute for a bug rolling around a ball of poo."

She closed the bathroom door with a bang. She hadn't appreciated my compliment of her broach the night of my father's party, either. The ancient Egyptians, who'd revered the dung beetle as a symbol of rebirth, must have had a better sense of humor than Pam.

"I'll keep an eye out for your scarab," I promised.

Through the door, she said, "Gather up your things from the spare room before you go."

"Am I being kicked out as a houseguest?"

"I don't want you here," she said. "I mean, I don't need you here. I'm quite capable of looking after myself, and I'd rather have my space, thank you."

I shook my clenched fists at the closed door. *You get out! This is my house*, I wanted to say but didn't.

I finished getting ready for the day, making some toast for a quick breakfast and then gathering up my things from the spare room. On my way out, I wished her a good day through the bathroom door. She didn't respond, but I could practically feel her seething through the door.

It took me another five minutes to get away because Jeffrey had arranged himself to be irresistible. He lay on his back, in the crack between two sofa cushions, tempting me with the cuteness of his belly. In a low voice, I told him how much I'd miss him when he moved out. He twisted and stretched, luring me into his pet-my-tummy trap before grasping my wrist and gnawing my thumb.

I extricated myself without a scratch and was on my way.

Outside, the chilly winter air was bracing.

I paused on the porch to zip up my jacket and noticed movement next door, at Mr. Michaels' house. A man with dark hair was standing on the lawn where the snowman had been, taking a picture of the house. The man had a beard and looked familiar, but it wasn't my new tenant or anyone whose name came to mind.

I called over a hello.

The man looked over at me and then turned and started walking away briskly.

Was this the bearded man Pam had reportedly seen in the neighborhood weeks earlier? What was he up to?

I pulled my phone from my purse, set it to take photos, and started following the guy.

CHAPTER 36

I FOLLOWED THE BEARDED MAN to the end of the block and around the corner. I stayed a safe distance back, pretending to be reading something on my phone, but my fine detective work was wasted. He didn't even glance back over his shoulder, let alone notice me taking pictures as he got into a car and drove away.

As I walked back to my own car, I called Officer Tony Milano and gave him a full report.

"Slow down," Tony said. "You're getting yourself all worked up, just like you did over the girl who calls herself Harper. I talked to her this morning, and you're lucky she's not pressing charges against you for assaulting her."

"She's mad at me?" I asked. "Over the laundry detergent?"

"Not exactly," he answered cagily. "But I saw the bruising on her forearm, and she told me what happened last night."

I groaned. "That was a misunderstanding. She had a scary hammer. Plus the lighting in that laundry room was super creepy, like the kill room in a serial killer movie. You would have been jumpy, too."

"Good to know," he said sarcastically. "I'll make a note here in the file. Creepy lighting. Yes, this is very damning. Thanks for calling it in. Oh, and I'll get right on running the license plate for this new suspect, the one who very suspiciously took a photo of a house."

I told Tony what I thought of his sarcasm and his casual dismissal of my help.

The call did not end well.

After he had hung up on me, I jumped into my car and drove around the neighborhood. I searched for the bearded man and his car, but he was long gone.

I considered calling in my license plate tip again, this time to Officer Wiggles, but I needed a moment to get my temper under control.

Coffee. I wanted coffee. Pam's brew had been weak, and I needed the real stuff. I drove to House of Bean.

My least favorite House of Bean employee was working. Chad took one look at me and prepared for combat. He turned to me, chest thrust out, shoulders squared, smug face begging to be punched.

"Good morning," he sang.

"And a good morning to you," I said evenly. "I'll have the third item on the menu, please."

He gave me a ferociously happy smile. "Do you mean the Teenie Weenie Beanie Steamer?"

"If that's the third item on the menu, then I suppose I do." I pointed to the stack of large cups. "This size."

Chad's nostrils flared big enough for flames to shoot out. "Mountain size," he said.

"Sure," I said with a deliberate shrug. "I'm easy. That sounds great."

I paid for my coffee and put a generous tip in the cafe's tip jar. This generosity was met with suspicion, just as I'd anticipated.

I took my vanilla latte to a corner table and enjoyed it along with a copy of the *Misty Falls Mirror*, which I read from cover to cover. Their coverage of the Murray Michaels case included a two-paragraph obituary and a statement from the police asking citizens to come forward with information. I called the phone number listed and asked to remain anonymous. I passed along the description of the bearded man I'd seen at the house, along with his vehicle make and plate number. Tony hadn't taken me seriously, but perhaps someone else would.

Feeling the satisfaction of one task completed, I tipped back the last of my coffee, checked the contents of my purse, and continued on my way. I would visit Leo Jenkins at Masquerade and return his stolen cufflinks. Then I would get out of the costume shop as fast as I could, before Creepy Jeepers got grateful enough to hug me with his spider arms.

CHAPTER 37

ON MY WAY TO MASQUERADE, I stopped at my reflection in Ruby's big mirror on the corner. I ruffled up my spiky hair and smiled. I liked how I looked with the postcard-pretty view of the small town and mountains behind me.

Was Ruby was sitting on the other side with a cup of tea? I waved, in case she was.

I turned away, walked down the street, and entered the costume shop with a bounce in my step.

Leo Jenkins, who was standing on the platform for the window display, greeted me with a dismayed look on his face and a decapitated foam snowman in his arms.

"Now you've done it," I said jokingly.

He sighed. "Busted."

"You've killed that snowman," I said.

"He was asking for it," Jenkins replied, rotating the snowman's face so it looked right at me.

I laughed. "You'll have to kill me next. You can't go around leaving witnesses."

"But I'm so busy this afternoon. I have to change this window display myself and then get to the bank for coins." He gave me a thin-lipped grin. "This will be our little secret."

"Sure." I stepped back and let him by with the foam snowman, which he placed in a cardboard box that advertised its contents as DAPPER SNOWMAN.

"I'm glad you stopped by," he said. "I've been meaning to apologize for the other night. I'm so sorry if I gave you a scare. Breaking and entering is just about the craziest thing I've done in my whole life, and I feel dreadful about, well, everything."

"People make mistakes," I said. "Those cufflinks must have meant a lot to you."

He continued loading the snowman into the box, avoiding eye contact. He'd gotten his glasses fixed, but he still bore a small red cut on his angular cheekbone, where he'd gotten injured during the arrest.

I pulled the cufflinks from my purse and held them out. "Here you go," I said. "I happened to come across these at a pawn shop, and I wanted to get them back to their rightful owner."

He frowned at the cufflinks, his thin face look practically skeletal.

"You can toss those on the counter," he said without so much as touching them. He continued his work in the window display, rolling up the white felt carpeting.

I walked over to the cash register and set the cufflinks down with a clink. Was he too ashamed about the break-in to let on he was happy to get the cufflinks back, or did he genuinely not care? Had the cufflinks been a cover story for the police?

Stalling for time, I pretended to be interested in the circular display of masquerade masks.

Mr. Jenkins continued changing the window, pulling snowflake decals off the glass with his long fingers.

Something was definitely odd about the man. He'd been released by the police after providing an alibi for the entire window of time during which Mr. Michaels must have been killed, but wasn't that, in itself, odd? Was there even another person in the entire town who had an alibi for that exact same period?

I grabbed my phone and set it to record a memo. I used the memo function often, to take down worries that hit me while I was driving or falling asleep. Our voices would be muffled by my purse, but if the costume shop owner said something damning, I could pass it along to the police. Tony couldn't ignore my help forever.

"I set your cufflinks by the cash register," I said. My voice sounded squeaky, compressed by the tightness in my throat.

He didn't even glance up. "Thanks for doing that. I wish you wouldn't have."

"Oh? Why?" I edged my way around the shop's displays so I had a clear escape route to the door.

He didn't answer my question, so I pressed on. "Why shouldn't I have gotten your cufflinks back? Didn't you want them?"

He answered, "They're not worth much."

"But you wanted them, didn't you? Why else would you break into Mr. Michaels' house?"

He turned his body so his back was to me, and I couldn't even see the edge of his face to gauge his expression. He slumped over and groaned.

I took two more steps toward the door. "You can tell me," I said.

Softly, barely loud enough for me to hear, he said, "No. I can't tell anyone. It's too disgusting."

My skin prickled, and the urge to run for the door became almost unbearable. But I had to stay calm, stay present. I'd been in stressful situations before, on the brink of losing huge financial deals, and I knew that the secret to success was pressing on beyond the point where most normal people would give up.

Just a little further. Just another nudge.

I took a risk and bluffed, "I saw what you were doing inside his house. I already know everything. Why don't you let it all out? Tell someone. You'll feel better."

"Okay," he said softly. "Please don't tell anyone else."

I casually tugged my purse open wider. I wouldn't tell anyone, but I would certainly share the recording. With the police.

"Start at the beginning," I said.

He reached for something on the platform next to him. A box cutter. My heart pounded. I could make it to the door in five steps, but he had such long legs, he could make it there in three. I held still, ready to bolt if he so much as twitched in my direction.

"The weight loss started in the summer," he said. "I didn't mind because it was swimming season. My wife actually admired me and said I was looking younger."

"Okay," I said, waiting to hear what this had to do with killing Mr. Michaels.

"By the fall, though, I kept losing weight, and I finally went in to see my doctor. They ran all the tests, so many tests, but there wasn't much they could do. I must have had a bad reaction to some medicine I took earlier this year for an ear infection. They said it could take years for my digestive system to recover, but there was an experimental treatment."

"How experimental?" While I listened, I kept a lookout for people entering the shop. I hoped someone would come in but not before I got a full confession.

"I had to fly to a special clinic," he said. "It was very expensive, not covered by insurance, and when I got there, I'm ashamed to say that I couldn't do the treatment. I stayed in the hotel the whole time and then flew back home. I told everyone I was feeling better, but I wasn't. I kept losing weight. So, I had to pay for the trip a second time, and off I went. The second time, I managed to go through with it."

"And… did Mr. Michaels know about this? Is that why you had to silence him?"

Jenkins straightened up and slowly turned to face me. He blinked, looking sad and confused. I almost felt sorry for him but not sorry enough to stop my phone from recording his confession.

"Murray didn't know," Jenkins said. "Nobody knew."

"So, you broke into a crime scene to retrieve some cufflinks you don't even care about?"

Jenkins deflated, looking skinnier than a popped balloon.

"I was searching for my wedding band," he said. "It slipped off my finger the day I banned Murray from the store. I was sure he'd taken it, but I didn't want to cause a scene on the sidewalk in front of the store. I thought I could reason with him eventually, but then I was out of town for a spell, and he never came around again."

"But you didn't tell the police about your ring. You told them you were looking for cufflinks."

His face went pale. "A good man doesn't take off his wedding band unless he's up to no good. I didn't want them to think I'd left my ring behind on a previous visit to the man's house. Now, I've got no problem with people who are gay, and I stay out of other people's business, but I couldn't bear to have everyone thinking something that wasn't true."

"Right," I said, the picture coming into focus. "Was Murray gay?"

He shrugged. "I don't know. But if word got out that my wedding band was in his possession, I guarantee you wouldn't be the last person to ask me that question."

"I understand," I said, and I did. A wedding band conveyed more than other types of jewelry. Whatever testimony Jenkins gave the police was supposed to be private and confidential, but the fact that I, an ordinary citizen, knew about his cufflinks story was evidence to the contrary.

He continued, "At least my treatment worked. I've gained a pound already. You must not tell anyone, though."

"Okay," I said slowly. "But why is it such a secret if you're feeling better?"

He gave me a look of annoyance. "I guess the whole town's going to know eventually, so I might as well tell you. After being suspected of murder and arrested for burglary, my reputation can't exactly get worse. People still need their tuxedos. They'll have to come here and rent them from the poo-poo eater."

I staggered back. "Pardon me?"

He rubbed his forehead with one long-fingered hand as he explained the procedure. The treatment for his digestive problem involved him ingesting live bacteria cultures, harvested from living donors. Apparently, waste was taken from healthy subjects and then processed in a manner that, upon hearing it described, made me question if I could ever use a blender again.

The funny thing was, even though he'd seemed so horrified about the treatment, the more he talked about it, the more animated he became. Almost proud.

I had only myself to blame. I had, after all, encouraged him to open up and talk about it to someone.

He kept talking, waving for me to follow him around the store as he tidied the display and gathered new materials. I lost track of how many times he used words that should never be uttered during normal retail interactions.

Finally, when I thought I was going to have to fake a medical emergency to get out of there, the door opened.

He walked over to greet the customers, who were the same mother and daughters I'd seen in the store four days earlier. The group of them blocked the exit. I stood near the counter and bided my time, studying the dimly-lit corkboard on the back wall as I waited for my chance to escape. Jenkins and the mother talked about the town's recent homicide and how it was so troubling the police hadn't made their arrest yet. The woman cited the statistic that most murders are solved within forty-eight hours, or never. Her daughters made faces at each other, and the older one distracted the younger one by trying on an assortment of sparkling hats.

The door jingled again, and a man with the beginning of a snowy white beard came in to ask about Santa Claus suit rentals.

Jenkins responded, "Mr. Lake, you know I always have one reserved for you!"

The door opened again, and a couple came in with a sandy brown dog with soft-looking curly fur. They asked if it was okay to bring in Stanley, who had separation anxiety and would cry if left on the sidewalk. Leo Jenkins assured them it would be fine, and the two girls cooed over the Labradoodle while the adults continued to gossip, speculating about possible motivations for the recent murder.

Ten minutes later, I moved out of the way to let the jolly-looking man arrange his costume rental.

I gave Leo Jenkins a friendly wave and practically ran out of the shop.

Breathless with excitement, I marched up the sidewalk.

I knew who killed Murray Michaels.

Now I just needed proof.

CHAPTER 38

ARMED WITH TWO dozen miniature cupcakes, I pulled open the spotless glass door for Ruby's Treasure Trove and went inside. Hayley, the young girl cleaning the display cases, looked exhausted.

"Hello," she said with a sigh. "May I help you with anything?" I looked into her pale blue eyes and saw the family resemblance to her half-sister, Harper.

"Is Ruby in today?" I opened the bakery box and set it on the counter between us. "We can't eat all these cupcakes by ourselves."

She hesitated, but I urged her to help herself to at least two, if not more.

"You need the calories," I said. "Ruby's been working you to the bone, hasn't she?"

"Nonsense," said Ruby, who'd just emerged from the back room. "I'm no more ruthless as a boss than anyone else in town, including you."

I rotated the cupcakes to face her. "These would go well with some tea," I said lightly.

Ruby laughed, her purple-red curls bouncing in every direction. She wore a plain cream blouse under a smart-looking leopard print vest. Her skirt was purple, matching her purple-framed reading glasses.

She waved for me to follow her, back through the doorway. I walked past the filing cabinets and on to the secret tea room. Ruby pushed over a stack of invoices and a sleek laptop on the round bistro table nearest the circular window. While I sat, she took the box of cupcakes over to the kitchenette and started filling the kettle.

I gazed out the window for a moment before checking the photos on my phone.

Ruby returned with hot tea and cupcakes, artfully arranged on a platter.

"You have good timing," she said. "I needed to take a break anyway." She patted her laptop, which wore a protective cover the same shade of purple as her glasses. "I don't know about this technology. It used to take much longer to do the bookkeeping the old-fashioned way, with the paper ledgers, but what have we done with the time we're saving? Pile on more work, that's what."

I asked, "What else are you up to on that laptop?"

"More like what am I not up to." She opened it and turned the screen to face me as she did a rundown of all the social networking sites she was involved with. There were a few I hadn't even heard of. Ruby was on all of them, posting inspiration photos and style tips. The woman was thirty years older than me and more up-to-date than most people my age.

"Wow," I said. "You make me feel like a slacker."

She pursed her full lips. "I seriously doubt that." She poured two cups of Earl Grey tea. "Well? You didn't come here for computer tips, so let's have it."

I blew over my hot tea and asked, "Who do you use for monitoring your cameras? I'm planning to upgrade the security at the gift shop."

Her brow wrinkled. "I'll have to look them up. I can't remember the name, but I'm sure they're in the local phone book."

I nodded, set my tea down, and leaned across the table to show her the picture I'd taken at the pawn shop.

"Ruby, I believe this panther charm is from your store. Murray Michaels was selling some smaller items through a pawn shop in Portland."

"Yes," she said heavily. "I figured as much."

"But you never talked to the police because you don't have any security footage of him stealing, do you?"

She gave me a guarded look. "What makes you say that?"

"All three of your cameras are dummies. The third one is more convincing than the others, but your employee left a feather from her duster on the lens the last time I was here, and it's still stuck up there." She didn't respond, so I continued, "A lot of retail theft is done by employees, so you lie to your workers, to trick them into thinking they're being watched."

"It's for Hayley's own good," she said.

"And what else is for her own good?" I asked. "Why are you being so tough on her?" I waved my hand at the other bistro tables. "And what exactly have you been getting up to back here, anyway? Last time I was here, you kept saying we. Who is this we? Are you going to tell me, or do I have to figure it out the hard way?"

Ruby sighed. "I make young Hayley clean all the display cases, then when she's not looking, I put fingerprints on from the inside and make her clean again." She sat up straighter in her chair. "That young woman needs to be in high school. We are in agreement that she needs to quit this job and get her education. We know she's on the run from something, but that's no excuse to throw your life away."

I picked up my tea and waved for her to continue.

"The Secret Tea Room Ladies are a group that meets here," she said. "We try to set things right, but in an unobtrusive way. If a person needs help but is too proud to ask, we might arrange for a door of opportunity to open at exactly the right moment. People are stubborn. They usually have to believe it's their own idea."

"Were you trying to help Mr. Michaels?" I asked.

"Not very well," she said sadly. "We hadn't gotten past the evidence-gathering stage. The panther charm was sort of a trap. There are only two of them in existence, and I put one out when he was in the store, hoping he'd take the bait." She frowned as she gazed at the street beyond the round window. "We wanted to see where the items were going, so we could present everything to the police and then get him some help for his compulsions. One of our ladies has connections to excellent psychiatric support, but of course we couldn't get him to take it if he wouldn't admit to having a problem."

"It sounds like your group does good work," I said.

"We try," she said. "We were making progress with Murray and thought we had plenty of time.

Then he went and got himself killed. And we don't have the foggiest idea by whom."

"No theories?" I asked. "Not even any little suspicions?"

She looked down at the cupcakes. "Nope," she said, one eye twitching behind her glasses. "Nothing I'd want to concern you with, anyway."

I touched my finger to the round window. "Is this really soundproof? I'd like to share something with you but just between the two of us."

Her expression brightened, and she pushed her purple-framed glasses up her nose as she leaned in.

I told her my theory, and when I was done, the look on her face told me everything I needed to know. Well, almost everything.

CHAPTER 39

I EMERGED FROM Ruby's tea room to find her young employee cleaning the top of a display case furiously, her cheeks red and her forehead shining with sweat.

I leaned over and commented, "Those fingerprints are on the inside."

"How would they get in there?" she sputtered. She opened the case and cleaned the inside. This time, the fingerprints came off easily. She took a step back and put her hands on her hips, breathing heavily and looking very much like a person on the verge of quitting. Just one more nudge, I thought.

"You and your sister live in my friend Jessica's building," I said.

She gave me a sullen look. "Yeah? So?"

"Harper told me why you're in Misty Falls."

"Great," she said sarcastically, every bit the rebellious, moody teenager. I worried that no matter what I said, she was going to find me old and out-of-touch. If Ruby hadn't been able to crack her, what chance did I have?

Ruby had sent me out with the remainder of the cupcakes in their original box. I set the box on the counter again and opened it.

"These are all yours," I said.

She muttered a thank-you and shoved one into her mouth.

"Your sister must really care about you," I said.

Around the mouthful of cake and icing, the girl said, "She wants me to go to school, but high school is boring."

I picked up the spray bottle. "More boring than wiping fingerprints off stuff all day?"

She frowned. "I dunno."

"Do you have any hobbies?"

She shrugged.

I kept going, asking, "Do you play any musical instruments?"

"The guitar but not really. I only know five chords."

"They've got a fantastic music program at the high school. I was in the school band, but there are less geeky options, too. We've got a lot of talent here in Misty Falls. Maybe you could get yourself into a local band."

"Really?"

"You might want to learn more than five chords."

She gave me side-eye. "You're not just saying that to trick me into going to high school, are you?"

I shrugged. "You got me. The high school pays me a bounty for recruits. Sometimes I drive around neighboring cities in a van covered in candy." I let my expression turn serious. "You should call the school's office, or just show up and ask for a tour. I could even go with you, if you'd like. I wouldn't mind saying hello to some of my favorite teachers."

"Hmm." She pretended to be more interested in licking the frosting off a cupcake than in what I was saying.

I walked over to the window and made a palm print on the smooth surface. "But I can understand how high school doesn't measure up to the thrills and chills of wiping fingerprints off these windows."

I left a dozen more streaky handprints before leaving her to think about what I'd said.

Outside, I turned the corner to find a redhead in a hot pink jacket checking her hair in the round mirror.

Jessica gave me a big smile. "I love that you live here now, and I can just bump into you. What are you up to? You look a bit lost."

"Lost?" I laughed. "Maybe a little bit."

She closed the distance between us and linked her arm through mine. "Don't be lost. Let's go window shopping. I'm meeting my friend Marcy at the Golden Wok later, but I have the whole day off. Are you free? You're invited to dinner with us, of course."

I checked the time. Shopping and eating a big meal were the furthest things from my mind, but it would still be a few hours until I could do what I had planned.

"Sure," I said. "You can show me the sights. Since I look lost, you can be my tour guide. Pretend I've never been here before."

She tugged on my arm and, without hesitation, began the tour. "Over here is our beautiful Central Park. Some people call it Central Bark, to distinguish it from the one in New York, and also because it's usually full of dogs, and people in small towns love their puns."

"Oh, dear," I said with mock horror. "If I stay here much longer, will I start loving puns?"

"It's just one of many exciting transformations you can expect. Don't fight the quaintness, Stormy. Let it steep through you, and everything will be fine."

Laughing, we crossed the street and made our way toward the park.

For the next few hours, we enjoyed the mild winter day, walking through the park and then shopping along Broad Avenue. We stopped in at Blue Enchantment, where, with Jessica's squealing encouragement, I bought everything off the mannequin again.

We had a late lunch that turned into an early dinner at the Golden Wok with some other friends of Jessica's. I could have sworn I wasn't hungry, but then the sweet and sour chicken balls came to the table, and my mouth actually watered for them. As I stuffed my face and laughed along with the group, I got a warm feeling that spread through my whole body.

Maybe the feeling was contentment.

Or maybe the Golden Wok put booze in my non-alcohol piña colada.

When we parted ways, the droopy winter sun, barely brighter than the moon, was disappearing.

In the expanding darkness, my fear grew, surrounding me in a cloud of whispering doubts.

On the drive toward my destination, I considered calling Tony about a thousand times, but I could hear him mocking my theory, so I didn't. I thought about calling my father to talk me out of my plan, but then a calmness washed over me.

Sometimes, when you know exactly what you need to do, you can stand still in the eye of the hurricane.

I pulled the car into the driveway of my house.

My new tenant hadn't stayed late at work. Logan Sanderson was already home, judging by the lights in the windows on his side of the duplex.

With my purse on my shoulder, I stepped out of my car, silently reciting the first part of the prayer I'd heard my father say countless times.

Lord, I ask for courage. Courage to face and conquer my own fears. Courage to take me where others will not go.

I knocked on the door.

CHAPTER 40

LOGAN OPENED THE DOOR and did a double-take.

"Surprise," I said. "It's me."

"The cute girl from the vet clinic," he said. "And then from the Fox and Hound. Thanks for the drink the other night. I would have thanked you at the pub, but you seemed to be having fun with your girlfriends, and I didn't want to intrude further." He chuckled and looked down at his feet. "Actually, I did want to intrude, but I figured you'd shoot me down." He looked up into my eyes. "What brings you to my door?"

I put my hand on my hip. "You don't know? Aren't lawyers supposed to be smart?"

"A good lawyer never reveals exactly how much he knows."

I crossed my arms. "And a good landlady keeps tight tabs on her property and her tenants."

He cocked his head to the side. "Did my landlady send you over here? I haven't met her yet, but I hear she's a little bit kooky."

"She's more than just a little bit kooky," I said. "Also, she's me. I'm her. I'm Stormy Day."

I shook his hand as he gave me a convincingly shocked reaction.

"Come on in," he said, waving for me to enter. "It's your house, after all." He stood aside, the door wide open.

I stepped in, clutching my purse strap with both hands to keep them from trembling visibly. My prayer had given me courage everywhere except my hands. I glanced around the room, admiring the furnishings and artwork.

"You've decorated the place surprisingly well, all things considered," I said.

He cut in, "For a bachelor."

"I meant considering it's a rental. Most people won't put in much effort if they don't own the place."

He walked over to the kitchen that was a mirror image of my own and started filling a kettle. "Home is like anything else in life," he said. "You get out what you put in." He clicked the kettle onto its appliance hub. "Tea? I'd offer you something stronger, but what I've got in the cupboard would offend a woman of your fine taste."

I stayed in place on the mat by the door. "What makes you think I have fine taste?" Nervousness stretched my voice thin, making my words sound more adversarial than I'd intended.

He looked at the wood floor halfway between us and scratched the side of his head. "Let's start over," he said.

"How do we do that?" I asked. "I have an excellent memory."

"You don't have to forget to forgive," he said. "Would you consider accepting my apology for the things I said when we first met? I didn't mean to offend you. I could see you were having a rough day, and all I wanted to do was make you smile. I figured we could share a laugh at the expense of my landlady. It was just my bad luck she was you." He looked up, his expression sweet enough to make my teeth hurt. "Not that I consider it bad luck anymore. I'm glad I live next door, so that I get more chances to make a better impression."

"If that's your apology, I accept it," I said. "Hang on, that's my phone buzzing."

He cupped a hand around his ear. "No, I think that's my kettle."

I pulled my phone from my purse and pulled up an old message from Jessica, from the day before.

"Oops," I said, feigning alarm. "I've got to be going."

He circled around me, getting closer to the door handle. "So soon?"

I held up my phone and snapped a photo of him. The picture application made a clicking shutter sound, and the flash temporarily blinded him.

Logan rubbed his eyes, grumbling, "Who tipped off the paparazzi?"

"Sorry about the flash," I said. "I needed your picture for my contact list. What's your phone number? I'm sure it's on your lease agreement, but you might as well give it to me while I'm here."

He gave me his number and I punched it in, and then I made sure he had mine.

The kettle came to a boil and whistled.

While he went to the kitchen to shut it off, I said a quick goodbye and let myself out.

CHAPTER 41

WHEN I GOT TO my father's house, I rang the doorbell rather than using my key to let myself in.

Pam yanked open the door and scowled at me.

"Oh, good. You're still up," I said.

"And I'm busy," she said. "I don't have the time or inclination to entertain Finnegan's offspring."

I put my foot in the doorway and peered in. "Busy with what? Cleaning up to throw Dad a welcome-home party?"

Her scowl twisted into something like a grin. "You could say that." She pointed to a pile of flattened moving boxes leaning against the wall in the hallway. "I'm moving out. Given how things have been lately, that should be all the welcome-home he needs."

"Oh?" I played dumb. "Where are you going? Moving in with your friend Denise?"

"I don't know," she snapped. "I've rented a truck, and I think I'll get in and just start driving. See where the road takes me."

"Sounds fun," I said. In Pam's eyes, under the anger, I could see the heartbreak and forced bravery.

She got a wistful look. "I've always loved to travel, but your father never wanted to leave this town. That's why I'm done with him. Yes. It's because I need to travel."

"Pam, I'm sorry it's ending this way," I said. "You know I can't take sides, but, as a woman, I want you to know, from the bottom of my heart, I'm sorry."

As her eyes glistened, an uncomfortable silence stretched out between us. She stepped back from the door and waved me in. I gave her a hug. She pulled away from me quickly, as though repulsed.

I felt a paw on my foot. Jeffrey looked up at me, his green eyes beseeching me to rescue him. I reached down and scooped him into my arms.

"Pam, when you go on your road trip, how about I take care of Jeffrey?"

Her eyes flashed for an instant, and she replied, "He'd love that. You're young and energetic, and you spoil him with too much fatty food and letting him do whatever he wants."

I winced inwardly as I bit my tongue. Jeffrey liked me better because I spoke nicely to him and fed him regularly.

"I've never been a cat owner," I said. "You could give me some tips."

"I'll think about it," she said. "Why are you here? Did you forget something?"

"Not exactly," I said, setting down Jeffrey and kicking off my boots on the hallway mat. "I suppose I should come clean. I've been investigating what happened to Murray Michaels, and I've located some facts the police aren't aware of yet. I was hoping to run some theories past you." I coughed dryly and fanned my face. "Wow, my throat is sore. Do you think we could have some tea?"

She gave me a sour look but waved for me to follow her into the kitchen. Ignoring her, I trudged to the sofa and flopped down on the cushions, moaning tiredly.

As soon as she left the living room, I started hunting around for the item I'd come to collect. I couldn't tell Pam what I wanted, or she'd never let me out of the house with it. I searched high and low, even under the couch cushions, and came up empty. I returned to my floppy position on the couch when I heard her returning.

"You don't look well," she said. "Maybe you should sleep here tonight."

"Good idea," I said, sitting up and reaching for one of the mugs on her tray. "Which one is mine?"

"Take your pick," she said. "They're both decaf."

I picked the one furthest from me and blew over it before taking a sip.

She sat on my father's recliner, watching me steadily.

"What's this theory you've been cooking up?" she asked.

I pulled out my phone and opened the photo of Logan before handing it over. "Do you recognize this guy? You said you saw a bearded man in the neighborhood."

She held one hand to her throat and made a choking sound. "Yes. That's him. That's the man I saw. Who is he?"

"He's a lawyer, and I believe he had Mr. Michaels' house under surveillance. He was gathering evidence about the man's thefts in preparation for a lawsuit. I believe he had cameras set up in one of the neighboring houses, maybe inside the attic across the street, behind that little circle window."

Pam studied the photo, frowning. "Inside Elizabeth Biggs' house? I don't think so. She would have told me if something like that was going on." She looked up at me, eyes wide. "What evidence do you have?"

I tapped the side of my temple. "All the evidence so far is up here, in my brain. But once I go to the police, they can issue warrants and get the rest."

"Remarkable," she said. "I'm very impressed. You are definitely your father's daughter."

I sat back on the sofa, rubbing my stomach and groaning. "And I have my father's propensity for eating too many sweet and sour chicken balls at the Golden Wok." I groaned again. "This heartburn is killing me. I already crunched some antacids in the car, but I guess all this detective work makes a person's stomach acidic. Do you happen to have anything stronger?"

A smile spread across her face. "I might have something. But you should get into the tub, in a nice, hot bath. The water relaxes all your muscles while the heartburn pill goes to work on the rest."

I looked at my phone, which was still in her hand. "Maybe I should phone Tony and get it over with. He's going to be so annoyed, but he'll be glad when he catches this killer."

"We'll all be glad," Pam said. "It's not that late. You go have that bath now, and I'll try to remember which days I saw this horrible man in the neighborhood, and then we'll call Tony with all the information."

She got to her feet, grabbed my forearm with her free hand, and led me toward the floor's main bathroom, which was the only washroom in the house with a tub.

"You're so tense," she said in a caring manner. "Let me take care of you this once. You poor dear. Growing up without a mother, taking whatever scraps of comfort you could from the weekly whore your father had running through here."

"It wasn't easy," I said.

Pam turned on the water for the bath and adjusted the temperature for me.

"A nice bath makes everything better," she said soothingly.

"Pam, I really hope things work out for you. I hope you get what you deserve."

Without turning around to face me, she added scented bath oil to the water. "Don't you worry about me, dear. Once I set my mind on something, I make it happen."

Jeffrey walked into the bathroom and announced his presence with a meow. He jumped onto the counter, where he gathered his paws together neatly, wrapping them in his dark gray ribbon of a tail.

Pam said she'd be back in a few minutes with my antacid and left me to my bath.

Jeffrey watched the tub water rise with his bright green eyes. He let his eyelids droop, pretending he was relaxed, but he was faking it. The swirling water had him very concerned, but he was staying cool on the surface, just like me. Faking it.

I got undressed and climbed in. I settled back into the hot water. The soaker tub did have the perfect angles for relaxation.

Pam knocked on the door and came in with a glass of white wine. She held one hand along the side of her face to preserve my modesty.

"I've got your antacids here," she said. "This is the kind you swallow. Don't chew. And you should probably take both of them."

"That drink doesn't look like my tea," I said.

She laughed. "I just opened this bottle to have a tipple while I pack my things. You must drink a glass. You can't let me drink alone. Reach out your hand and I'll give everything to you."

"Hang on," I said. "I've got shampoo in my eye. You can set the pills on the counter."

"I'll wait," she said.

I turned the tap to cold and splashed water on my face. "It's really stinging. This could take a while."

She hesitated but finally did as I asked, setting the pills and wine on the counter next to Jeffrey. Then, instead of leaving, she started gathering up my clothes from the floor.

"Don't take those," I said.

"I'm starting up a load of laundry with these colors," she said.

"But those don't need washing. I just put them on before I came over."

She said, "Now you're being silly. You were wearing this outfit when you left here this morning. Remember, I have a keen eye for fashion."

I nodded and let her take my clothes.

As soon as she left, Jeffrey caught my attention with a tail flick. He looked me right in the eyes as he used one paw to knock one of the two pills off the counter. The white pill sailed over the wastebasket and toilet and straight into my tub water, making a tiny plopping sound before sinking from sight. It was followed, mere seconds later, by the second one.

As I stared at him in shock, he sat up straight, looking very pleased with himself. I reached into the water and groped around in search of the tablets, but the first one had already dissolved, and the second one melted under my touch.

I whispered to him, "Now what?"

He hooked his paw around the stem of the wine glass and gave it a nudge.

Shaking my head, I grabbed the wineglass before he ruined everything. I lifted the toilet seat, sloshed the wine into the water, and set the empty glass next to the tub. I settled down into the water to re-think my plan.

Fifteen minutes had passed when Pam returned, rapping softly on the door.

Groggily, I mumbled for her to come in. I couldn't have stopped her since the handle for the room hadn't been lockable for years. As kids, my sister and I had driven my father crazy with our indoor games, so he'd dismantled the interior locks on all the doors to cut down on door-kicking battles. Never before had I regretted my childhood antics more than now.

Pam came in, still with her hand at the side of her face to preserve my modesty. "You can borrow my bathrobe," she said, setting a garishly-patterned monstrosity on a hook on the wall. "Feeling sleepy?" she asked.

"Yeah," I said, closing my eyes. "Gimme a few minutes more in here with my eyes closed, then I'm going to crash in your guest room, if that's okay."

"Of course it's okay," she said sweetly.

I kept very still as she hovered over me. She wasn't much bigger than me, and she was a lot older, but she had one huge advantage.

Pam was a stone-cold murderer.

She'd killed Murray Michaels, and if I didn't do something, she was going to kill me next.

I breathed steadily, even though her close proximity made my skin crawl.

In hindsight, I shouldn't have taken off my clothes and gotten into the tub. It was too dangerous a risk, just to get a couple of sleeping pills to use as evidence. What I really wanted was Pam's sketchbook, but I hadn't found it in the living room and had hoped to buy myself more time.

She leaned in over me, her body a growing darkness I could sense, as well as see through my closed eyelids. Were those her hands coming toward my throat?

"Chicken balls," I said sleepily, licking my lips. "Never again."

She made a groaning sound as she backed away from the tub and finally left the bathroom.

My eyelids flew open.

I had to get out of there, empty-handed but alive.

The ceiling above me creaked. My heart pounded. It wasn't just any old creak. I knew the creaks of that house, thanks to hours and hours of playing hide-and-seek with my sister and anyone else we could draw into our games.

The creak had come from directly overhead, from the squeaky floorboard that had once been in my childhood bedroom and was now in my father's den, right in front of the safe, where he kept his gun. If Pam knew the combination, which wasn't that difficult to guess, as he'd used his birthday, she could be retrieving the gun and loading it.

The creak sounded again overhead.

Just when I thought all I had to worry about was sleeping pills and strangling, the neighborhood killer had to go and get herself a gun.

CHAPTER 42

LEAVING THE PLUG in the drain, I slowly withdrew from the tub, making the smallest movements so I didn't alert Pam with splashing sounds.

Pam had taken my clothes, so I grabbed the only thing available, which was her bathrobe, and slipped it on. I stood at the bathroom door, listening. Now what? My boots, purse, and phone were at the front of the house, but if she was in the living room with a gun, it would be safer for me to sneak out the back door then around to the front, where my car was parked on the street. It would be embarrassing to be seen running around in a housecoat but preferable to being shot dead in a housecoat.

As I reached for the door handle, I heard movement nearby.

She called out, "If you want more wine, it's here in the kitchen. Come get some when you're done in the tub."

I tied the robe's belt. She sounded so friendly, which I hadn't anticipated. Was I wrong about everything? The story about Logan doing surveillance next door had been pure fiction on my part, a lie I'd told to test her, to push her into doing something to silence me. Now I was defenseless, trapped in the bathroom, and unsure what to do next. Had the floor upstairs really creaked? Did she have my father's gun? Or was it all my overactive imagination?

Something scratched behind me. I turned to find Jeffrey swatting at the bathroom window, trying to catch a tiny bug. That gave me an idea.

I undid the latch and pushed the window open. Cool air rushed in, clearing my mind. The bathroom was on the ground floor, and the window wasn't the most graceful way to leave the house, but I could do it.

I hated the idea of jumping into the snowy bushes below wearing nothing more than a bathrobe, and I hated the idea of doing so without evidence even more. What could I do? I really wanted Pam's sketchbook. Where had I seen it last? I'd written a note on a blank sheet for Pam while she was on the phone, and she'd snatched it away and hid right here, in the bathroom.

I crouched down and opened the cupboard doors under the sink. The sight of the spiral binding made me squeal inwardly. Unfortunately, the book was a good twenty inches long, which was too bulky to hide within the bathrobe even if I did dare to sneak out past her. I leafed through the pages quickly, saw what I'd hoped to find, and tossed it out of the window. Jeffrey snapped to attention, eager to play the new game I'd just invented. He jumped out of the window after the book.

After another quick prayer, I did the same.

I landed in the snowy bushes, scratching my legs and shredding my dignity. My robe gaped open, and there I was, mostly naked in the snow, for anyone to see. Nobody screamed, so I had to assume I hadn't been spotted by a neighbor… yet. I pulled the robe shut, gave the belt a quick tying, and grabbed both the book and Jeffrey.

I walked quickly between the two houses. To say my bare feet were uncomfortable on the crunchy, cold snow would be an understatement. After a minute, though, the ice numbed them, and walking wasn't too painful, thanks to my elevated temperature from the hot bath plus the adrenaline.

I ran up the steps to the neighbor's house and rang the doorbell. Nobody came. I rang it a few more times. No answer. A pile of mail and flyers sat by the door. The family was out of town. I looked up and down the quiet, dark street. It was late, and the nearest homes were all dark.

Jeffrey meowed that he was bored with this game and wanted to be set down. He jumped from my arms and raced away, running toward my car.

"Good idea," I whispered.

I shoved Pam's sketchbook under the neighbor's pile of mail and ran after him, toward the car. I didn't have my purse or my keys, but I didn't need them. The fancy, expensive car I'd been embarrassed about driving in town was now my salvation, with its luxurious keyless entry. I'd never used the feature, but in theory I could open the door and start the engine by punching in a code.

I crouched down by the driver's side door, so the keypad was at eye level, and so I couldn't be seen if Pam noticed I was missing from the bathroom and popped her head out of the front door.

...s the code? I hadn't used it since I'd ...e car a couple of years earlier. The guy at ...ership suggested the name of a child or a pet. ...n't have either, but as I recalled the conversation ... the car dealership, I remembered making the salesman laugh when I made my selection.

I punched in the code: JEFFREY BLUE.

The door unlocked, and the engine purred as it came to life. My code was the name I'd given to my childhood imaginary friend. Now I just had to grab the cat I'd named after him.

I whisper-yelled, "Jeffrey. Here, kitty, kitty, kitty."

Movement on the porch caught my eye. Jeffrey was at the front door, done with our game and ready to go inside again.

The curtains on the living room window were drawn, but shadows shifted as Pam moved around inside the house. It was only a matter of time before she opened the door. Ignoring all my self-preservation warning bells, I cinched the bathrobe tighter and walked in a crouch toward the porch, where the silly cat was sitting.

The door swung open, and there was Pam.

"Stormy Day!" she sputtered. "What the devil are you doing outside in the middle of the night, in my bathrobe?"

She was backlit, the front of her face only dimly lit by the street lamps, but I could see her expression contorting as she worked through what was happening. Here I was, awake, which meant her sleeping pills hadn't worked.

"Pam, you're going to laugh at this. I fell asleep in the tub, so I opened the window to get some fresh air, and the cat jumped out. I heard something outside, and I was worried a dog had cornered him, so I went out to rescue him. Silly me, right?"

She wasn't laughing. "Stormy, get inside before you catch your death of cold."

Obeying her, I walked up the steps slowly. Her posture changed, and suddenly she was a monster standing in the doorway of her lair, commanding me to come in so she could kill me.

I stopped and took a step backward.

"Actually," I said. "Since I'm already outside, I'll go run an errand. Can you believe I left the stove on at my duplex? I won't be long."

Coldly, she said, "At least get some shoes." She slowly backed up, toward the hallway table and my purse. She kept one hand behind her back the whole time. I caught a glimpse of her hidden hand in the hall mirror, and the glint of something metallic.

My heart pounded louder than my thoughts. I held still, my face neutral. She didn't know that I'd seen the gun. She didn't know how much I knew.

"That wine was great," I said. "I've got a nice bottle at the duplex that I'll grab when I'm there. I'll come right back and pop it open while I help you pack."

"You've lost your mind," she said. "Come inside and lie down on the sofa. You need some rest. I'll take care of you."

She sounded so convincing, so caring. I wanted to believe her, but I couldn't.

She said, "Don't be scared. Come inside and let me take care of you, the way a mother would."

"Pam, did you do Leo Jenkins' window display at Masquerade?"

She tilted her head to the side. "Of course I did. Why do you ask?"

"Why didn't you go in again and change it for him? I was there today, and he said he had to change it himself. Are you avoiding him? Or are you avoiding standing inside a display window, handling a snowman somewhere the whole town can see you? Is there a reason you don't want anyone to make a connection between you and professional-looking snowmen?"

She slumped against the side of the doorframe as though tired. "Not that it's any of your business, but I've been busy," she said.

"Busy trying to set my father up for killing his neighbor?"

She let out a laugh that sounded like a fender collapsing. "You certainly do have a wild imagination," she said.

I continued, "You were planning to be long gone by the time the snow melted in the spring and the body showed up. You were going to watch from a safe distance while the police turned my father's life upside down. That was your revenge for him breaking your heart."

She made a tsk-tsk sound. "He didn't deserve me, anyway. Neither do you."

"What about Murray Michaels?" I asked. "Did he deserve to be drugged with your sleeping pills and then strangled to death? What did he ever do to you, Pam? Did he steal your newspaper one time too many? Was that a good enough reason for you to kill him?"

"You saw him," she said. "He had that smug, self-satisfied look on his face. He'd found himself a young woman who didn't know any better, that little wisp of a waitress. I saw how she looked at him when she refilled her coffee at the Olive Grove. She didn't know what a filthy old fool he was. She was falling under his spell."

I shook my head. "She was his daughter, Pam. She was his daughter. And now, thanks to you, she won't ever get to know him."

"Good riddance," she said.

Jeffrey rubbed against my shin. I leaned down and scooped him up.

Pam said, "Give me back my cat."

"No." I stepped down the porch steps until I was on the cement walkway. My feet were so numb; I had to use my eyes to check that I was on solid ground.

She drew herself up tall and brought her hidden hand into view. She pointed the gun at my head. Pam didn't have police training, or she would have pointed it at my chest, giving herself a broader target. I didn't point this out to her.

"Pack a bag quickly," I said. "I've called the police, and they're on the way now. You've got a head start. If you get in your car and drive, you might be able to get away, or you might be able to concoct a defense they'll believe. But if they show up in a few minutes and I've got a bullet in me, that's going to be a tough one for you to talk your way out of."

She kept the gun aimed at my head. "You're bluffing. You don't have your phone. You couldn't have called the police."

"Do you really think I came over here without a plan? Does that sound like me?"

She made a growling sound. “And do you think I won’t shoot you?”

I continued backing away steadily. “I’d rather be shot on the front lawn than shot in my father’s living room.”

The night cracked with the sound of Pam’s first shot. She missed my head, as far as I could tell, but even a lousy marksman can get lucky.

I turned and ran toward my car, zig-zagging to keep my head from staying in a straight line of sight. Another shot rang out as I pivoted again, hard.

Breaking glass tinkled. She’d hit a window of my car.

I dodged and crouched down low, putting the car between me and Pam.

She screamed, “Stormy! Get back here!”

“I changed my mind!” I yelled back. “I’d rather not be shot at all!”

I huddled behind the back tire. She fired off another bullet, which shattered the window of another car, across the street.

“Young lady, get back in the house right now!” she screamed.

“Why? Am I grounded?”

She answered by firing off another shot.

Jeffrey squirmed in my arms. He didn’t know what a gun was, but he knew better than to come to the house when Pam was screaming for him. So did I.

CHAPTER 43

I DOVE FOR the driver's side door, which was thankfully already unlocked. I tossed the cat in first and followed, keeping my head down low. The engine had been running since I'd punched in the code, and was warm and ready to go.

I threw the car into gear and punched the gas with my half-frozen foot. Another gunshot cracked through the night.

Drive, I thought. Just drive.

The car accelerated with a purr. I sailed through three intersections before I even considered touching the brakes.

I kept checking the rear-view mirror. My feet were numb, and the rest of my body felt equally strange, as though all the atomic particles that were part of me were ready to go elsewhere, separately.

The streets were nearly empty, but I kept looking over my shoulder. I expected to see Pam, whipping out from behind a building, careening after me in a monster truck, leaning out of the window with a roaring chainsaw. She would be screaming about giving me a really short haircut.

I saw her in every shadow, my imagination making up for all the time I'd spent with her, not knowing she was a killer. I'd actually felt sorry for the woman. I'd eaten the french toast she made with her murderous hands.

Jeffrey was also on edge, and without the restraint of a pet carrier, he was free to act out his anxieties. He'd started off underneath the passenger-side seat, out of sight but howling. After a few blocks, he emerged and scaled the back of my leather seat, all the better to meow loudly in my ear.

Cold air whistled through the car, thanks to the bullet hole in the rear window. I shoulder checked. A vehicle was approaching from behind, its bright headlights preventing me from seeing the driver. I breathed easier when I made out the shape of the vehicle as that of a truck. Pam's vehicle was a car. Unless she'd learned the fine art of hot-wiring, the person behind me wasn't her.

Jeffrey howled in my ear. Either he was picking up on my panic, or he thought we were going to the vet again. He was not happy, in any case.

"We're safe now," I told him.

He responded by singing me the song of his cat people. For an encore, he jumped onto the dash interior and wedged himself against the windshield, still meowing about the evening's horrible ordeals.

A traffic light up ahead turned red. I tried to tap the brakes, but my tingling foot stomped the pedal. The car lurched to a graceless stop. Another vehicle pulled up next to us. Jeffrey hissed. I turned my head slowly to the left, following Jeffrey's fearful gaze. I fully expected to see Pam with the gun, or a chainsaw, or perhaps both.

Much to my relief, I found the bearded face of Logan Sanderson.

I lowered my window and croaked, "Hello."

Logan lowered his passenger-side window and leaned over to say, "Is it considered normal in Misty Falls to drive around in a bathrobe with a cat on your dashboard?"

"Yes," I said. "But if you don't have a cat, you can use a dog or a ferret." I gave him an I'm-not-crazy smile before checking over my shoulder for Pam.

Logan said, "I don't know what you're up to, but you look like a woman who knows how to have fun."

"Thanks."

"Do you need chocolate?" he asked. "I wasn't going anywhere in particular, but I had a massive craving for road trip food. I am currently in possession of five kinds of chocolate, plus potato chips, pretzels, and something the gas station clerk recommended personally." He held up a bag of gummy worms.

"I'd love some, but I have to go turn in my father's girlfriend for murder. Pam Bochenek killed Murray Michaels."

His eyebrows raised higher and higher. "You did it. You found the snowman killer."

I nodded. "If you'll excuse me, I should get to the police station to give a statement."

"Do you think you'll need a lawyer? I'm asking you seriously."

"I didn't kill anyone, but I can pass your card along to Pam."

He rubbed his beard thoughtfully. "I have a better idea. As the town's newest lawyer, I should get better acquainted with the local law enforcement. You'd be doing me a favor by letting me come along."

I couldn't argue with that, but I did have one important question. "Will you bring the gummy worms?"

"Of course." He pointed to the traffic light above us. "Light's green. I'll follow you to the police station."

CHAPTER 44

I WALKED INTO THE POLICE STATION with nothing but a colorful bathrobe and an irritated cat. The night receptionist didn't even pause to say hello before paging for an on-duty police officer.

We were met by Officer Peggy Wiggles, who ushered the three of us back to an interview room. She asked what happened, and I had a tough time slowing down enough for her to understand me. I did communicate that they needed to send cars to Warbler Street for Pam Bochenek, who was armed and dangerous.

Officer Wiggles didn't doubt me for an instant. If anything, the expression on her face conveyed satisfaction that she'd suspected the killer was Pam all along. She had, after all, been the one who'd commented on how professionally made the snowman had appeared.

She left us in the interview room while she went to coordinate with the other officers.

Jeffrey sat on his own chair, having a personal grooming session. I patted his soft gray head, and he gave me a look of annoyance. He'd already cleaned that spot, and now he would have to wash it again.

I turned to Logan. "Thanks for coming with me. You don't have to stay for the whole thing."

"Did you say something?" He shook his head as though waking up. "I couldn't hear you over that bathrobe. It's really loud. Are those pelicans or flowers?"

I looked down at my ensemble. "The pattern is rather spectacular."

"At least it brings out your pretty eyes."

I snorted. "How would you know? You're colorblind."

He gave me a funny look. "How did you know I was colorblind?"

I gave him a Mona Lisa smile. "The same way I tracked down the killer. I'm clearly a brilliant detective." I tried to close the front of my bathrobe and appear more respectable, but there was no use. "And I'm humble, too," I added. "Be sure and mention that to Tony Baloney when we see him."

"Tony who?"

"Officer Tony Milano. You met him already, for all of about a minute, at the vet clinic. Why were you there, anyway? Do you have a cat? A dog? A fish?"

"None of the above," he said. "What's your connection to this Tony guy?"

"My father's a cop. Well, he was. He's retired now. Tony trained with him and was his partner for a while. I've known him forever."

"Ah," Logan said with a nod. "I thought maybe he was your boyfriend."

"Yuck. Tony's old and gross."

"Hmm." Logan looked at me with the cool expression of someone skilled at detecting lies.

His cool blue eyes tracked down, moving languidly along my neckline. I adjusted the bathrobe's overlap to preserve my modesty as best I could.

"What about you?" I asked. "Did you move to Misty Falls by yourself, or will someone be joining you at the duplex?"

"Are you inquiring as my landlady?" he asked cheekily. "Will I have to pay more than a fifty-five-percent share of the electricity bill?"

"To be fair, you should pay more if you have excessively long showers."

"I'll keep that in mind." He sorted through the pile of junk food he'd brought in and opened a bag of pretzels, offering them to me first.

"These are good," I said, reaching for another handful.

"I'm glad to see a smile on your face," he said. "You've had a tough night, and it's part of a good lawyer's job to put his client at ease so she can function."

"So, you're just doing your job?" A squeak of disappointment made its way into my voice.

In a serious tone, he said, "I might joke around at times, but I take my work very seriously. Stormy, if you ever need me again in a legal capacity, please don't hesitate to call." He smiled warmly. "Or knock on my door."

"For legal matters," I clarified.

"Or to borrow a cup of sugar," he said.

"A cup of sugar? That won't happen. I never bake."

He raised his eyebrows. "Never say never."

Wiggles came back into the room, interrupting our exchange. "Everything's under control," she said. "Pam Bochenek is in custody, and we're going to get a psych evaluation."

"Good," I said. "Something is not right with her. My father mentioned something about her losing her sense of humor, and he wasn't wrong. She actually found me amusing at some point, and I know I haven't changed, so I did a little research online. Apparently there's a type of corticobasal degeneration that could explain some of her personality changes. It's rare, and I know it's not the sort of thing that turns regular people into killers, but it could have clouded her judgment."

Wiggles nodded. "We'll leave the mental assessment to the professionals. When did you know it was her?"

"I'm embarrassed I didn't figure it out sooner," I said. "Back at my place, sitting on my coffee table, is a vase she made for me at the paint-your-own ceramics place. It has the exact same crooked grin as the snowman she built around Murray Michaels, but it's a different face from the one that was in the window at Masquerade because that was a store-bought snowman. I saw Leo Jenkins putting it away, and I was thinking what a shame it was the snowman hadn't given us more of a clue, but then my eyes wandered over to the cards posted on his corkboard. I saw Pam's business card for her window display business."

Logan interrupted, "And her card has a hand-drawn snowman on it."

"No." I shook my head. "Flowers. But the flowers have faces, and they all have the same crooked smiles."

"That's not much to go on," he said.

Wiggles shushed him. "Let her talk, Mr. Lawyer."

"The other thing was Pam's scarab broach."

They both nodded, and Wiggles asked, "And where did you find that?"

"I didn't, but it may show up at the pawn shop Murray was using, or inside his house. You see, Pam claimed she hadn't seen the victim since his appearance at my father's party, and I remember that when I was leaving, I pulled on her jacket by accident. I made a comment about her scarab broach, which she didn't appreciate. But then this morning, she was sure that he'd swiped it. Either she was mistaken, or she had seen him after the party."

"These are good clues," Wiggles said. "Not exactly bulletproof as evidence, though."

"That's why I went in to get proof. I bluffed her by making her think I had information that would point back to her, and then I practically invited her to drug me with sleeping pills. I was going to bring the pills in as evidence, but then Mr. Not-So-Helpful over here knocked them into the tub." I pointed to Jeffrey, who blinked innocently.

"Good cat," Wiggles said, leaning over to pat his head. She cooed at him, "Your heart was in the right place, and you were trying to protect her." To us, she added, "They know more than they let on."

"At least I got her sketchpad," I said. "Not on me, but it's hidden in the neighbor's mail. You'll find some very interesting drawings, including one of a snowman in front of Murray's house, dated before his disappearance. She may claim she wrote down the dates wrong, or that it's just a coincidence, but that's not bad for evidence, is it?"

"Not bad at all," Wiggles said. "It certainly doesn't hurt that we have her red-handed for trying to shoot you tonight."

Logan leaned forward and asked, "Was anyone else hurt?"

Officer Wiggles shook her head. "Lucky for the boys, Pam was out of bullets by the time they arrived, and was packing a bag." She took a breath and let it out noisily. "Which is good, for obvious reasons, but also because we can't afford to have anyone out with an injury. I'm still a rookie, but I've been thrown into the deep end here. Between the snowman murder and complaints about the voodoo lady, I've been running around like a house mouse with a backpack full of catnip."

Logan's eyebrows raised. "Voodoo lady?"

"Nothing to be concerned about," she said, tapping away on the laptop keys. "Let's start again from the beginning."

We went through the basics, with me slowing down to explain everything from the beginning, point by point.

Logan continued to sit in as my legal counsel and official junk food supplier. We left the door to the room open so that Jeffrey could prowl around the nearly-empty police station.

Officer Wiggles pulled up the previous statement I'd made, the one after I'd found the body, and we picked up from there. When I got to describing how goofy Jeffrey had been after his surgery, I got the giggles and kept apologizing.

"It's good to laugh," Wiggles assured me. "My cat keeps me sane. He loves playing table hockey, and when you described Jeffrey knocking the sleeping pill into the tub, I could see it clearly since my Peekaboo does the same thing. Mostly he breaks my favorite mugs."

"What kind of cat?"

"A chubby ginger with a stubby tail. His name is Peekaboo because he actually plays peekaboo. And he hides in laundry baskets."

"That is so cute! Do you have a photo?"

She did, and we took a few minutes to appreciate Peekaboo in all his ginger glory before returning to the serious business of finishing my statement.

Time passed, and while I didn't see Tony, a familiar face in the form of Officer Gary Gomez popped in to say hello.

"Thanks for making us look bad," Gomez said, grinning under his big mustache. "Just kidding, Stormy. I'm glad to see you continuing your father's legacy for whipping this town into shape."

I smiled tiredly. "You can have the next one," I said. "This was a one-time deal."

"Good," he said. "By the way, your cat is working the Case of the Mouse Who Nibbled the Snack Room Crackers."

"Will that be all?" Wiggles asked him with a tone of dismissal.

Gomez waggled his eyebrows at her and left without another word.

We continued with my statement until I was hoarse.

"We're done, and it's either late or early," Wiggles said with a yawn. "I've got some spare shoes and socks in my locker that you can borrow to get home."

"Thank you." I looked down at my bare feet. My mind went blank. It had been a long night.

She excused herself and returned with the shoes and socks. I pulled them on while Logan made jokes about carrying me to my car. He was funny, but I was too tired to laugh.

CHAPTER 45

"IT'S OVER," Logan said as we walked out of the police station together. "You and your father are safe now, thanks to your detective skills."

I held Jeffrey tightly as we walked out into the snowy parking lot. The sky was pink, casting a warm glow on our surroundings. The long night had passed. I was still wearing the ridiculous bathrobe I'd arrived in, but thanks to Officer Wiggles' athletic shoes, I wasn't barefoot in the snow.

We reached my vehicle, where I handed Logan the cat so I could punch in the keyless entry code for the door. When I turned back, Jeffrey had his paws around Logan's neck and was rubbing his whiskered cheek against the man's beard, as though it was a kitty grooming brush.

"Somebody likes me," Logan said. "Go easy on the beard, Mr. Kitty."

"His full name is Mr. Jeffrey Blue."

"Good to know." With a formal flair, he added, "I shall henceforth address my landlord by his full title."

I pried Jeffrey away from his new friend and loaded him into the car. He snaked under the passenger seat. The crime scene investigators had put a makeshift plastic covering over my shot-out rear passenger window. I climbed into the driver's seat, shut the door, and lowered my window.

"Logan, thanks for everything. Let me know if I can ever repay you."

"I promise I will." He patted the roof of my car. "Get out of here now. I've got a new spot I like to drive to for the view, so I'm going to head there for a bit. It should give you thirty minutes, more than enough time to get settled before I show up."

"I understand," I said. "That's always so awkward, when you say goodbye to someone and then you see them again right away."

"Yeah, awkward." He gave me a flirtatious, sidelong look. "After a night like this, you don't need to be contending with the likes of me one more time."

"That would be horrible," I said.

He patted the roof again, turned and left.

I leaned over to peer under the seat at Jeffrey, who was all eyes in the darkness.

"We're going home," I told him. "By the way, I'm adopting you. Any objections?"

He had none. I sat up, clicked my seatbelt on, and started driving us home.

I clicked on the radio. The local station was playing the usual morning routine. I smiled as the joke-cracking host told his tall tales.

"Morning commuters, you'll want to steer clear of the rush hour traffic in the downtown core. We've had some reports of a staggering three-car lineup at the red light by Ruby's Treasure Trove. Ladies, if you need to check your hair and makeup while you're driving, that's what the rear-view mirror is for! You're listening to the Misty Mountain Man's Morning Mugga. It's none of my business what's in your morning mugga, but you should know mine's full of herbal tea, brewed with the sparkling clear water of our own Misty Falls, plus a handful of the Mountain Man's personal stash of special mushrooms. Coming up on the hour, we'll have news and weather and a report on those late-night fireworks some of you heard last night. Spoiler alert: those weren't fireworks. Stay tuned through this next song, and don't you dare change the station!"

When we got home, Jeffrey prowled around his new home with his tail held high. He seemed to understand immediately that everything mine was now his. He trotted from room to room, rubbing his cheeks on anything with a corner.

We didn't have any cat food yet, but I set out some canned tuna, and he seemed impressed. I already had kitty litter, left behind by the previous homeowners with a note that it was good for absorbing oil spills on the driveway. I used a plastic storage bin to set up facilities for Jeffrey, and then I brushed my teeth.

The cool-white sun of a winter morning was now streaming in the windows. I considered brewing a pot of coffee and staying up, but I couldn't stop yawning.

I heard a vehicle pull into the driveway. I checked the time. I'd been home for exactly thirty minutes.

I walked down the hall toward my bedroom. The bed was crisply made with fresh sheets, and the room itself was welcoming. After being away for a few days, I appreciated all my things even more. I hadn't taken much time to decorate, or even paint the walls anything other than eggshell cream, but the duplex had a vintage style I found comfortable.

I slipped off the bathrobe, tossed it in the hamper, and changed into a favorite pair of soft pajamas.

"Time for bed," I called to Jeffrey.

He came running and jumped up on the bed, as though he'd understood every word.

"You can stay up if you want," I said. "I was just letting you know that I'm going to bed."

He gave me two slow blinks as he softened up my pillow with his front paws.

"That's my side," I said.

He stretched and settled down in the center of my pillow.

"Fine," I sighed. "I guess I can make some allowances for the new man in my life."

I walked around to the other side of the bed, pulled back the duvet, and climbed in. I set the alarm clock on my bedside table for five hours because I didn't want to miss the entire day. I lay my head down, facing my newly adopted Russian Blue cat.

"Jeffrey, I have to ask you a question. Are you afraid of big spiders?"

In response, he yawned. His yawn crossed the species barrier and made me yawn, too.

I wondered, was Logan also drifting off to sleep in his bed on the other side of the wall? How would Jessica react when I told her everything? And what would Ruby and the other Secret Tea Room Ladies say?

Jeffrey reached out and gently bopped me on the nose.

"Sleepy time," I said.

He let out an adorable cat-sigh and curled up fetchingly on the pillow. I curled my arm around him.

Sleepiness rolled up like a comfortable blanket of fog. My limbs grew heavy and warm. The tension I'd been holding for days in my neck and shoulders melted away.

I closed my eyes and started to drift.

CHAPTER 46

ONE WEEK LATER

OUR CHRISTMAS-THEMED CENTERPIECES were disappearing from the gift shop faster than we could unbox more.

"You're a magnificent salesperson," I told my employee during a quiet break, when it was only the two of us in the store.

"This is all you, Boss," Brianna said. "Everyone's coming in to see the person who single-handedly solved the town's most notorious murder."

"But once they get in the door, you're the one who directs their energies toward purchasing home decor items and gifts."

Brianna smiled. "That's my job." She tidied up the display of napkins and napkin rings. "How are things going with your tenant these days?"

"Logan paid his December rent on time," I said.

"And?"

"And give it some time, girl! We thirty-somethings are not like you twenty-somethings. Some of us have a few city miles on our hearts, plus the baggage to go with it."

Brianna gave me one of her sassy looks. "Well, when he does get around to doing something cute, you'll have to let me know. I always need material for my webcomic."

I shook my finger at her. "You leave me out of your webcomic."

She gave me half a shrug as she continued tidying up the displays.

A minute later, Brianna asked, "Remind me again, who was the guy you saw taking photos next door to your father's?"

"That was my real estate agent's husband, Michael Sweet. He must have run off because he was embarrassed about moving in like a vulture, planning to pick the house up cheap at auction and flip it."

"You should buy the house," Brianna said.

"And live next door to my father?"

"Or flip it," she said.

"I'll suggest it to my father as a project for him. At the very least, we can put in a bid and make sure Michael Sweet pays market value." I rubbed my chin and considered the idea for a minute. The property value was depressed due to the hoarded contents, not to mention being the site of a homicide. Then again, scooping up an investment the Sweets had an eye on would put the three of us on adversarial ground, and I liked working with his wife.

I found it funny that investments in Misty Falls were no less complicated than the deals I'd overseen at Fairchild Capital.

Brianna interrupted my thoughts. "I saw Chip yesterday," she said.

"Who?"

"The mail carrier who works in your father's neighborhood. The big guy who wears shorts all winter." She held up a sunset-hued napkin. "He wasn't quite this shade of orange, but his skin is showing signs of excess beta-carotene consumption. Since he's my second-cousin, I figured I was within my rights to talk to him about it. He says he's lost twenty pounds on his mostly-carrot diet, but he's going to switch things up before he gets as orange as those things in the movie. Oompa Loompas."

"He'd make a great Oompa Loompa," I said. "You could put him in your webcomic."

She quirked one eyebrow. "What makes you think I haven't already?"

The door chimed, and Jessica came in. She pointed to my elbow, which was resting on a display rack. "Stormy, if you've got time to lean, you've got time to get a coffee. Come on, it's my treat."

I turned to Brianna, who said, "Go! Get out now while it's quiet. I'll hold down the fort."

"I'll bring you back a mocha," I promised.

"You're spoiling me, Boss." She held open the door and waved us out.

On the sidewalk, Jessica gave me a hug. Her bright red hair smelled of fresh cinnamon buns.

"Do you think you can handle House of Bean today?" she asked. "Chad's working today."

"Perfect," I said. "There's something I need to do."

Jessica sighed, probably imagining the worst.

We walked into House of Bean. Chad took one look at me, and rather than puffing up like a pufferfish, he deflated. Waving one limp arm, he muttered, “Good morning,” with none of his usual enthusiasm.

“Hi Chad,” I said. “May we please have two of your fine Teeny Weenie Beanie Steamers? Mountain size. And a Choco Loco Hobo Mocha in a takeout cup.”

Chad’s eyes flitted between my face and Jessica’s. “Are you sure?” He pointed to a can of sign-painter’s paint on a counter by the wall behind him. “I’ve been thinking that our coffee names are too creative, and I was just about to change them.”

“Don’t you dare,” I said. “People can get a vanilla latte at any chain coffee shop, anywhere in the country, and it’s exactly the same. What makes Misty Falls special isn’t just the mountains and the beautiful four seasons, it’s the people and all the details. Please don’t change anything. I’m the one who needs to change, and that’s why I moved here. It would defeat the purpose if the things I did changed the town to be any different from how it is now, which is perfect.”

Chad blinked. “Perfect?”

“Don’t change a thing,” I said.

He eyed me with suspicion as he prepared our beverages.

Jessica paid, and we took our seats at a corner table, where Jessica asked, “What you said to Chad, did you mean it?”

“Absolutely.” I took a sip of my Teenie Weenie Beanie Steamer and smiled. “I’m embracing small-town life, as of right now. This whole adventure I’ve had has given me a lot of perspective. People get so worked up about what others are going to think or say about them. Pam didn’t want people to know about the breakup. Creepy Jeepers wouldn't tell the truth about his wedding band because he was worried about rumors. And I've spent way too much energy getting upset over the rumors people tell about me. From now on, I'm just going to be grateful that people talk about me because I'm part of something, part of this town."

She nodded slowly. "So, you don't mind that people say you walked away from billions of dollars?"

"It's more interesting than the truth," I said. "I did work in venture capital, and I was responsible for investing large sums of money in startup companies, but it was never my money. Fairchild Capital wasn't even an angel investor. We used other people's money to finance investments using a pool of money. The profit got reinvested or paid out to the investors. It never went to me, Stormy Day. Sure, there were some bonuses, and I did get paid nicely, but I would have gotten the same working for any other large company."

She smiled. "Since you're not rich, I suppose it's a good thing you're lucky."

I laughed. "And don't forget smart," I added.

She nodded solemnly. "And good looking."

"Not to mention humble."

"So humble," she agreed.

"Cheers to that." I clinked my coffee mug against hers.

TO BE CONTINUED...
IN STORMY DAY MYSTERY #2

DEATH OF A CRAFTY KNITTER

ANGELA PEPPER

www.angelapepper.com

TURN THE PAGE FOR A PREVIEW OF BOOK 2

DEATH OF A CRAFTY KNITTER
CHAPTER 1

VOULA VARGA WOKE UP on New Year's Day and went about her usual morning routine, not knowing it would be the final day of her life.

As she stood in her kitchen, waiting for the coffee maker to release her coffee, she scowled and tapped her long, black-lacquered fingernails impatiently.

Soon, she told herself, she would live in luxury and have a maid to bring her coffee in bed and fix her manicure. When that day finally came, all of the drudgery of hustling for a living would be behind her. Her humiliation would be over.

She couldn't wait to see Misty Falls in her rear-view mirror. The postcard-pretty little town, nestled in a scenic mountain valley, was a nice enough place, except for the people. The residents all bored her to tears with their terrible, awful, horrible, tedious niceness. On top of that, they failed to recognize her as any different from the rest of them.

Voula Varga should have been a star. If those Hollywood casting agents knew how to spot genuine talent, they would have seen it. But they were fools. Instead of giving her the lead roles she deserved, they cast her in small parts. Some actresses would have been happy to get a few speaking lines and a regular paycheck, but for Voula, each assignment was a personal insult. She was always cast in the same pathetic role: fortune-teller.

By the time she left Los Angeles, Voula Varga had been credited as the gypsy fortune-teller or psychic or voodoo priestess in more than forty feature-length films and an equal number of television dramas. Her closest thing to a breakout role had been in a fantasy epic, playing an evil sorceress who summoned the dead. It was to be her big break. Unfortunately, the film tanked at the box office and went on to become a joke. There were regular viewing parties around the country now, where people gathered to watch the movie and make fun of it, yelling out Voula's lines of corny dialog at the screen.

Her movie career had flatlined after that film, along with the careers of all but a few people associated with the failed endeavor. She fled Los Angeles and wandered from town to town, working odd jobs here and there until she stumbled upon a way to use her particular curse for her own gain.

Voula Varga was utterly perfect at playing a fortune-teller.

So, instead of fighting it, she embraced her curse and *became* her typecast role. Even before she'd fully mastered the tricks of the trade, people who visited her booth to have their palms read thought she was the real thing. From her dark, curly hair to her golden eyes, Voula looked the part of a mystical psychic, and now she played the part for real. It was the role of a lifetime, and she would soon be wealthy and powerful.

She had a plan.

She'd moved to Misty Falls six months earlier, in the summer. It was the warmest day of the year for the little town, and she was overdressed in her layers of dark scarves and flowing dresses. People eyed her uneasily on her first walk through town, as though they could tell she had a plan to suck the life savings out of all the gullible townspeople before disappearing again.

On the first day of the new year, Voula Varga poured her morning coffee, unlocked her front door, walked upstairs, and stood at one of the windows that overlooked the entire unsuspecting town. She stood there and she cackled her evil, malicious laugh, not unlike a witch in a bad movie.

Two hours later, the doorbell rang. Voula quickly changed out of her silky nightie into one of her everyday long dresses. She pulled on her winter jacket, grabbed a box of bullets, and answered the door.

"I have a little treat for us," Voula told the visitor as she held up the bullets. "Give me a minute to gather up some old cans, and we'll see if that lovely antique still fires."

The visitor was surprised by this suggestion, but reluctantly agreed to go along with the plan.

Of course her visitor had agreed to her suggestion of target practice. Voula always got what she wanted from regular people who weren't as sophisticated or as smart as her.

Voula smiled as they walked through the snow, down the sloping hill of the backyard. The visitor fretted that people would hear the gunshots, but Voula said, “They'll think it's just illegal fireworks, left over from last night.”

They put foam earplugs in their ears, loaded the old gun, and took turns firing at aluminum soda cans lined up on a fallen log. The shots were loud, but the house was secluded, just outside of town, so Voula didn't worry about the town's bumbling police force showing up to snoop around.

Voula laughed freely as she fired shots at the cans. She missed every shot, but liked the feeling of the gun's kick in her hands. She loved the power. She couldn't get enough of it.

The visitor, however, wasn't as excited by target practice and began to grumble about cold hands.

Voula stopped shooting and pulled out one of her earplugs to re-mold it. She tilted her ear toward the house. “Do you hear something? Like crying?”

They listened in silence for a moment, but the only sound was the whistle of a breeze that had just picked up.

“Never mind,” Voula said. “Must have been a stray spirit whimpering in the wind. Sometimes they get shy and stop talking when you actually listen.”

They walked back up to the house, made a second pot of coffee, and went upstairs to the room where Voula hosted the knitting club and did readings.

As they talked about how last night's performance had gone, Voula tried to focus on what her visitor was saying, but it was all so boring and beneath her. She nodded and pretended to be listening as she sorted through her basket of knitted dolls. These dolls were her own invention, and she'd learned to knit just so she could make these little voodoo dolls.

Even before they were dressed in their clothes, they seemed to have their own personalities. Sometimes, when she was finishing a doll, she imagined that she really *was* a witch, and that these objects held magical powers.

She picked up the green and purple masquerade mask she'd been given the night before. With a few snips of her sharp scissors and a dab of glue, she would be able to create a miniature version of the mask.

She smiled, because out of everything, the crafts were probably her favorite part. While knitting or creating miniature outfits, the rest of the world disappeared.

"What about you?" asked the visitor.

Voula looked up and blinked as she tried to recall the last few seconds of conversation.

"Sorry," Voula said as she pushed away the basket of dolls and crafting materials. "The spirits were speaking to me, and I didn't hear you over their noises." She made an elaborate hand gesture and uttered a nonsense spell before hissing, "Hush, foul spirits. Hush and be still."

The visitor fixed her with a steady look and repeated the same question Voula hadn't heard the first time. "Are you dating anyone? Your cheeks have the glow of a woman in love."

Voula snorted with contempt. "A wise woman doesn't confuse a few moments of vigorous exercise for love." She let out a mean-spirited cackle. Firing the gun had unleashed something in Voula. She felt raw and energized, and for once she wanted to say what she really felt instead of uttering the lines from a script.

"Vigorous exercise? Do you mean… a lover?"

Still warm from her witchlike laughter, Voula continued, "Men are only useful for two things, and the most pathetic of the lot are only useful for *one* thing, and that's paying the bills. Of course, you have to make all the right noises to let them think they're competent at the other thing, or you'll have to deal with the sulking." She rolled her eyes and groaned.

"I'm sorry I asked." The visitor frowned and pushed back their chair. "Never mind."

Voula sensed her control over the situation evaporating and quickly went into damage-control mode. She shook and convulsed, pretending to be fighting an internal battle with spirits. Gasping, she gripped the edge of the table and said hoarsely, "That wasn't me. That was a man-hating spirit." She convulsed, then waved her hands as though shooing away ghosts. "That wasn't me," she repeated.

The visitor didn't push the chair away and leave, but didn't seem comfortable, either. They looked down at the gun on the table, equal distance between them. The box of bullets sat alongside.

"Voula, tell me the truth," the visitor said gently. "Were you really possessed by a spirit just now? Is any of the stuff you do real? Do you even believe in the power of love?"

"What does it matter?" Voula spat back. "Don't act like you're better than me. Who were you thinking about shooting in the eye when you fired off those bullets in the backyard just now?"

The visitor gasped. "Nobody! I'd never think about killing a person."

"What if you could make it look like an accident?" Voula grinned and tapped her long, black-lacquered fingernails on the table. “Don't act like you haven't been planning the perfect murder ever since that first night we shared a bottle of wine and I said too much.”

The visitor reached for the gun on the table. “This was a bad idea.”

Voula reached for the gun at the same time. “Don't you dare wimp out.”

CHAPTER 2

THE DAY BEFORE
(NEW YEAR'S EVE)
STORMY DAY

I WAS DEALING with what felt like the biggest decision of my life when my friend showed up at my front door.

"You're not dressed yet," Jessica said.

I clutched the colorful robe closed at my neck and chuckled. "And to think… the people of Misty Falls say *I'm the one* with the keen powers of observation."

Jessica arched her delicate red eyebrows and smirked. "People say that? You mean when they're not clucking their tongues over that fancy car you drive?" She nodded toward my car, parked in the snowy driveway and added, "Speaking of which, I see you got the window fixed, but not the bullet holes."

"Bullet holes add character." I waved for her to come in, and shivered as the cold air swirled up the interior of my robe.

"Character, huh?" She looked for an instant like she might cry, but shrugged it away. "Better those bullet holes are in the car than my best friend, I suppose."

She wasn't moving fast enough, so I grabbed her arm and playfully yanked her in. It was snowy and cold that night, and she was letting out the heat, but more importantly, I didn't want my tenant to see me in the bathrobe. *Not again.*

Jessica narrowed her pretty blue eyes as she looked me up and down. "Stormy Day, what's going on here with this clown outfit? Are you having a meltdown because of the gift shop? Retail isn't for everyone, but you can tell me if you're not up for the party tonight. You *have* been through a lot lately."

"I'm fine," I said, and I meant it. Now that Christmas was done, I was almost looking forward to doing storewide inventory. *Almost.*

"You're not fine. You're wearing the bathrobe of a murderer, and it's not even a *nice* bathrobe." She leaned in to examine the fabric. "Are those smudgy things flowers or pink flamingos?"

"They might be fish." I smoothed out a section of the robe and used my finger to trace a shape that could have been a fish. "If you don't want to be staring at this magnificent work of art all night, help me pick out something better to wear. I've got three dresses, but they're all wrong."

"Then wear jeans."

"That's my backup plan!"

Jessica hung her jacket by the door and proceeded into the adjacent open-plan kitchen, where she stuffed groceries into the fridge, then followed me down the hallway to my bedroom, where the *real* owner of the house was relaxing on *his* bed.

"Jeffrey McFluffy Trousers," Jessica cooed as she jumped on the bed and smothered her face in his dark gray tummy.

I watched, smiling, as Jeffrey, my new Russian Blue cat, pretended not to enjoy the attention being lavished on him.

"Let's see your dresses," Jessica said, her voice muffled by Jeffrey's soft fur as she gave him what we called *schnerfles*. With the back of her head facing me, I got a good view of her fancy hairstyle. Her naturally red locks were gathered into a twist, with small braids of red hair woven through.

Seeing her cute braids made me miss my long hair, but only fleetingly. I didn't miss all the time I used to spend using a blow drier or flat iron to straighten my naturally curly hair. My short pixie cut was much more sensible and easy, which was perfect. Moving back to my hometown and giving up my executive lifestyle in the venture capital business was all about simplifying.

I gathered the dress options for Jessica's opinion. All three had been in the window of Blue Enchantment before I dropped in and bought them all. Undressing window display mannequins was becoming a guilty pleasure of mine.

Jessica tore herself away from her noisy *schnerfles* on the cat just long enough to say, "The black and white stripes."

"Won't I look like a zebra?"

"Sure, but I don't think there'll be any lions or tigers at the Fox and Hound. Steer clear of the watering hole, just in case."

I couldn't argue with her logic, so I slipped off the warm bathrobe and finished getting dressed. I went into the washroom to fluff up my hair, where I was surprised to hear a muffled woman's voice.

"Jessica," I hissed from the bathroom doorway. "Come here. Quickly. I think Logan's got a woman over."

She came running, her blue eyes wide and her pale cheeks flushed. "Is he allowed?"

I smiled. Technically, yes, Logan Sanderson could have anyone he wanted over. He paid his rent on time, and whatever he did over there was his business, but I still felt like I'd caught him at something.

I held my finger up to my lips as I pressed my ear against the wall separating the two bathrooms.

"He can't do this to us," Jessica sputtered as her freckled cheeks became even redder. "I mean, he can't do this to you. He's supposed to be your date for tonight."

"He's not my date," I said softly. "I asked him to be our chauffeur."

Jessica shushed me and pressed her ear to the wall. The muffled sounds were a real woman's voice, and not the TV or radio. Unfortunately, the walls of my duplex were just thick enough to prevent me from making out any of the words she was saying.

"Maybe it's a client," I whispered. "Some after-hours legal emergency."

Jessica grabbed the water glass from my bathroom counter and held it between the wall and her ear. "Nope. Still can't hear what she's saying." She pulled away from the wall and set the glass back on the counter. “Stormy,” she said slowly. “What did you mean, about Logan being our chauffeur?”

I used my hands to shoo her out of the bathroom and away from the shared wall. The rest of the house had better soundproofing, so I chased her all the way to the kitchen, where I offered her some of the fancy crackers and soft cheese I'd set out.

She crunched on the snacks, then demanded an answer. “Why doesn't Logan know he's your date tonight?”

“It's not a date. I can't exactly date my tenant.”

“So, why take him to a New Year's Eve party? What happens at midnight when everyone's kissing?”

She had a good point, but now I was thinking about kissing Logan, feeling the tickle of his beard on my cheek. To stall, I stacked some delicious, creamy soft cheese between two different kinds of crackers and stuffed my mouth.

Jessica waited patiently for me to swallow and answer.

“We could kiss,” I said. “But it's not a date, because dating my tenant would be a disaster. I've got a whole series of activities in mind. Come spring, we can work on the garden together. I was hoping that if things went well, neither of us would notice we were dating until we were already married.” I let out a self-conscious giggle. “By the way, we're eating goat cheese.”

“This is goat cheese? Who knew goats made such delicious cheese?”

“It's called chèvre.”

“Great. We can serve chèvre at your wedding to Logan, when you surprise him with that. Just a tip, though. If you're wearing a big white dress, he might get suspicious."

"Good tip."

Something dark streaked by the edge of my vision. Jessica and I made jokes about surprise weddings for the next few minutes, not noticing that Jeffrey had jumped up to sample the goat cheese. We were oblivious to his forbidden feasting until he got too enthusiastic and knocked some cutlery off the counter.

I grabbed him and set him back down on the floor, laughing. "Nice try, little man. You nearly got away with the perfect crime, but you got greedy."

Jessica asked, in a serious tone, "Do you think it's possible to plan the perfect crime? To get away with murder?"

"Is your boss making you triple-wash the pre-washed spinach again?"

"Very funny." She smiled wanly and handed me a cracker sandwich that may or may not have been pre-licked by a gray cat.

"I just have a bad feeling," she said. "I lie awake in bed thinking about stuff. After what happened to Mr. Michaels, it's all everyone wants to talk about. Everybody's got their own theory about where the killer went wrong."

I snorted. "The killer went wrong by getting on my bad side."

"Then it's settled. You can never move out of Misty Falls again. We need you to scare away those would-be murderers."

"Who said I was thinking about leaving?"

"Sometimes you get that faraway look, like a kid who wants to run away from home."

"So, I'm a runaway?" I asked in a light tone.

She fixed me with her bright blue eyes, which were just as lively as I remembered from when we were little kids, bonding over loose teeth and favorite comic books.

"Jessica, I'm not going anywhere. I moved back here for a reason."

She kept giving me her skeptical look.

To change the topic, I opened the container of herbed olives. "These aren't garlic-stuffed," I assured her. "Just fresh herbs, in case *you* want to smooch someone at midnight."

She helped herself to the plump, glistening olives with a happy sigh. "Good. I'll crash here tonight, and I'll have decent breath for smooching Jeffrey McFluffy Trousers."

There was a knock at the door.

"Logan's here," I said. "Quick, refill the cheese tray and make it look like we haven't touched it."

"Of course," she said as she spread out more crackers. "We are *dainty ladies* and we'd never eat the guest food before the guests arrive."

I ran to the door, nearly tripping over Jeffrey, who seemed to think he was a dog sometimes, eager to see who was at to the door when someone knocked softly, but not if they knocked loudly. He pawed the door impatiently.

I opened the door, bracing myself for the possibility Logan would have his own date for the evening, the woman whose voice I'd heard through the bathroom wall.

To my relief, he was alone. To my disappointment, he wore jeans and a college sweatshirt, both well worn. I'd seen him in suits, so I knew he owned good clothes, but this casual attire didn't bode well.

"Stormy Day in a dress," he said gruffly. "For a kooky cat lady, you clean up real nice once the bathrobe comes off."

"Logan Sanderson, for a hotshot lawyer, you resemble an unemployed drummer on your days off."

He looked down my body. "Those are some nice stripes. Black and white. Very eye-catching."

Logan's blue eyes took a second and a third tour of my zebra stripes, and he flashed me his perfect teeth. His dark beard made his teeth look even brighter, and his lips redder.

Despite the cold air coming in the open door, I was feeling warmer and warmer.

He nodded down at Jeffrey, who was sniffing and rubbing his face on the frayed hem of Logan's jeans. "May I come in, or are we waiting for the cat to finish claiming me? You know, they rub their cheek glands on things they like. He's saying I'm *his* now."

"That would be funny if humans did that."

He laughed. "It would make life easier." He scooped up Jeffrey, gave him a manly kiss on the forehead, then handed him to me.

I stepped aside and nodded for Logan to come in. As I clutched the squirming cat to my chest, I noticed how rapidly my heart was beating. The night wasn't going as planned, but it did promise to be memorable.

* End of Preview*

Stormy Day Mystery Book 2,

Death of a Crafty Knitter,

is available now!